COBB

LIGHTHOUSE SECURITY INVESTIGATIONS

MARYANN JORDAN

Cover design: Cosmic Letterz

ISBN ebook: 978-1-947214-80-4

ISBN print: 978-1-947214-81-1

In many ways, the gala was similar to other black-tie events that Cobb had attended over the years. The men were in tuxes, most of them designer labels that had been tailored to a perfect fit. The women were in swirls of elegant evening wear, their gowns complemented to perfection with the jewels they wore about their necks and wrists, hanging from their ears, and adorning their fingers. Most of the attendees were middle-aged or older, but as the wealth distribution in New Mexico had shifted over the years, younger affluent people mingled in the crowd. After all, the invitations had been sent to persons who had the social standing and money to not only attend but also be willing to make large donations to the charities represented.

A string quartet sat on a small balcony, the delicate notes drifting in the background over the gathering, neither drowning the noise of people chatting nor too soft so the musical entertainment couldn't be enjoyed. A few couples swayed to the music while others smiled with indulgence as they continued to converse.

A long table was against one wall holding silver warming trays as the waitstaff, wearing the requisite white shirt and black pants, stood nearby to assist guests as they placed the hors d'oeuvres and delicacies onto the small crystal plates. Other servers moved unobtrusively among the gathering, balancing trays filled with champagne flutes and more hors d'oeuvres. More staff glided around the room, whisking away the empty plates to ensure the invitees weren't standing with a half-eaten cheese and salmon puff ruining the effect of their appearance.

His gaze continued about the room, and he stifled the snort ready to erupt. The venue was massive, the main room reaching over forty feet, although there were plenty of shadowed nooks and crannies as pathways meandered throughout. He could honestly say that despite the similarities, he'd never been to a gala quite like this. Unlike most black-tie events, the room was not brilliantly lit. There were no crystal chandeliers dangling from the ceiling. Instead, bones were suspended from wires hanging from the dark, cavernous ceiling. Ancient bones. Prehistoric bones. Bones that had been meticulously connected in an intricate puzzle, creating a whole from the many parts.

Dinosaur bones.

And instead of expensive floral arrangements in glass and silver vases on marble pedestals, the guests wandered through the multiple exhibits filled with dirt, palm trees, large ferns, and more massive dinosaur skeletons.

It seemed a curious place, but in the back corner, tucked under a twenty-foot-tall Tyrannosaurus Rex, was the open bar, making sure the guests were well-lubricated, hopefully encouraging them to open their pockets when it came time to make donations to the local charities.

Cobb remembered the first black-tie event his parents allowed him to attend when he was sixteen years old. Of course, if it had been held here, he would've loved it. Instead, that event, like so many of the others his parents attended throughout the years, was held in an expensive ballroom. He'd been excited, feeling like a man, only to have been sorely disappointed when he discovered the gala was filled with adults and the only other young people were the college-aged servers. At least there had been the one dark-haired beauty that caught his eye. While she wouldn't risk getting fired by openly flirting, he'd followed her subtle invitation and met her down the hall and inside one of the coat closets. That alone made it one of the more memorable galas.

As soon as he'd joined the military, he'd left his parents' world behind to serve in places that would never know such luxuries and served with men and women who didn't give a fuck about crystal goblets, brie pastry, and foie gras.

Even though he was an attendee and probably expected to hobnob, he preferred standing to the side, his attentive gaze roaming about the darkened room. It was a habit born of many years of always looking for the unexpected.

Now, he watched the familiar greeting dance that always occurred at events like this. People who were meeting with good friends offered handshakes that included a pat on the shoulder for men and cheek kisses for the women. If someone was chatting with an acquaintance that could not improve their social standing, it involved a shorter handshake, no shoulder pat, and only air kisses for the women. If someone was approaching an acquaintance that they hoped would be beneficial either socially or financially, a hearty smile followed a robust handshake and a cheek kiss for the woman if she leaned forward. If she offered only her hand, then it behooved the greeter to not make an assumption and attempt to kiss the woman. *Woe be to those who didn't follow these intricate greeting rules.*

"Jorge, what are you doing over here by yourself?"

He'd been aware of the woman who approached as he was aware of everything around him, but hearing her voice always made him smile. Dropping his chin, he shook his head and tried to hide his grin. Turning, he bent to kiss her cheek.

"Grandmother, it's good to see you."

For him, she abandoned the necessary greeting protocol and accepted his hug, patting his back with true affection.

The petite woman staring up at him was as lovely as ever. Her silver hair was pulled back into an elegant chignon. Her long, blue designer gown was highlighted by the diamonds in her ears and around her neck, wrist, and fingers. The jewels were not showy but pieces that his grandfather had gifted her over the years and held emotional significance. "You look as beautiful as always," he said, his words truthful even if she looked completely out of place standing underneath the skeleton of a Triceratops.

She pursed her lips as she twisted her head and glared at the offending prehistoric creature at her shoulder. He was not surprised to see that she attempted to ignore the ridiculous skeleton and turned her gaze back to him. Drawing herself up, she lifted a brow. "Instead of wasting your compliments on me, why aren't you out of this dark corner and socializing?"

"I've already wished Dad a happy birthday when I got into town yesterday. And he's surrounded by those that either need to suck up to him, want him for something, or came for the free food and drinks."

His delicate grandmother barked out a laugh and shook her head as though surprised. "I would fuss at you if you weren't speaking the truth." She cast her gaze about the room, slowly shaking her head, finally addressing the elephant—or the dinosaur—in the room. "Your father certainly outdid himself this year. When he told me that he'd decided to have his annual charity birthday event in a museum, I was picturing something a little more… elegant. Perhaps the Art Museum or the Turquoise Museum."

"Just be glad he didn't choose the American International Rattlesnake Museum." He watched her shudder again, and he chuckled. "I confess that just before you came over, I was thinking that this was the most unusual gala I've ever attended."

"I wonder what Selena thinks."

"You know Mom. She and Dad are having a blast."

She shifted her gaze back to him. "How long are you staying in town?"

"I'll still be here tomorrow when we all gather for the family birthday celebration. Then I'll have to leave the next day. It was just a long weekend for me."

She lifted her chin as she eyed him carefully. "You look well, Jorge. Although why anyone would want to live in Maine with the cold and snow, I have no idea. But it must agree with you."

He wouldn't mention to her that after some of the hellholes he'd served in around the world, the thick woods, ocean coastline, clear skies, and the camaraderie that he found in Maine had no equal. Looking beyond her shoulder, he smiled as his grandfather approached. The two men hugged tightly, affection evident before his grandfather slid his arm around his grandmother.

"Maria, are you behaving yourself amongst the dinosaurs?"

His grandmother rolled her eyes and replied, "There are times that I think our son takes after me, and then he pulls a stunt like this. And at his age! Seeing the venue for this gala, I'm sure he must take after you."

He laughed as his grandfather pretend-glared at her. Soon, with promises to catch up tomorrow at the family gathering, his dad's parents walked past one of the many palm trees to greet more friends.

He sighed and looked at his watch. As interesting as

it had been to see the event in this tropical venue filled with the bones of the extinct, the truth of the matter was he was bored. He moved along the wall, avoiding small talk with those who only wanted to greet him as an attempt to curry favor with his father. He politely nodded at a few acquaintances but didn't stop, having no desire to start a conversation.

A flash of silver-blue like the pearlescent scales of a fish leaping from the waters off the coast of Maine caught his eye. Moving to a more advantageous position, he observed a young woman standing alone. Her face was turned in profile, but that gave him an opportunity to admire her dress. The front fell only to her knees, then the material swooped down toward the back where it ended at the top of her stiletto heels. The dress was shimmery, seeming to change from pale blue to silver depending on how the light caught the silky folds. Her reddish-blonde hair was thick and wavy, falling beyond her shoulders in the back, the top held by a clip that glistened with crystals. Small diamond drop earrings hung from her ears, and a diamond bracelet encircled her wrist.

As she turned slowly, a heavy sigh left her lips, her chest heaving slightly with the exertion. Her lips barely curved into a smile that appeared to take all her effort to remain polite. In her hand was a champagne flute, untouched as though she had been offered the drink and holding the crystal gave her something to do with her hand even though she had no desire to partake of the bubbly alcohol. She stepped backward, slipping a bit further into the shadows, and the desire to go over to her rocked through him, not an emotion he normally felt.

Before he had a chance, a hand clapped him on the back, and he startled, surprised that he hadn't realized someone was coming up behind him. Turning quickly, he smiled as he greeted his parents. His mother was beautiful in a deep burgundy gown, wearing her signature silver and turquoise jewelry. His dad's silver hair was neatly trimmed but not overly styled, and he appreciated his parents' ability to present an elegant picture without being affectatious. "Dad, you really outdid yourself for your sixty-fifth birthday. I've been standing here looking at all of these people surrounded by dinosaur skeletons, having to pinch myself to see if it's real."

His dad threw his head back and laughed, his arm wrapped around his wife. She winked and said, "When your dad told me where he wanted to have his party this year, I couldn't believe it. But isn't it wonderful?"

While *wonderful* might not be the word he'd use to describe the gala, he was glad his parents were happy. "As long as it gives you lots of donations to the charities you're sponsoring, it'll be great."

Another couple approached, and his dad swung his arm out to greet them. "John, Betty, come meet my son, Jorge. This is John and Betty Rector. John is our State Senator."

He shook hands with the Rectors, making the requisite small talk that he hated but was necessary at these events. He occasionally glanced beyond his father's shoulder to see the young woman still standing alone.

She had now turned in his direction, although her gaze had not rested on him, and her beauty almost made it impossible to focus on what his parents and the Rectors were saying. Glad when he could say goodbye as they all moved away, he began walking toward the woman, hoping to avoid any other interruptions. He approached her from the side, careful to not startle her. She appeared to be lost in thought and nonetheless jumped slightly when he reached her.

When she turned her pale blue eyes up to him, he almost stumbled at her beauty. He was no stranger to attractive women whether in ballrooms or barrooms, but she was an ethereal vision. Her dress continued to shimmer as she moved, the ever-changing silver-blue material accentuating the diamonds at her ears and wrist, causing them to glitter even more. Around her neck was a simple but elegant silver cross necklace.

"May I take this?" He reached up and gently slid the champagne glass from her hand, setting it on a server's tray.

"What—"

"You've been holding that drink for a long time, and I don't think you really want it."

Her head tilted to the side as her gaze moved over his face, and he thought she was going to refute his assumption. Instead, she surprised him. "You've been paying attention?"

"You are the only person here to hold my attention. Please, come dance with me."

She opened her mouth as though to refuse his offer, then pressed her lips tightly together. If she'd given resistance, he would've stepped back, but after assessing him for a long moment, she placed her hand in his, and they walked around the pillar. Now, partially hidden by the Ankylosaurus skeleton, he pulled her close. With one hand on her waist, still leaving a socially-polite space between them, he took her other hand and held it close to his chest. Moving slowly, they began to dance. The delicate scent of orange blossoms filled his nostrils, and he fought the urge to bury his nose in her hair and inhale.

She was taller than his grandmother, but he knew without her heels she would be staring at his chest instead of his chin. Her dress dipped in the front, giving a hint of perfect cleavage. His hand rested on the material in the back, his fingertips able to slide along the soft skin at her shoulder.

"I should apologize for being so forward, but you looked quite lonely standing by yourself pretending to drink champagne."

Her clear-eyed gaze never wavered. "You're right, you should apologize for being so presumptuous, but I notice you didn't actually say that you're sorry."

Her voice was as soft as he imagined but her lips still had not formed a smile.

"Then I do apologize if you were, in truth, drinking the champagne that you'd been holding. Or if you weren't standing by yourself."

She tilted her head slightly to the side. "I'm afraid that's not a good enough apology. I was choosing to stand there with the champagne in my hand."

"But isn't it more fun to dance than to stand all alone?"

"And you think a woman standing by herself needs to be rescued? Perhaps I was waiting on someone."

He gently rubbed his thumb over her fingers and pressed them closer to his chest. "If you were waiting on someone, they should have been there. I assure you that if you were supposed to meet me, I would never have been late to leave someone as beautiful as you to stand alone."

He hoped her lips would curve slightly or that she would glance up at him through her eyelashes, coyly offering a silent invitation. Instead, she merely lifted an eyebrow. He had the strange sensation that he was back in school having offered a smartass comment that was overheard by a teacher. He'd never had to work so hard to get a woman to smile at his charm.

Clearing his throat, he confessed, "I'm afraid my attempts at being suave have fallen short. Do you think perhaps we can start over?"

"That would probably be best, and may I suggest you begin by taking your foot out of your mouth?"

Unable to keep from laughing, he shook his head. "Good evening, I'm Jorge."

"Just Jorge?"

Wanting to get to know her without revealing that he was the son of the governor, he smiled. "Yes. And I completely understand about standing off by yourself. I've done it many times."

She shook her head slowly as she continued to hold his

gaze. "I have to admit you certainly don't look like the others here. For one thing, you're much taller and broader than any other man in the room." She blinked suddenly and tilted her head as her eyes narrowed. "Are you a bodyguard? Is there someone here you're keeping an eye on?"

"Yes," he said smoothly. Since he worked for a security company, his deception didn't seem so bad.

An adorable crinkle formed along her brow. "I find it quite odd that you're dancing and flirting with me instead of guarding whatever body you're supposed to be attending to."

"There's no one right now that I have to keep an eye on other than the woman that's in my arms. Which, by the way, I still don't know your name."

"Josie."

Hating that he'd not been entirely truthful, he continued to move slowly to the sounds of the music, maneuvering them so that they could enjoy the music privately. "So, Josie, what brings you to an event like this?"

"Why is anyone at an event like this unless they have to be here?"

"For many people, it's to see and be seen," he offered as a glib reply.

"Perhaps that was my reason."

He shook his head slowly, drowning in her pale blue eyes. "I doubt it since you're the most beautiful woman in the room, and yet you were standing off to the side."

She offered a delicate shrug. "Perhaps there was just no one here I cared to talk to."

"That I could believe." Finally, her lips curved ever so

slightly. Josie was an enigma, but he knew anyone at this event was wealthy, usually with an agenda. *Who was she and why come alone if she was just going to stand in the shadows?* She didn't appear to be there to enjoy a night out but neither did she seem to be making connections. But right now, with her body close to his, he knew exactly the connection he'd like to make. "I don't suppose you're ready to make an early exit, are you?"

Her body stiffened slightly. "With you?" she asked, her brow lifting again.

"I thought we could get a drink somewhere… something other than champagne."

She inclined her head toward the Tyrannosaurus Rex. "There's a bar over there."

"Okay then, how about somewhere that doesn't include prehistoric relics?"

Finally, she laughed. He'd never worked so hard to get a woman to smile, but now that he had, the effort was worth it. If he'd thought she was beautiful all alone with an I-wish-I-was-somewhere-else expression on her face, with her in his arms and laughing, she was exquisite. Pressing his luck, he said, "No expectations. Just drinks… and a chance to get to know each other better."

As her mirth slowed, she looked to the side before shifting her gaze back to him. He forced himself not to squirm, although her penetrating gaze reminded him of his grandmother when he'd knocked over one of her crystal vases.

"Well, Jorge, I've got a long drive home and have to get up early tomorrow for work. As tempting as it is to say yes to drinks and the possibility of knock-my-socks-off sex—if our getting to know each other was going to lead down that path—I don't think I'm your type... or you mine. Nor is it safe to go off with a man I don't know, even if he is a bodyguard. So, I'll politely decline."

In a few sentences, her explanation caused whiplash. Yes, she was right to be cautious with a stranger. But her description of what she thought sex with him would be like made his already-erect cock twitch painfully. But then her comment about not being his *type*... he had no idea what she was referring to. Was it because she thought he was a hired bodyguard instead of a wealthy invitee to the gala? Or was it that his multicultural heritage was written all over his face? He'd thought her to be shy, but perhaps she was simply conceited. As though one of the ice buckets chilling the champagne had been dumped over him, he stepped back, dropping her hand. Offering a slight bow, he said, "Thank you for the dance, Josie. I wish you a pleasant evening." Turning, he weaved his way through the guests and the mocking Triceratops skeleton. Walking out into the cool evening, he jerked his tie off as soon as he exited the building and shoved it into his pocket.

Beautiful, well-spoken, reticent... she was an enigma, a mystery he would have liked to have solved. *But on the other hand, perhaps I wouldn't have cared for what I discovered.*

2

Cobb pulled into his parents' driveway, meandered around the front circle, and parked outside the garage. The large Spanish revival home always sent a feeling of calm throughout him. The tanned stucco exterior with the red-tiled roof had an old-world ambiance while the interior combined modern with the past. His parents had bought the house when his father was a U.S. Senator with plans to run for governor.

Twelve-foot ceilings throughout, paired with wide, sun-reflective windows gave it a light, airy feel along with wide verandas, a backyard that featured lush, green grass, a swimming pool, and a Tiki bar. And situated on a hill, the views of the mountains in the distant background were spectacular. Tiled and oak floors, exposed wooden beams, and sandstone brick complemented its heritage. Large yet cozy. Exquisite yet comfortable.

He walked into the kitchen and headed directly to the refrigerator, pulling out a bottle of water. The room was spotless, but he knew the family's cook, Mrs. Sanchez, would have everything ready for tomorrow's breakfast when she arrived early. Spying carefully wrapped slices of apple pie, he grabbed one and set it on the counter. He turned, hearing a slight noise, and watched as Mrs. Sanchez approached. "It's late, Mrs. Sanchez. Are you all right?"

"Jorge? You're home early."

When back home in New Mexico he went by his given name, Jorge, although since the military he'd been referred to by his last name, Cobb. His last name had meant nothing to those he served with. The fact that his grandfather had once been the governor of New Mexico and his father had been in politics for years was not recognized by anyone. And that was perfect. He'd been treated differently his entire childhood and adolescence, and the military offered an equalizing opportunity for him to just be whatever he chose to make of himself. And he'd found himself not wanting Josie to recognize that she was talking to a relative of the governor. He swallowed a snort. *For all the good it did me.*

But, with Mrs. Sanchez, like his family, he would always be Jorge. Smiling down at her, he replied, "I had socialized with everyone I needed to."

She walked over and patted his arm, her head inclined toward the slice of pie. "I'll wager that's better than any of the fancy food they had at the party."

Taking a large bite and not having to fake his enjoyment, he nodded, moaning in delight as he swallowed. "You're right. Nothing's better than your cooking. But why are you still here? Do you need a ride home?"

She shook her head and smiled. "I wanted to make sure everything was perfect for your father's family birthday party tomorrow. Since I was working late on the cake, your mother suggested I stay in the downstairs guest room overnight so that I wouldn't have to travel back and forth. I was almost going to bed when I heard someone in here and thought I would check to see who was sneaking in." Patting his arm again, she turned and began walking out of the room, calling over her shoulder, "Enjoy your pie, but make sure to rinse your dish before you go upstairs."

Shaking his head, he grinned. "Yes, ma'am," he said with affection. Finishing the pie and dutifully rinsing the dish, he headed to his bedroom. He pulled out the tie that had been shoved into his pocket and draped it over a hanger. He did the same with the tuxedo, knowing his father's valet would have it cleaned and pressed tomorrow, ready for it to be taken back when he left New Mexico. Stalking into the en suite bathroom, he stripped while letting the shower water heat.

The delicate scent of orange and flowers hit him just before he stepped into the water. It was the scent he'd noticed with Josie, and for a second, he hated to wash it off. But knowing he'd never see her again, he scrubbed his body and hair, although he couldn't scrub her from his mind. Beautiful, elegant. *I'm not her type... she's not my type... what the hell did that mean?*

Stepping out of the shower, he toweled off before pulling on a clean pair of boxers. As the condensation lifted from the mirror, he stared at the reflection. Black hair. Dark eyes. Full lips. Broad nose. Heavy five o'clock shadow. His features were formed from a variety of genetics. His mother's mother was Native American, and her father was Mexican American. On his father's side of the family, his grandmother immigrated from Italy as a child, and his grandfather was of German descent.

He had no idea what *type* Josie was referring to but decided he didn't give a fuck. When his father had served as a U.S. Senator, Cobb had certainly experienced times when racial slurs had been directed toward him and his mom. But seeing it, knowing it exists, and living through it were different things. Thinking back to his days in prep school, he shook his head. Some experiences had been wonderful, but other days he'd rather forget.

Walking back into the bedroom, he twisted off the cap to the bottle of water and drank deeply. Tired, he was ready to go back to his house in Maine, although he looked forward to the next day. His father's annual birthday charity gala would be over, and it would just be the family at home. All of his grandparents would come along with some other relatives, and he knew he'd have a good time. But still, New Mexico was no longer home and hadn't been for many years. He longed for the cool forests and ocean waves of Maine.

Two Weeks Later

Moose's Bar was quite different from the gala event Cobb had attended earlier in the month. It was run by a crotchety veteran who'd served in Desert Storm, and his father had started the bar when he came home from the Vietnam War. Cobb was fairly certain that the interior hadn't changed much in the past fifty years. The scuffed wooden floor and dented bar were original. It wasn't fancy and some weekend nights got rowdy, but it made for a great place to unwind.

Sitting with his group of coworkers and friends, the laughter and camaraderie reminded him why he was so much happier here.

After serving as a SEAL, he'd been recruited for CIA special ops. That's where he and the others had met their boss and iconic leader, Mace Hanover. Mace had started his own business, Lighthouse Security Investigations, hiring men and women who'd served with special operations in the military or CIA. Known as Keepers, Mace worked relentlessly, recruiting only the best and those that fit his idea of the team. Cobb counted himself lucky to have been chosen.

Looking around the table that was now filled with almost as many women as men, he could not help but be envious as well as happy for his friends. They'd found love, something that so far had eluded him. Of the original ten Keepers, there were only three that were still single. Mace had increased their ranks with Knox, Rick, and Abbie, all siblings of various original Keepers who'd served in the military or CIA special ops.

They were also single, and for some inexplicable reason, Cobb was glad. It made him feel less conspicuous.

"Are you okay?"

He startled and turned to his side, seeing Christina, now married to one of his closest friends, Clay, next to him. He cocked his head to the side, wondering why she asked.

"You're here in body, but I'm not sure you're here in spirit."

He laughed and shook his head. "I'm fine." When she continued to hold his gaze, he added. "I was just thinking that I'm glad I made Maine my home."

"So, how was it when you went back to New Mexico for a visit?"

"Always good to see my parents and grandparents. But I think there comes a point where you realize that the place you were born and raised is no longer your home. For me, I'm lucky. It's a great place to visit and filled with good memories for the most part. But it always makes me appreciate what I have here."

Tate, another Keeper sitting across the table from him, nodded. His arms wrapped around his wife, Nora, both having left their home in Wyoming, Tate when he joined the military and Nora more recently when she and Tate reunited. "Yeah, it's nice to go back and visit the family, but it no longer feels like home."

As Cobb finished his beer, several of the couples made their way to the back where an old jukebox kept the music lively. A stacked blonde with painted on jeans left the bar and walked slowly toward their table. Her gaze moved around the single men before landing on his. Interest flared in her eyes, and she sauntered over. Leaning closer, her breasts on display, she winked. "Care to show a girl a good time on the dance floor?"

There was no doubt she was a beauty, and it had been a while since he'd been with anyone. Standing, he nodded and took her hand, leading her toward the back. "Can't think of anything better than dancing with a beautiful woman." As soon as those words left his mouth, the memory of Josie jumped into his mind.

She laughed as he gave her a twirl and pulled her in closer, his hand on her waist. She appeared not satisfied with the distance between them and wrapped her arms around him to pull him in tight. Her method of dancing was more grinding, which would've excited him years before but now felt a little desperate. Shoving those thoughts away, he looked down at her and smiled. Her straight blonde hair was long, hanging in a sheet down her back. Her curves were evident in her jeans and tight, low-cut T-shirt. And she was tall. In heeled boots, she almost looked him in the eye. *She's much taller than Josie.*

Blinking, he hated that Josie was still in his thoughts, but in truth, she'd popped into his mind numerous times over the last several weeks. Deciding to exorcise all thoughts of Josie, he gave the blonde a twirl again, hoping to enjoy his night at the bar with friends and dancing with a beautiful woman.

She plastered her body against his front. Dancing this close, he felt her breasts press against his chest. She whispered against his ear, "I'm Rochelle," then pulled his earlobe between her teeth. He jerked back, but she quickly maneuvered so her legs were straddling his thigh, continuing to grind herself on him in the middle of the dance floor.

A shockwave of embarrassment hit him. Aware of his friends and their wives nearby, he shot his gaze around but saw they only had eyes for each other. Regardless, he was glad when the song ended. She clung to his arm as they walked off the dance floor, her breasts still pressed tightly against him.

"You want to buy me a drink first or should we just head back to your place? Or my place... whichever is closer."

He swallowed a sigh... this just wasn't doing it for him. Especially when pale blue eyes haunted his thoughts. Hoping to let her down easy, he offered, "I can buy you a drink, but I'll be heading home by myself." He tried for a heartfelt smile, but it was as fake as the boobs pressed against his arm.

She cackled loudly and the nails-on-a-chalkboard sound grated on his nerves. "Oh, you're so funny." Peering up at him through half-lowered eyes, she said, "I know a man like you won't go home alone. You look like just my type."

"Your type?" *Am I going to be stuck wondering what that word means?* "Just what type is that?"

"You know... all big muscles... and I'll bet you're *big* everywhere." Her hand snaked down his abs toward his crotch, and he snagged it quickly as she continued, "You look like the kind of man who knows he can satisfy a woman."

Still holding her wrist, not willing to see what else

she wanted to grab, he held her gaze. "You're not afraid of going off with a man you don't know?"

She barked out a laugh again. "I've seen you in here before. You don't look like a serial killer to me. Anyway, the only woman who wouldn't want to take you for a spin is one who doesn't have what it takes. Hell, handsome, I'm ready for you."

He stepped back, his mind no longer on the blonde in front of him but the beautiful Josie. Rochelle tried to move her hand toward him again, but he stopped her. "Not trying to be an ass, but seriously... we danced. That's all. I'm not looking for more."

As his refusal sunk in, her eyes narrowed. "Well, aren't you just full of yourself?" she snorted as her hands landed on her hips. "Bet you've propositioned a shit-ton of women over the years after nothing more than a dance." Shaking her head, she stomped off toward the bar, leaving him alone, her words slamming into him.

Propositioned a woman after nothing more than a dance. The air left his lungs in a rush. *Exactly what I did with Josie.* Shit, fuck, damn. He still had no idea what she'd meant by saying he wasn't her *type*, but it didn't matter. He'd done the same thing to her that Rochelle had done to him.

And the realization tasted bitter in his mouth.

3

TWO MONTHS LATER

Josie stared at the sheaf of papers in front of her, reviewing the columns of numbers and tabulations, matching them with names, and comparing them to the last six months of reports. She hated this part of her job but was not comfortable turning it completely over to someone else.

Reaching into her top desk drawer, she pulled out a stretchy headband, slipping it over her neck before pushing the front past her forehead. *That's better.* She appreciated her thick hair except when it fell into her face while she was trying to concentrate.

A flash of Jorge gently tucking a strand behind her ear when they had danced moved through her mind. She resisted the urge to drop her head down to bang on her desk. Anything to dislodge the image of the gorgeous man from her mind.

Jerking upright, she pinched her lips. *No, just no.* Sucking in a deep breath, she squirmed in her chair, trying to stretch the kinks out of her back before turning her attention back to the numbers swimming together on the page.

Her office was small and utilitarian but neat. Several plants graced a small table near the window, adding a splash of nature. The room was painted a calming lilac and colorful pictures adorned the walls. Anything to make the clients more comfortable.

The clinic she ran provided free or sliding-scale services for the elderly. There were several other clinics in the Las Cruces vicinity that provided services for all ages, but her area of specialty and interest was with the aging population. Considering this area of New Mexico was one of the poorest, she had no shortage of people in need.

Her staff was small but efficient and compatible. She felt fortunate to have a physician who worked three mornings a week. Doctor Mark Forbes was able to lower his medical school debts through this part-time position, and the rest of his time was spent at the local hospital. She was thrilled to have a full-time registered nurse, Laurie Mitchell, who was also her best friend. A full-time nursing aide, Mario Rodriguez, and a full-time receptionist, Charlene Porter, rounded out her staff. And for several months, she'd had a social work intern, Sally Garcia, who had settled into the clinic with ease, making Josie wish she could hire her full-time after Sally graduated.

Turning her attention back to the report, she sighed. Her desk was normally free of clutter, but right now it was covered in papers.

Hearing a noise outside her office, she glanced up and saw the person she wanted to speak to as he hurried by. "Caesar!"

The clinic's part-time bookkeeper popped his head around the doorframe and smiled—at least until his gaze dropped to the report spread out on her desk, and then she could have sworn he winced before covering it up quickly. Now, it appeared his smile was forced.

"We need to go over this together, Caesar. This month's reports are not making any sense to me."

He sighed as though realizing his hasty departure was thwarted and walked into her office, sitting heavily in one of the chairs facing her desk. Small and wiry, his hair was still black, no streaks of gray visible. Whenever he came into work, he always wore a dark suit, white shirt, and dark tie. Laurie once joked that he looked like a mortician. Josie had hushed her, sure that he simply preferred a severe professional appearance.

"Josie, I told you that donations were up recently. I would think you'd be happy about that."

"Yes, but first of all, I don't understand why they've tripled in amount."

"Perhaps it was from the Governor's charity event a couple of months ago. I'm sure that helped."

"I've considered that, Caesar. But most of these names don't match up to anyone that I know or recognize. And what causes me more concern is that the clinic's spending hasn't changed, and yet the amount that's in the bank isn't any more. If our donations are going up, why aren't they in the account?"

He lifted his hand and wiped a trickle of sweat from

his brow, smiling as he mumbled, "I should see about us lowering the temperature on the air conditioner so that we're more comfortable." He chuckled, but it was as forced as his earlier smile.

Caesar Castiel had been the clinic's part-time book-keeper for almost a year after the sudden retirement of the person who had worked there since its inception. He owned his bookkeeping business, and she'd been glad he was able to take them on as clients. She had no reason not to trust him but knew that human error could make a huge difference in the running of the clinic if accurate records were not kept. Considering much of the clinic's finances were supported by dona-tions as well as grants, she felt a strong need to make sure every dollar was accounted for.

Looking back down at the list, she sighed. "Did it not strike you as unusual when you looked at some of these donors? Did you make any calls to check on them? ILT international. Stubbs Contracting. CORE, Incorporat-ed." She lifted her gaze and pinned him with his stare. "I mean, who are these? There's no notation by them at all as to who actually made the donation. A couple of them don't even have tax identifications. I'd like you to take this list and go through every single donation made. Find a name, number, address. Call each one and, if nothing else, thank them for the donation and then ask them all for the identification that we need to have to keep our records straight. And then go back to our expenses over the last several months and see why things are not adding up."

Another bead of sweat rolled down the side of Caesar's face despite the air conditioning blasting throughout the clinic. He jerked his head up and down, and she was unsure if he was agreeing or simply wanted to get out of her office. He stood and reached for the papers on her desk.

"You can use your own copies," she said. What had started as a trickle of suspicion was now growing. "I made these for myself so that we're both looking over the figures at the same time. After all, we don't want the clinic to get closed down for not having accurate records."

"Yes, yes, Josie. Yes, I'm sure that's the right thing to do. I'll go back through everything, don't worry about anything." A tight smile crossed his face as he walked out of her office.

She slumped back in her chair, uncertainty filling her. Looking down at the reports, she pondered her options. *Make some calls myself. Hire another bookkeeper to work alongside Caesar. Go ahead and send these to our accountant.*

Deciding that before she spent the money to hire another bookkeeper or contact their accountant, she turned to her laptop. *I'll do a little digging on some of these donation sources then make a few phone calls myself. If I have to track down every one of these donors and find out who they are and why our records don't match up to tax IDs, I will!*

By the end of the day, her frustration had grown, but then so had her suspicions. Stepping out of her office to grab a water bottle from the kitchen, she walked down the hall, spying Caesar hovering at her doorway. He turned, his smile drooping. "Um, I was just ready to leave but thought I'd see how you were doing."

Her curt response had him shifting from foot to foot before he nodded his goodbyes. Her gaze followed him out the clinic, a hound dog expression plastered on his face. Entering her office again, she carefully looked at the papers on her desk, now suspicious of him being near, but they were all as she had left them.

Ready for the day to be over, she gathered the records, shoved them into her bag, and waved goodbye to her staff.

The next week, Caesar didn't come by the clinic on his regularly scheduled days. When she attempted to contact him, his phone had been disconnected. Finding his address, she drove by to check on him, but he didn't answer her knock at his apartment. None of his neighbors had seen him nor had they seen his car.

And for Josie, it was only the beginning as the threats began. The first was innocuous... a note on her car, secured under the wiper blade. She dismissed it as having been left for the wrong person. The second one instructed her to stay quiet, and a trickle of fear ran through her. The third one was more sinister, and her heart pounded as she dialed her father. "Dad, I have a problem. Someone is threatening me... and I think I know why!"

The early morning run along the trails and through the woods near his house had invigorated Cobb. Now, showered and caffeinated, he parked outside the lighthouse that housed Lighthouse Security Investigations. LSI's compound was located deep in the rocky caves beneath the decommissioned lighthouse that Mace had purchased years ago.

Climbing out of his SUV, he watched as Horace Tiddle drove by in a utility vehicle, the back filled with fence posts and wire. Horace, a former SEAL from years ago, and his wife, Marge, a former CIA Operator that Mace once worked with, had taken positions with Mace when he opened LSI. They ran the buildings and grounds as well as looked after all the Keepers. "Looks like you're going to be busy today."

Horace pulled off his ball cap and wiped his brow before resettling it on his head, aiming his friendly smile toward Cobb. "Marge has been wanting to start a garden with Sylvie between their property and here, and the deer keep getting in. I thought I'd put a fence around and see if I can keep 'em out."

"I'm surprised you don't shoot 'em, and then Marge can fix her venison stew."

"Don't think I haven't thought about it, but Mace would have my hide. David really likes the deer, and I think Sylvie does, too, as long as they stay out of the garden."

Mace had met Sylvie and David on a mission, falling for the beautiful single mom and her son. Now married and having adopted David, he'd do anything for either of them.

As Horace drove off, he called over his shoulder, "Marge is already out at the garden this morning, so you'll have to get your coffee downstairs."

Cobb walked through the empty kitchen and made his way down the hall toward the base of the lighthouse. Flipping the hidden panel by the wall, he tapped in a security code and then stood still as the retina scan took place. Adding his hand on a finger scanner, he waited until his digital prints had been taken before a door swung open and he entered the elevator. At the bottom, he entered a hallway with another door and once again went through the motions of the security systems.

Finally, he walked into the cavernous main room of LSI. He'd been working here for several years and always thought he would become accustomed to the interior of the caves, but they never failed to strike him as utterly awesome. The walls and ceilings were reinforced with steel beams and panels, and the concrete floor retained the original look of the cave. The room was sealed and environmentally protected and filled with computer equipment, tables, stations, wide screens, and specialized printers. Multiple doors opened from the room leading to weapons rooms, bunk rooms, a gym, and back stairs that led away from the lighthouse down toward the rocky shore.

Josh and one of the new Keepers, Knox, were at their stations, scrolling through the chatter coming in from the local, state, and national police monitors. Rank and his brother, Richard, were working security duty, sitting at a bank of monitors.

LSI was involved in designing and installing security for those needing something beyond run-of-the-mill systems. Mace subcontracted the monitoring of those cameras and systems, but a few of the Keepers would periodically check in to make sure the security was running properly.

Passing by Sylvie's desk, Cobb winked. "I hear Bambi's getting on your nerves."

She laughed and rolled her eyes. "I'm perfectly happy for Horace to put up a fence, but I'd better not hear a gunshot that doesn't involve the Keepers' weapons practice."

Babs, one of the Keepers, pointed her finger and made a firing motion. "I can take care of that for you, Sylvie."

"That's my babe. The Bambi killer." Babs' husband, Drew, laughed as he walked by, kissing the top of Babs' head.

Sylvie gave a visible shudder. "Oh, you two," she moaned, glaring at the fun-loving couple.

Babs shook her head, smiling. "Nah... I'm just kidding. I love the deer as well."

Cobb walked to the counter where the industrial coffee maker sat. He may have caffeinated at home but felt the need for more. Josh liked it strong, and that worked for him. Pouring a mug full, he noticed Marge had made several large quiches and was thankful there was any left. Grabbing a plate, he helped himself to a slice, wolfing it down quickly.

Mace called the group together, and everyone made

their way around the large circular table. As their group had grown in numbers their chairs barely fit, but the newcomers tended to sit back in deference to those who'd been Keepers since the beginning. But with Walker and Blake out of town on missions, they all managed to squeeze in.

"Walker is in Canada, keeping an eye on the situation with the Minotaurs." He looked toward Clay and added, "He says he's fine for now, but I told him you're itching to get back up there to help. I'll let you know if he needs you."

The Canadian motorcycle gang had been dealing in drugs, and Clay's fiancé had been caught in the crosshairs, saved when the Keepers rescued her when she'd been kidnapped. Cobb knew Clay would have no problem going up to work with Walker to help bring the gang down.

Continuing, Mace said, "Blake is in California, assisting the local FBI in a case involving one of our security clients." He continued for several moments, allowing some of the Keepers to respond to questions and report on the cases they were working on.

Finally, he pinned Cobb with a stare and said, "Something new came in. Something I'd like to give to you because this is your skillset and geographic area of knowledge."

"Okay, boss," Cobb spoke without any hesitation. It never entered his mind to refuse. He'd taken every mission that came his way, and if Mace stated that he was the right person for the job, that was good enough for him.

"I talked to your father this morning."

Nothing Mace could have said would have shocked Cobb more. Bolting up straight, his heart pounded at the thought that something had happened to his family. "What the fuck? Are they okay?"

Mace threw his hand up, rushing his assurances. "They're fine. I'm sorry, I didn't realize how that was going to sound. Your family is fine, but your father has an acquaintance that needs our help. He didn't go straight to you because he wanted to follow the right chain of command. I hope that doesn't piss you off because I consider that to be appropriate as well."

He'd just spoken to his parents last week and couldn't imagine what had happened that made him contact Mace, but if it was official for LSI, he had no complaint about how Mace wanted to handle the situation. Nodding, he remained quiet as he tried to swallow his heart back down after it had leaped into his throat.

"His friend, State Senator John Rector, contacted him because he's concerned about his daughter's safety. She's a social worker who runs a small clinic out of Las Cruces, New Mexico. She's not involved in the finances other than grants and pushing for charitable donations. There's a bookkeeper who's been taking care of the books for the clinic. Caesar Castiel. She examined the records and found discrepancies and things that concerned her. She made phone calls to some of the unknown companies whose donations seemed excessive and were not well documented. It seems that she may have poked a hornet's nest. Now, the bookkeeper has disappeared. She grew concerned when he didn't return her emails, but it appears he left the area."

"Fuckin' hell," Cobb murmured under his breath. "Money laundering?"

"Right now, we don't know."

"It would be best if she had a forensic accountant or certified fraud examiner," Cobb continued. "Regular tax accounting does not always have the investigative skills to follow the money trail."

"Her father's looking into that, but his fear right now is for her. After she made several phone calls, she began getting threats. Notes on her car. Harassing phone calls. Her father's afraid that things are escalating."

"He wants protection for her? I met the senator and his wife several months ago when I was home for my dad's birthday. I know they're friends of my parents, but I've never met the daughter."

"I thought you'd be perfect for the protection detail and on-site investigative mission. You know the area. You know the people. And you understand the finances. There is a warning, though. Her father doesn't think she'll take well to having someone trailing after her."

Cobb chuckled, "Don't worry. I can be very charming." He opened his tablet, knowing that Josh would be sending the mission information to him. "And the missing bookkeeper?"

Mace held his gaze for a few seconds before saying, "Don't know. Levi will coordinate with the local FBI there. My guess... either he disappeared, or someone got rid of him. And that's what Senator Rector is afraid of for his daughter."

"What's the daughter's name?"

"Josephine. Josephine Rector."

Just then, Josh sent the picture of Josephine to his tablet, and all the oxygen was sucked out of Cobb's lungs. *Josephine. Holy shit. Josie.*

4

_____

By lunchtime, Cobb had pored over the information Josh had sent him on Josie. The more he read the more antsy he felt, discovering that his conceptions about her didn't seem to add up to the reality presented. Deciding to take a break, he gave in to the urge to pound the trails around his house to clear his head. Saying goodbye to the Keepers that were still in the compound, he headed home.

He pulled into his driveway thirty minutes later, embarrassed to acknowledge he'd made the whole trip on automatic pilot, barely remembering anything. He slammed his SUV door shut and stalked inside. Changing clothes, he headed out the back door to the deck and down to the lush green grass, starting his run toward the beach that was at the back of his property. When he'd moved to Maine to accept a position with Mace, he searched for properties. Like many of the other Keepers, he preferred to be near the water and liked his privacy.

When the real estate agent said she had a cottage for him that included five acres of woods, he laughed when he met her at the property. The *cottage* was a large red and white house built on a slight hill surrounded by woods with a back deck that led to the rocky coastline below. A dock was built over the water, giving him easy access to his canoe, kayak, and small motorboat.

His feet pounded the dirt as he dragged oxygen into his lungs, hoping to clear his mind. But he should have known—the only thing on his mind was Josie. The pictures he'd perused confirmed she was as beautiful as he remembered although rarely in a gown at a gala. Her social media was limited, but there were photographs of her wearing basic slacks and blouses while standing in front of a small brick building that housed her clinic or at charity meetings. Her smile was easy, and he could see her comfort when standing with some of the elderly persons at the clinic. Her pale blue eyes always shone in the photographs, and he remembered what it felt like to be on the receiving end of her smile.

Turning away from the water, he weaved through the trees on the path he'd created. By the time he'd circled to the other side of the house, he ran down his pier and dove into the water, swimming around the bay that was at the mouth of the ocean.

The cold water brought all his senses back into line, years of SEAL training returning as he focused on the current. By the time he climbed up the ladder to the pier, his body felt refreshed even if his mind was still muddled.

"Did it help?"

Looking up, he grinned at the sight of Clay, Tate, and Levi standing on the pier. With water sluicing into a puddle on the wooden planks, he shook his head. "Not as much as I would have liked." Walking past them, he said, "Come on up to the house. Cold beer is in the fridge."

While his friends made themselves at home, he took a quick shower and changed into sweatpants and a t-shirt. Running his fingers through his hair, he joined them after grabbing his beer. The outside of his house had a traditional New England appearance, but the inside was anything but. The kitchen, dining room, and living room were open, one space flowing into the other, with two-story vaulted ceilings and a wall of windows that overlooked the water. While there was nothing southwest about his house, a great deal of exposed wooden beams, hardwood floors, and a stone fireplace gave it even more appeal.

The four men spread out on the comfortable sofas overlooking the water, drinking their beer quietly for a moment. He wondered when one of them was going to break the silence... his money was on Clay. He wasn't wrong.

"So, are you going to tell us why your eyes nearly bugged out of your head when you saw the picture of Josephine Rector?"

With his head leaned back against the comfortable cushions of his reclining sofa, he only had to roll his head to the side to peer at his friend. "Guess my poker playing days are over if I wasn't able to hide that reaction."

Tate snorted. "Hell, man, you couldn't have given away more if you jumped up and screamed, 'Holy fuck, I know her.'"

Levi had been quietly observing him. "To be honest, I was surprised you didn't recognize her name with both your parents being in politics from the same state."

He shook his head and took another swig of beer. "My grandfather was governor years ago, but with my dad working in embassies during his younger years, we were all over the place. I spent time in elementary and middle school in Greece, Spain, and Italy. By the beginning of high school, my dad was a U.S. Senator, and we were in D.C. Now, he's Governor, but I'm no longer around."

Levi nodded. "Makes sense."

"Yeah, but what doesn't make sense was your reaction," Clay prodded.

"Jesus, don't your women gossip enough? Didn't know that had been passed on to you," he quipped, knowing they wouldn't let up until they got what they wanted.

"Fuck, Cobb. We gotta know your head is screwed on straight before you head off on a mission."

He speared Tate with a glare, a stinging retort barely held back from flying out of his lips. Blowing out a deep breath, he sighed. "My head is screwed on straight. I met Josie once when I was back there the last time. It was at my dad's birthday charity gala. It was boring as shit as they always are—until I saw her. I didn't tell her who I was. She thought I was a bodyguard because I wasn't socializing, and I didn't correct her assumption.

We had a dance. Chatted a bit. End of story. I only knew her name was Josie and had no idea she was related to Senator Rector. Hell, I'd just met him for the first time that night."

"You say *end of story*?" Clay held his gaze, a question in his eyes.

"If you're asking if there was more, no." The other men relaxed before he continued. "But I tried."

Clay's eyes widened. "Shit."

"Nothing happened. She shot me down." Seeing the continued wide-eyed stares, he groused, "I just asked if she wanted to go for a drink and intimated that more could be on the table. She said I wasn't her type."

Tate sputtered from the sip he'd just taken, breaking the moment with his coughing. Finally gaining control, he stared. "Not her type. Did she say what her type was?"

"Truthfully? I figured she meant my heritage or that she assumed I was just a hired bodyguard who was there working. Neither supposition sat very well with me, so I said good night and left. Since then, I've thought it over and felt like I owed her an apology. I left abruptly, so it did make me look like an ass."

"What about now? Do you feel like you can work with her?" Levi asked.

"I can't imagine that you were happy with every FBI assignment or mission you were given, but you did your best. Same with me. I have no problem working with her but realize she may not be overly keen to work with me. Her father's the one hiring us, and I want to make sure she's safe."

Cutting straight to the mission, Clay asked, "Have you learned anything?"

He finished his beer and leaned forward, placing it on the coffee table. Staring out the window for a moment at the peaceful scene of green trees and blue water, he sighed. "She's an enigma, that's for sure. Public school upbringing, then she left New Mexico to attend university in Boston. Four years later, she attended graduate school in New Mexico. Social worker. Works in a clinic in Las Cruces and makes a very modest salary. Seems to live off her own money, but then…"

The others looked at him when he paused, and he hated the blush that he knew was coloring his tanned face.

"So, she's not a rich daddy's little girl?" Clay prodded again, already grinning. "And that's exactly what you expected when you met her at your dad's big-ass event."

"Fuck you." He slumped deeper into the sofa cushions, hating but knowing Clay was right. "Yeah. Her clinic was one of the ones being supported by my dad's charity event. I checked into her dad. He was an attorney before running for state senator. Not wealthy, but not hurting."

"So, how are you going to handle it?"

"First up… I'll talk to her dad. Then, when I meet her, I'll apologize. Let her know what I need to do to keep her safe while we try to find out who's sending the threats. She's a smart woman. She'll be fine with it."

The others finished their drinks, and with good lucks called out as they left, he headed into his bedroom to pack. Sylvie had his travel arrangements completed, and he'd leave on a flight to New Mexico the next morning.

That night, sitting in bed with his tablet open, he continued to study everything he could about Josie Rector. But it was her photograph that kept drawing his attention. Red-blonde hair. Light blue eyes. He remembered the flash in those eyes when he curtly ended the evening after she turned down his invitation to get drinks. *Oh, yeah... I need to apologize.*

Cobb stared out the window as the plane began its descent into the Albuquerque airport. The scene was familiar, having flown in and out over the years. The land was flat, with mountains in the background. Dry and arid, it resembled a dustbowl from the air until they neared the city. Upon arrival, Cobb took possession of a large SUV that Sylvie had reserved for him. A big man, he enjoyed the legroom while driving and liked the protection the vehicle afforded.

For his first stop, he headed downtown and parked near the capitol. Senator Rector's office was in a building nearby, and he found it easily. Walking into the reception area, he noted two desks, one closer to the door and one just outside the senator's office. Stepping to the closest desk, he smiled at the young woman who stared up at him, her eyes wide. He stepped back slightly, knowing his size could be intimidating.

"Jorge Cobb from LSI to see Senator Rector, please."

The woman blinked, and her silence was interrupted by another woman's voice.

"Carla!"

Turning, Cobb's lips twitched at the reproving gaze the older woman sitting at the next desk was throwing toward the younger woman. She looked up at him and said smoothly, "Mr. Cobb, you are expected. Welcome back to New Mexico, sir."

He didn't bother asking how she knew he'd been there before. The last name Cobb was not common in New Mexico, and yet with his grandfather and father's political careers tied intrinsically to the state, he had no doubt she knew exactly who he was. Inclining his head, he returned her greeting. "Thank you. It's nice to be back."

With a final searing gaze toward the young woman who was now blushing furiously, the older woman ushered Cobb down a short hall with several doors opening from it. One appeared to be a large workroom where a group of people at small desks busily typed at their computers or were on their telephones. Another door opened to an empty conference room. Turning onto another hall there were two offices on opposite sides, both doors open, exposing small spaces with only one desk each. Finally, he was ushered into the senator's comfortable office. Not opulent by any stretch of the imagination, it was well appointed with thick carpet underneath his feet, a wall of bookcases, and a wooden desk with the requisite wood and leather chairs in front.

Senator Rector jumped up from behind his desk and rushed around, his hand outstretched. "Mr. Cobb, I cannot tell you how glad I am that you're here. As soon as the threats started coming in, I immediately remembered that your father said you worked in security. I had no idea if this was something you could help with, but I gave him a call."

"Yes, sir. To my friends and ever since the military, I just go by Cobb, but if that's confusing, then you may certainly call me Jorge. Mr. Cobb always makes me think of my father and grandfather."

The senator laughed and nodded. "Please, you may call me John."

He moved to sit behind his desk, and Cobb settled into one of the chairs directly in front. The leather and wood gave the familiar squeak as he sat down, and he was reminded of the old furniture in his grandfather's office.

"I read everything that you forwarded to my boss, and we've already started the investigation. I want to make sure that I understand exactly what your expectations are. I'm prepared to serve as both the protection detail for your daughter as well as offer on-site investigation. My coworkers back at the LSI office will also be investigating."

John nodded, his head jerking up and down rapidly. "Yes, yes to all the above. Josie hates the idea of needing protection, but I know the threats rattled her. She does such good work but is now concerned since the bookkeeper, Caesar Castiel, has disappeared. While Las Cruces does not have the most crime in New Mexico, its rates are higher than the national average. The population can be worrisome."

"What specific population are you referring to? Her actual clients or those close to where the clinic is located?"

"She works with many people, but specifically the elderly. They are harmless enough, but the area she is in is rather... um... rough."

"I understand. And besides the missing bookkeeper, she made specific calls to determine the sources of some of the money coming in. If the threats are tied into the calls she made, then I'm not sure her clients are relevant to the threats, but perhaps the area she works in has people who would be willing to commit threatening acts for easy money."

John continued to nod. "Yes, this is what I fear. As far as the financial reports, I contacted my accountant. He recommended a forensic accountant that's here in Albuquerque, but I haven't given them her books to work on yet. I wanted a chance to see what your father recommended and what your boss wanted to do. The situation is all out of my element, and I'm willing to turn it over to those who know best. My main concern is my daughter's safety."

"I appreciate that, John. I'm going to drive to Las Cruces to meet with her. Does she know to expect me?"

"I told her that I had contacted Governor Cobb because his son worked for an investigative company and that someone would be in contact with her. She's nervous but doesn't want everyone to know what's going on. She's afraid the clinic will suffer and cares greatly about the clients." He cleared his throat, his gaze dropping for a moment before he looked back at Cobb.

"She didn't know what to tell the other clinic employees because she was trying to keep everything low profile. I... well, I suggested that she pretend she's dating whoever the investigative company sent, just to give her an easy excuse as to why you'd be around so much. She doesn't socialize much, so I figured no one would be the wiser."

Cobb rubbed his chin, his thoughts swirling at the knowledge that she wasn't going to know he was the person coming and yet they were supposed to be dating. Unable to come up with an alternate scenario, he sighed. "I'll go ahead and warn you, sir, that my protection detail will include scoping out her work and residence. I'll install security cameras and take precautions that she may find intrusive."

John waved his hand dismissively. "Jorge, do whatever you need to do to keep her safe. She might find them intrusive, but she's a smart woman. She'll see reason."

Standing, he reached over and shook John's hand and said, "I'll let you know what we find out."

A knock on the door sounded, and Cobb looked over his shoulder as a man and woman entered. Both appeared to be in their early thirties. The man had ditched his suit jacket and had his shirt sleeves rolled up. The barest edge of a tattoo peeked from underneath his sleeve. His features hinted at Native American, and his dark eyes shot between the senator and Cobb. The woman's black hair was pulled back into a tight bun, but her deep red lipstick emphasized the wide smile that did nothing to soften her severe appearance.

"Oh, Carmen. Tahoma. Come in, come in."

Standing, Cobb turned to the newcomers.

"These are my two senatorial aides, Carmen Martinez and Tahoma Starr. They are my right-hand assistants and work tirelessly for me, my office, and the state of New Mexico."

Cobb shook their hands, noting Tahoma's intense scrutiny behind his smile. Carmen held his hand a few seconds longer than necessary, her smile hiding a calculating assessment in her eyes. Cobb wondered if the senator had confided Josie's concerns to them even though Mace would have advised against it. As far as Cobb was concerned, no one was above suspicion, but his expression remained neutral.

"I'm so sorry to intrude," Carmen said, her voice smooth. "But we heard that Governor Cobb's son was here. I know you had business with the governor and didn't know if you needed us."

"Well, in fact—" John began.

"Just a social call." Cobb easily interrupted what he felt sure was going to be John's admission of his daughter's difficulties. "I had the pleasure of meeting Senator Rector at my father's birthday event a few months ago, and since I was visiting my parents, I thought I'd take the opportunity to say hello."

Carmen's red lips curved even more. "I do hope you'll consider meeting us for drinks while you're here in Albuquerque."

"I'm afraid I'm leaving right after this."

Her lips stayed curved into a smile, but the rest of her face was hard as she inclined her head. "Maybe another time." Turning to the senator, she said, "I'll be leaving for lunch soon, sir, and then have an appointment this afternoon. I'll see you tomorrow." With a last long glance toward Cobb, she walked out of the office, followed by Tahoma, whose tight jaw and narrowed eyes were noted by Cobb.

Mentally adding the two aides to his list of people to investigate, he shook hands again with the senator, who leaned close and whispered, "I realize you didn't want me to say anything to my aides."

"I think the fewer people who know what's going on is best. It makes it easier for an investigation to not be hampered by *anyone*, regardless of who you trust."

John held his gaze for a long moment, thoughts working behind his eyes before he finally nodded slowly. "I understand. I won't call Josie and tell her you're coming. I now realize that I need to step back and let you handle it, even though that goes against my instincts as her father."

"You're doing the right thing, sir. I'll be in touch," Cobb repeated from before their interruption. He walked out, nodded to the two receptionists, and climbed into his SUV. Turning onto the highway leading to Las Cruces, he had a feeling that while Josie Rector was smart, she was not going to like seeing him again.

5

"Mark, I'm telling you all I know. My dad says that he'll have the police check to see if they know where Caesar is." Josie tried to keep her voice steady, but her nerves were stretched taut and she was afraid of snapping.

Sitting at the small table in the break room, she rubbed her head as she spoke to the general practitioner who came into the clinic three mornings a week. He was young, tall, and thin, with bright red hair. He always seemed to be in a good mood and the elderly patients loved him.

"Well, if we knew where he was, it would be nice. For him to just take off makes no sense."

Josie pursed her lips but remained quiet. She'd expressed her concerns to her dad about Caesar's absence in light of her questioning the suspicious donations and the subsequent threats but had kept them from the others in the clinic. At first, it was because she was uncertain of the donation reports and the threats were aimed only at her. But with Caesar's disappearance, her father talked to an investigator, and she was advised to remain quiet until someone from security came to her. But she'd already told her nurse and best friend, Laurie Mitchell, before being cautioned to stay silent.

As for Mario, the nursing assistant, and Charlene Porter, the receptionist, she had no reason to involve them in the clinic's finances. Mario was in his mid-forties, married with four children, and he was dedicated to the clinic as well as his family. Charlene was young, pretty, and dressed in skirts that were a little too tight, heels that were a little too tall, and full makeup, but she was friendly, and the patients liked how she made a big deal over them when they came in. The only other person who worked in the clinic was Sally Garcia, the social work intern that only had a few weeks left on her rotation before she would be leaving, almost finished with her social work degree.

Rubbing the tight muscles in the back of her neck, she stood and left the break room, heading to her office. Laurie stopped her in the hall, a concerned expression on her face as she studied Josie. Her friend was a beautiful brunette, tall and leggy, always smiling, and engaged to be married in the fall.

"Hey, are you okay?"

"Yeah." She knew her voice sounded tired but didn't feel the need to pretend with her friend.

"Heard anything?" Laurie kept her voice low.

Shaking her head, she whispered, "No. Dad said that

I can expect to have an investigator come talk to me about what's happening. I assume I'll get a phone call or an email to let me know when he'll arrive, but I haven't heard anything yet. I just don't want anyone else here to know what's going on."

"You should take the afternoon off. You look tired."

"I admit that I haven't been sleeping well. Christ, Laurie, I haven't even told you this, but Dad said to pretend I'm going out with the investigator to give credence as to why he'll be around so much. It'll probably be an older, bald man with a big gut."

Laurie snorted but shook her head in sympathy.

"I mean, it doesn't matter. It's not like I've got some kind of dating reputation to uphold. But still, it's weird."

"Yes, but if it keeps you safe, that's all that matters."

"Well, at least it's already Thursday, and I only have a few home visits to make tomorrow. I might stay in bed all weekend with the covers pulled over my head."

Charlene popped her head around the door frame, her smile huge and her eyes wide. "Oh, my God, Josie! There's a gorgeous man out here to see you!"

She glanced at her calendar, wondering if she had forgotten an appointment. Seeing it blank, she glanced toward Laurie, who simply shrugged. Sighing, she followed Charlene out to the reception lobby. Her feet stuttered to a halt as she stared at the man who had crept through her mind over the past few months.

"Josie." He stepped toward her, a smile on his face.

His voice was just as deep as she remembered. Blinking, she stared, dumbfounded. "Uh, Jorge?"

"I took a chance that you'd still be at the clinic. I hoped you'd have dinner with me."

"Dinner?"

"Jorge," Laurie repeated, her eyes wide as she looked at Josie. Then, suddenly, her brows lowered as she turned back to him. A slight gasp slipped from her lips before she breathed, "Oh... Jorge Cobb."

"Cobb?" Charlene squealed. "Like Governor Cobb?"

"No," Laurie huffed, rolling her eyes at Charlene. "Like Governor Cobb's son."

The air fled Josie's lungs at Laurie's announcement of who the man was that was standing... no, *filling* all the space in her vision. Even as the others moved into the room and Charlene preened, Jorge had not taken his eyes off her.

He stepped closer. "I couldn't wait to get back here. Please, say you'll have dinner with me."

"But... um..." The alternate dimension she'd dropped into continued, and Josie shook her head in an effort to ascertain why he was really here. Sucking in a gasp, it hit her. *Dad. Governor Cobb. Investigator. Bodyguard. Jorge. Well, fuck.* Glancing to the side, she observed her lobby now filled with all the employees of the clinic, their faces full of curiosity, and for the moment she was stunned silent.

Laurie stepped forward, and with great exuberance, greeted him. "It's nice to meet you. I'm Laurie, best friend and nurse extraordinaire." After shaking his hand, she turned and pinned Josie with a pointed glare. "You were just saying how much you were looking forward to dinner with him. Head on out, and we'll make sure the clinic is closed up."

Grateful that Laurie had a cool head and kept her wits about her, something Josie was lacking at the moment, she nodded, her head moving in jerks. "Yeah... sure. That sounds good. Um... see you tomorrow, everyone."

"I'll grab your purse," Laurie volunteered and hustled down the hall, returning quickly. Handing it to Josie, she offered a hug and whispered into her ear, "Girl, if this is the *bodyguard* Jorge you danced with and let walk away, fate has just given you another chance. Damn, he's fine... and the governor's son!" Squeezing her tighter, she added, "Let me know what's going on as soon as you find out."

With her head held high, Josie walked toward Jorge, not saying anything until they made it outside. Walking to her car, she noticed a huge, black SUV was parked next to her and wasn't surprised when he leaned against it. *No, this wasn't fate. More like a royal kick in the ass.*

Sucking in a deep breath, her eyes pinned him to the spot. "Jorge Cobb. Governor Cobb's son. I can imagine your reasons for not wanting me to know your full name when we met at the gala."

"My reasons are that I prefer to be known as myself and not who my father is. Although, Jorge is the name my family calls me. To everyone else, I'm just Cobb."

Her eyes narrowed. "Wouldn't that be rather telling?" He smiled, and she tried to ignore the tingles running rampant through her body.

"Only to people in New Mexico. Outside of my

father being the governor, no one knows or cares about the name Cobb. It's what I was called in the military, and it stuck."

Shaking her head quickly, she said, "I don't even know why we're talking about what name you want to go by. What I really want to know is why are you here? Are you a bodyguard or was that another deception?"

"There was no deception, Josie. I work for a security and investigative company. I'm qualified to provide protection detail as well as investigate suspicious activity and crimes."

That news was unexpected, and she chewed on her bottom lip as her eyes cut to the side for a moment before returning to his. "You're the person that my father said would be coming to help me?"

"Yes."

Inclining her head back toward the building they just left, she asked, "And we act as though we're going out on a date?"

"Right now, it's best if no one knows what's going on. As far as I'm concerned, no one is above suspicion. I take it, though, that your friend Laurie knows."

She nodded her head slowly. "She's my best friend, and I trust her. But I also admit that I said something to her before I talked to my father and was given the direction that no one else should know."

"She thinks fast on her feet and covered for you very well."

In the light of day, she noticed his eyes were as dark as she had remembered, only little flecks of gold-rimmed the irises. He seemed even taller, but considering she was now wearing comfortable flats, her five-feet-three-inches made her at least a foot shorter than him. While he had cut an elegant vision in his tux, seeing him in jeans and a dark-blue polo that stretched over his muscles, showing off arms that looked like they could chop wood, rope cows, and cuddle with equal prowess, she was struck dumb, something that rarely happened.

"Josie?"

Blinking, she jerked, feeling her face heat. "Sorry, my mind is… I'm distracted… a lot is going on."

His gaze was intense but kind. "I know. I'm sorry to just show up here, but it was necessary."

There was no impatient macho-vibe from him. Instead, he seemed genuinely concerned.

"Come on, Josie, let's get out of here in case someone is watching from the clinic. I'd truly be honored if you'd have dinner with me. There's a lot we need to talk about."

Licking her lips, she nodded. "Okay," she sighed. "I need to run home first to feed my cat—"

"I'll follow you."

Jerking again, she narrowed her eyes, but he continued before she could object.

"I'm going to have to assess your house for security anyway. I might as well get that started."

"My house?"

"Yes, my protection detail will include your house. But we can talk about that later. We should get moving."

Again, his words were firm but not high-handed. She wanted to argue but knew he was right. "Okay. I'm not dumb, Jorge. But let me just say that all this seems like overkill. If I've stirred the shit, I need to be prepared for the smell."

His smile widened before he leaned his head back and laughed. She stared and her heart pinged just a little. He was handsome, but when he laughed, he was gorgeous. Turning, she opened her car door, mumbling, "You can follow me." Climbing inside, she continued to grumble. *He's going to be trouble, I can just tell.*

The drive to her house did not take long, but her nerves were frazzled by the time they arrived. He pulled into the driveway behind her and parked. He'd alighted from his huge SUV by the time she walked toward him, and they followed the concrete path to her front door. Like most houses in the area, she had no grass. The front yard was decorated with colored gravel, mostly tan and dark brown. A few scrub bushes and cacti offered the respite color.

Opening the front door, she was surprised when he took her arm and gently maneuvered her next to the door. "Wait here." He entered quickly and walked through the foyer, through the kitchen, and into the living room. She lost sight of him when he walked down the hall and disappeared through the bedrooms. Her forehead wrinkled as she tried to remember if she'd left any underwear in the bathroom. She pursed her lips, irritated at the strange thoughts that had flown through her mind since Jorge had resurfaced.

He walked back, his face a mask, unreadable. "Is everything okay?" She hated the sound of fear that she could hear. "Christ, this is ridiculous."

He cocked his head to the side. "Yes, your place is clear. And what is ridiculous?"

"I feel like I'm in some kind of TV show."

"Your safety isn't playacting on my part."

She held his serious gaze, wondering if she'd insulted him. Nodding, she busied herself by slipping off her shoes. Leaning against the table by the door, she lifted first one foot and then the other, sliding on her slippers.

He watched her carefully, then asked, "Would you like me to take my shoes off?"

She walked past him on her way to the kitchen. "No, that's fine. I just prefer having slippers on when I'm at home. It's more comfortable for me."

She opened the refrigerator and called out, "Melon!"

"Not for me, thanks."

She turned around with a can of cat food in her hand. Seeing his chin jerked back and his brow furrowed, she couldn't help but laugh. Laughing was not something she'd done much of in the past week, but she felt lighter with her mirth spilling out. "I'm sorry, I wasn't offering melon. That's the name of my cat."

Now, his eyes widened. "Your cat's name is Melon?"

"The first day I got her, she jumped up on the counters and got into everything. The next morning, I'd sliced some melon and left the rinds in the sink until I was going to come back and clean them up. When I got back into the kitchen, she was up on the counter eating the melon rinds. I started calling her a melon eater, and then shortened it to Melon."

Retelling the story, she could only imagine how it

sounded to him considering that it sounded ridiculous to herself. But she watched in fascination as his lips slowly curved, a smile overtaking his already-beautiful face. Letting out a slow breath, she remembered why she'd wanted to go with him the first night they met. And why she didn't.

"Once you feed your cat, we'll take my car and go to dinner," he said with ease.

"Instead of going out to eat, why don't we order in?"

He held her gaze for a long, silent moment. She wanted to squirm, not understanding his careful appraisal, but remained steady. Finally, he nodded slowly. "Sure. That'd be fine. You choose. I'll eat anything, but I pay. And when it arrives, I'll answer the door."

A muscle ticked in his jaw, and she wondered if he preferred eating out that much more than eating in. Sucking in her lips, she nodded. "Okay. Um… I've been craving pizza, and there's a good Italian restaurant down the street that delivers quickly."

Gaining his nod, she turned and made the call. Once completed, she realized Melon hadn't come into the kitchen. Placing the canned food into the dish, she called out again. This time, the cat came slinking around the corner, her eyes wide as they stared between Jorge and the food dish, trying to decide if its fear over the newcomer was going to win out over its desire for dinner.

Squatting, she tapped the dish and held her fingers out. "Come on, Melon. You don't have to be afraid." Jorge walked into the living room, and the solid black cat with one white paw finally sauntered over, rubbing up against Josie's hand before diving into her dinner. No longer seeing Jorge, she continued to rub her cat. Keeping her voice low, she said, "I know he's a big guy, but he's here to help."

6

While Josie excused herself to her bedroom to change,
Cobb stood in the living room. His hearing was exceptional, and even though he was sure Josie had not meant
for him to hear her speaking to her cat, he'd heard her
words. *I know he's a big guy, but he's here to help.* He
wondered if she was already resigned to allowing him
to do his job.

Melon had finished eating and then walked out of
the kitchen into the open living room, moving silently
from the tile floor to the pale wooden planks. Stopping
in the middle of the floor, she looked up at Cobb before
lifting her paw and began to wash her whiskers.

When he'd first moved through Josie's house, he
appreciated the clean, simple lines. Now, he took a
moment to look around. He'd already discovered that
she was renting and could understand the house's
appeal. Pale walls, cream-colored cabinets and granite
countertop, pale floors, and tall ceilings all gave a sense
of space, even though the house was not large. Three

bedrooms, one requisite bathroom in the hall, and a well-appointed main bathroom connected to the largest bedroom.

The lot was large and surrounded by a stone fence, completing the desert-style home. From researching before he came, he knew there was a small, covered deck area on the roof that afforded spectacular views of the mountains in the distance.

He walked over to the fireplace mantle to get a closer look at the framed photographs. Family pictures graced most of the frames. Josie, her father and mother, and a young man that Cobb knew was her cousin, Bert Rector. In Cobb's investigation, he'd discovered Bert's parents died in a plane crash when he was in college. He'd spent a great deal of time at Josie's house with her parents over the years, and after his parents' deaths became even closer. There was also a photograph of Josie, Bert with his arm around a dark-haired woman, and Laurie wrapped up in another man's arms. It didn't miss his attention that Josie sat slightly back from the others who appeared to be camera hogging.

He had just stepped away from the mantle as Josie walked down the hall, now dressed in black leggings and a turquoise-colored tunic cinched at the waist. She still wore the black ballet slippers on her feet. Her hair was pulled back into a ponytail, making her look even more youthful. She might've been thirty but could easily pass for twenty.

Before he had a chance to speak, the doorbell rang. He stalked over, looked out her security peephole, fought the desire to roll his eyes at the poor lighting on her front porch, and threw the door open, startling the delivery boy. Taking the bags, paying and tipping well, he closed the door and bolted the locks. Glancing down at the bags in his hand, he grinned. "It looks like you ordered a lot of food."

"I like to eat. And, well… you look like you can eat a lot, as well." As soon as the words left her mouth, her eyes widened and she slapped her hand over her face. "I'm sorry, Jorge. That came out terribly rude."

He shook his head and laughed. "Not at all. It's true, you don't get to be my size without eating a lot."

She waved her hand toward the wide granite kitchen island, and he placed the bags on top. Together, they unpacked the food and he discovered she had not only ordered two pizzas but mozzarella sticks, a small dish of baked ziti, extra garlic bread, and two large servings of tiramisu.

Eyes wide, he shook his head. "Damn, Josie. This looks amazing."

She smiled and walked over to a cabinet, pulling out two plates. Placing them on the island, she turned and retrieved spoons and forks. Silently, they loaded their plates with food. She grabbed two beers from the refrigerator and handed one to him. He followed her to the dining room table and waited until she chose her seat first. When she was settled, he took the seat that was directly across from her, wanting to be close but not crowding.

The meal was as delicious as she'd indicated. She didn't pick at her food but ate heartily. He never cared how much another person ate but found that some women seemed to be terrified of a man thinking that they enjoyed their food. For him, food and family celebrations had always gone hand in hand, so to see Josie eat with obvious enjoyment was nice.

After finishing, she pushed her plate away and leaned back in her chair. Sucking in her lips, she glanced around the room, her gaze never landing on him.

"We need to talk, Josie," he said, and her attention snapped to his face. He gave her a moment, not surprised when she finally nodded, although her lips were tight. Her father was right... she was smart and knew she needed help.

"Let's go to the roof," she said. "I can breathe... think... up there when it's cool in the evenings."

They grabbed two more beers after putting the leftovers into the refrigerator, and he followed her up the steps near her bedroom to the rooftop deck. The indigo blue of the evening sky with the craggy mountains in the background was breathtaking. They settled onto the deep cushions of a comfortable settee, and he sipped his beer in silence for a moment, appreciating the view as well as the company.

"I like coming up here in the evenings," she said, sucking in a deep breath before letting it out slowly. "Sitting on the patio downstairs just reminds me that this property has no grass."

"Less mowing that way."

She barked out a laugh and turned her head toward him. Her eyes lit when she smiled, and just like the first time he saw her, it was like a punch to the gut.

"You're right about that," she agreed. "That's one way to think about it." She looked out over the vista again. "It's the one thing that made me decide this was the place to rent."

"I'm curious why you didn't purchase a home."

He held his breath for a second, almost afraid she would be offended at the question. Instead, she shrugged and sighed, immediately answering.

"I don't want to buy a house until I've found that one place that I can call home." She took a sip of beer, waited another moment, and then continued. "I don't just mean an actual house, but I mean a place."

This was unexpected. He'd already learned everything he could about her from his early investigation, but her reason for renting surprised him. She shifted in her seat, twisting her body around, and tucked her legs up under her, looking at him. The movement surprised him, but it wasn't unwanted. He mimicked her behavior, and they sat facing each other, their bodies now closer.

"Am I to assume that you've already studied up on me since you're offering security and investigating this mess I've found myself in?"

Again, he was struck with her *no-bullshit* attitude. Nodding, he said, "Yes. I've learned as much about you as I can. Your finances... solvent and frugal. Your education... New Mexico and Boston. Your work... dedicated. Your social life—" He heard a slight gasp from her but kept going. "Your personal life from social media accounts... you're very private." Again, he steeled himself for her indignant response, but she simply looked away, her jaw tight for a moment.

Taking another sip of beer, she finally said, "Since you know all about me, then you know I was born and raised in Albuquerque. Even there, we had a house that had grass and trees. And I loved going to the east coast for college." Her smile returned and she closed her eyes for a second. "I still remember the first, deep snow in Boston. The brisk breeze, the lush flower gardens in the spring, and the deep green trees in the summer. I was lucky enough during high school and then in college to be able to travel to several places with school groups. Canada. England. Switzerland."

Her voice was melodious, soft, full of emotion, and he hoped she continued to speak freely. "I think I understand what you're saying. I was born and raised in Albuquerque as well, but as a young boy, my father was assigned to several embassies. I was able to travel to Spain, Greece, Italy, just to mention a few. It definitely broadens your horizons."

A slight smile curved her lips. "Exactly. While I love the southwest, I've never considered it to be the only place I can live. When I graduated, I wanted to be close to my family and there was a position to work with the elderly in Las Cruces. It was a job opportunity. I love it, and I'm happy here. But I'm not ready to say this is my forever home, so I don't want to buy a house." She tilted her head to the side and asked, "But what about you? Do you own a house?"

Nodding slowly, he smiled. "Yes, I do. My employer is based in Maine. And I admit that while very different from New Mexico, I discovered that the weather, lush forests, the ocean crashing against the rocks... it's exactly where I want to be."

"That's nice that you found that."

Her voice was wistful and yet sincere. So far, Josie was as much an enigma as ever.

Her smile slid from her face. "So, where do we go from here? What do you need to know?"

"Talk to me. I know what I've read in the reports. I know what your father told me. I've seen the initial bookkeeping. I know about the threats you received. But what's missing is you. You're the one thing that's central to all of this, and I need to hear from you what you found, what you discovered, what you said to Caesar, what's happened since."

She nodded, nibbling on her lips again. "So, just talk?"

"Yep. I'll ask questions as needed but just start from the beginning. You might even discover something that you hadn't thought of before."

Leaning forward, she placed her beer bottle on the floor next to her feet before resettling back against the cushions. Her hands rested in her lap but her fingers were linked together tightly. Sucking in a deep breath as though to cleanse her mind, she began. "The doctor who began the clinic years ago finally retired and moved away. While it's part of the Las Cruces medical commission for the elderly, we get most of our funding from grants and private sources. Since my father became a state senator, I've been thrust into the world of private donations more than I'm comfortable with.

But money talks, and we need money to help our clients."

"That's why you were at the gala that night. You were one of the charities obtaining donations."

Nodding slowly, she scrunched her nose. "Yes. I hate those events."

"Is that why you were standing off by yourself?" Her gaze shot to his, vulnerability exposed in her pale eyes. Knowing more about her, it was no longer strange that such a beautiful woman desired to stay out of the spotlight.

"When I was growing up, my father was an attorney in Albuquerque. He and Mom belonged to one of the country clubs, but I rarely went. I was the shy, awkward child who grew into a shy, awkward teen. I didn't need a lot of friends, but the few I had were very good and loyal. But I've never been comfortable at a see-and-be-seen event. Bert loves going. He's my cousin and stayed with us a lot when he was younger. He's the crowd-pleaser. Easy to converse with, joke with. Easy to make friends. My parents always respected my choices, but I knew it would help the clinic if I showed up in person that night at your father's event, although Bert would have been a much better choice."

But then I wouldn't have met you. He was thankful the words had not slipped out. He'd wanted to avoid talk of their previous meeting until he had a better sense of who Josie Rector was.

She took another sip and continued. "I relied on Caesar to do the basic bookkeeping for the clinic, and we have an accountant that takes care of the clinic's final accounting to maintain its tax-free status. Actually, it's my father's accountant. Henry Begay. He's from the Acoma Reservation. He and Dad became friends in university. I don't normally study the accounts and records, but Caesar had mentioned that we'd gotten donations from your father's event, and I simply decided that I should take a look and see who had donated. If it were people that I or my family knew, then it would be smart to make a personal thank you instead of just one from the clinic."

"Was Caesar surprised when you looked at the records?"

"I have access to the program, so he didn't even know I was going to do that. I stayed late a few evenings, and it didn't take long to realize that something wasn't right. Please understand, Cobb, accounting and finances are not my strong suit, so I can't give you dollar amounts and tell you exactly what would go where, but I knew things didn't look the same. Several donations came in from corporations that I've never heard of. People who've never given to us before. Okay, in and of itself, that could be seen as good. But when I glanced at deposits that were being made into our accounts, none of it made any sense."

"When did you talk to Caesar?"

She scrunched her nose again and chewed on her lip, her eyes sliding to the side. "Um... well, it was about two-and-a-half weeks ago. I called him into my office and showed him what I was looking at. He was always so easygoing, but his body language was off. It was hard for him to keep his eyes on me. His fingers were twitching. And he was perspiring even though the room was not warm. He kept trying to convince me that everything was fine, and I told him that I was going to dig deeper to see who some of the donations were from. I knew he didn't like that, but I chalked it up to him being offended that I was essentially checking up on him."

The more she talked to him, the more at ease she seemed to be. Her fingers were no longer clenched together, and she occasionally waved her hands when she spoke. Her words were clear and articulate, and her memory of the details excellent. Nodding, he encouraged her to continue her recitation.

"The next day was Thursday, a day that he wasn't supposed to be with us. I started looking up the new companies that had made donations and found that I was running into difficulty figuring out who they were and where they were. I finally got hold of one of them. ILT International. I spoke to several people, being transferred from one person to another until I felt sure I was right back to talking to the first person who answered the phone. I identified myself and why I was calling. Essentially, I was told that there was no one person at the company that handled donations and that I should simply accept the charity and be satisfied with that."

She leaned forward, placing her hand on the cushion next to his leg, her eyes boring into his. "But this is where it got interesting."

His breath caught in his throat, and as much as he wanted to hear what she had to say, it was the closest she'd ever gotten to him on her own. At the gala, it had been because he took her hand. At the front door, it had been because he wanted her to step to the side while he performed a security sweep on her house. But now, caught up in her tale, she was leaning near. Without makeup, he could see a few freckles that scattered across her cheeks, each one capturing his attention. Her pale blue eyes held him mesmerized, and her tongue darted out to moisten her lips. Always focused on a mission, he couldn't believe how distracted he was. "What was interesting?" He realized his words were almost a grunt but was surprised he was even able to make a sentence.

She jerked, then leaned back slightly, and he was both glad and hated it at the same time. He needed to focus on what she was telling him but hated that she'd moved farther away. Trying to soften his voice, he prodded, "Please, you were saying?"

"Oh... um... well, when I called two of the other companies on the list, the phone numbers were different, but I could've sworn the same person answered the phone. When I identified myself and told them what I was doing, they hung up. When I tried to call again, it went straight to voicemail."

"You think it was the same person, don't you?"

"Absolutely. The more I thought about it, the more I'm sure. And that's when I knew I'd stumbled onto something that wasn't right. I have no idea what they're doing, but I'm sure somebody was using the clinic as a way to hide or move money around."

He leaned back against the cushions, a long, slow exhalation leaving his lungs. He had no doubt she was right. Whatever those companies were doing, either Caesar was part of it, or he had stumbled upon it. "Okay, Josie, you're doing really well. So, what happened next?"

She pulled her lips in and pressed down, her brow lowered. "I saw Caesar the following day. I told him what I'd done, and he looked like he was going to be sick. He left early and then didn't show up last week at all. When he didn't come in again this Monday, I tried calling his cell phone but there was no answer. When he didn't come in on Wednesday, I tried calling again and got no answer. Then I drove to his apartment. He didn't answer the door. One of his neighbors came out and said that she hadn't seen Caesar since the previous weekend and that his car hadn't been in the parking lot. That evening, I found a note on my car. It was a folded piece of paper that said, *Just do your job.*"

"I saw copies that had been provided by your father."

"All left on my car. The first two came while I was at work, and then the next one when I was in the grocery store. That scared me because I realized someone was following me. I called Dad immediately. I didn't know what else to do. *Just do your job. Stay quiet and tell no one. Curiosity killed the cat.*"

Tears pricked the back of her eyes, and her nose tingled over the last one.

"Fucking hell, Josie!"

Swallowing deeply, she continued, "I know you're going to wonder why I didn't go to the police at first, but that note wasn't threatening. I actually thought it was left on my car by mistake. Then, with the second one, I felt sure it was tied into what I was discovering with the books, but I had no evidence. It was just a note that the police wouldn't have even looked at. And just because Caesar left, the police don't consider him to be missing. By the time I got the last one, Dad said he'd contacted an investigation company, and someone was coming." Her hands clasped tightly together. "You surely must understand. Being the child of a politician, you know that scandal, even the hint of it, is to be avoided. I wasn't about to call the police for something that wasn't an immediate emergency without giving my dad a chance to decide how to handle it."

He nodded. "I don't doubt what you've done at all, Josie, and you're right, I do understand. I'm just glad I'm here now. My people are working with an FBI liaison and I'll be in contact with them."

Tilting her head slightly to the side, she held his gaze. "Thank you."

"That's not all, right?"

"No. I've had phone calls on my cell phone and at work where someone just hung up. Someone in a vehicle following too closely. I was afraid things were going to escalate." She rolled her eyes and a little snort slipped out. "Dad wanted me to immediately come to Albuquerque to stay with him and Mom. Obviously, that wasn't going to happen. Dad told me that Governor Cobb's son did investigations, so I figured someone would get in contact with me before things got worse."

"You just didn't expect the investigator to walk through your front door. Or for it to be me."

By now, the brilliantly painted sunset that had

surrounded them while they talked had settled into the deep blue of the night sky. Stars twinkled overhead, but there was a slight chill from the desert around them.

She shivered and stood after snagging her empty beer bottle from the tiled deck. "We should go in." Without waiting, she walked to the edge and began descending the stairs. He grabbed his empty bottle as well and followed. The thought hit him that as much as he wanted to stay with her for protection, he wanted to be near her just for himself.

7

Josie walked to the sink and rinsed out her beer bottle. Aware of Jorge's presence behind her, she turned and took his bottle from him. Rinsing his, she placed them into the recycle bin. Leaning against the counter, she folded her arms across her waist, the discussion of recent events making her feel exposed. "So, what now? How do you proceed?"

He leaned his large body against the opposite side, crossing one booted foot over the other, his hands resting behind him on the edge of the counter. "Now, I provide a protection detail and work with my crew back home to see if we can figure out where the money came from. That will indicate who's behind the threats while keeping you safe."

She rubbed her lips together, her mind a swirl of tangled thoughts.

"Hey, don't worry."

His words cut through the chatter in her head, and she snapped her gaze up to him. He pushed away from the counter but kept a respectable distance, not crowding her. She was glad. The last thing she needed was more muddled thoughts. A hot, gorgeous man standing in her kitchen was already out of her norm. Clearing her throat, she said, "I'm not sure how *not* to worry."

"Let's begin with the investigation side of this. I'll go ahead and warn you that it may feel a bit invasive because while there are people that you trust, I won't. I'll take a look at the people who work at the clinic to see if I can discover any suspicious behaviors."

"Why would you do that? None of the workers have that kind of money."

"I'm just saying that sometimes there's someone on the inside that provides information or access. I have no idea if that's happening, but since it's a possibility, I'll check into it."

Her head began to pound as she wondered how this situation was going to interfere with her life.

"Josie, I know what I'm doing. Trust me."

A long exhalation escaped as she tried to find an ounce of calm deep inside. "Okay... so, you'll be checking into the clinic. What else?"

"My coworkers will continue to pore over the financial reports and dig to find out who owns the companies that are hiding behind layers. Lots of ways to launder money through charities, so they'll work that angle." He hesitated for a moment then added, "And protection."

She imagined suited bodyguards on TV that stuck close by, little radio earpieces stuck in their ears, glaring at anyone who came close. Very much the way Jorge looked at the gala. As much as that idea chafed, a tiny part of her wondered what it would be like to have someone as handsome as Jorge with her all the time.

"I'll add cameras here and at the clinic to keep an eye on your vehicle and doors."

A strange trickle of disappointment slithered through. His gaze was intense and she felt like a bug under a glass. "Oh… sure. That seems like a good idea."

"And," he continued, "I'll have to stay close. I'll be in the clinic with you during the day."

"How are we going to explain that?"

He winked, and a smug expression curved his lips. "I'm your new bookkeeper."

"My new bookkeeper?" she squeaked, her eyes bugging.

"Finance major. I know how to read financial reports, and with Caesar missing, you need someone. Our families are friends, and I volunteered to help out."

She pondered his idea, nibbling on her bottom lip. "But Caesar wasn't around every day. How will we explain that?"

"You want the finances thoroughly reviewed. Plus, since we're dating…" His voice trailed off, but his gaze stayed steady.

"Dating." She blew out a breath, wondering how she would ever pull off that deception.

"That's the easiest explanation as to why I'm at the clinic all the time. It also covers if someone sees my vehicle in your driveway or we're out together."

"But won't that look strange to the people I work with?"

"No, we met a couple of months ago at my father's event. At least that's the truth. And we can say that your father suggested that I work for you. That's another truth."

She nodded absentmindedly while analyzing his suggestions but couldn't come up with a reason why it wouldn't work—other than the fact that they'd have to pretend to be dating when they were around others. "I'm not sure people would believe that we're actually dating."

Something dark passed through his eyes, but she didn't know him well enough to understand what it was.

He shrugged as though he didn't have a care in the world. "Then we'll just have to be good actors. I can be convincing, can you?"

"Yeah, sure. But I'm not always in the office. I make a lot of home visits."

He nodded, seeming nonplussed. "Okay. I'll go on the visits with you."

Her brow scrunched. "I don't know if that's such a good idea, Cobb. There's client privacy, confidentiality—"

"I'll stay in the car."

"Oh. Um…" She couldn't think of anything else to say.

"Same as here."

Now, her brows shot upward. "Here?"

"I'll stay in my vehicle until I get a security camera on your place, so I'll be close."

Her breath left her lungs, and she slowly shook her head as she stared at her clenched hands.

He leaned forward, dipping so his gaze could land on hers. "What are you thinking, Josie?"

"That my simple life has suddenly gone haywire."

He reached out, his movements tentative as he placed his hand over hers. She stared at the difference. His large and tanned. His finger pads rough. A few scars dashing across the skin. Hers pale and white and small. A strange sensation moved over her. The warmth from their connection made its way up her arm and throughout her chest. Their hands together seemed right. She knew it wasn't true, but for a moment it was nice to pretend.

Suddenly, she looked up, shaking her head. "You can't sleep in your vehicle outside my home."

A door slammed shut over his face, surprising her. "Afraid of the neighbors? I'm sorry, Josie, I'll be discreet, but until we know what the threat is against you, I'm paid to stay close to my mission."

The reminder that he was here because her father paid him jolted through her, freezing out the warmth that had settled around her heart. His sudden irritation made no sense to her, but she refused to let him call all the shots. "Neighbors? Who cares about the neighbors? But staying in your vehicle is ridiculous when there's room here."

He blinked slowly, mirroring her expression with a now-lowered brow. "Here?"

Snorting, she waved her hand around. "You did a walk-through. You know there's another empty bedroom and there's a bathroom just across the hall. Why would you sleep in the car when staying here makes more sense? You'd be closer to your *mission*." She hated the slight sneer in her voice but hated even more knowing she was just a job.

"You want me to stay here, in your home?"

Huffing, she glared. "Jesus, Jorge, is that such a bad suggestion? You might hate the idea, but for someone who's supposed to be so great at protection, it seems like the best plan. But hey, if you can't stand the thought of being that close to me, stay in your big-ass SUV." She blinked back the sting of tears threatening to fall. "I'm heading to bed. You can make yourself at home or not. Your call. Be ready to leave for work at seven-thirty in the morning. We'll stop by my office, and then I'll do home visits for the rest of the day."

With that, she walked away, determined to not look over her shoulder to expose the tears that pricked the back of her eyes. Closing her bedroom door with a resounding click, she sucked in a ragged breath. She leaned her back against the door for a moment, working to squelch the heat that blazed across her face. Finally, swallowing deeply, she pushed off the door and held her head high as she stomped into the bathroom, mumbling to herself. "*Whatever! It's not the first time a gorgeous guy walked away.*"

She remembered high school taunts... *bookworm, nerd, geek, plain, boring.* She sucked in a quick breath, blanking her mind from the adolescent rabbit hole everyone occasionally falls into.

But standing in front of the mirror, she sucked in her lips and stared at the reflection, acknowledging the sting of rejection was just as prickly for an adult as for an adolescent. Giving her head a quick shake, she flipped off the light.

Cobb stood in the kitchen, staring at Josie as she disappeared down the hall and into her bedroom, the door closing resolutely. He blinked, then jerked his chin back. *What the hell just happened?* He had been pleased ever since she invited him to her home for dinner. They had talked about the case and the threat. She seemed at ease with him once they sat on the roof. Then she intimated no one would believe they were dating... *fuckin' hell, not that again.* Then she suddenly became angry when he mentioned sleeping in his vehicle. *Hell, she's the one who said I wasn't her type.*

She was twisting him in knots, but he had a mission to do. *And I'm fucking going to do it even if she's hot and cold. She doesn't have to like me... just work with me so I can keep her safe.*

In the middle of his internal rant, he felt something brush against his leg and looked down at the black, sleek, green-eyed cat rubbing against his legs. Reaching down, he ran his hand along her back, finding the fur to be as silky as it appeared. "Melon, I keep fucking things up with your mistress. Think you can put in a good word for me?"

The cat simply stared up at him, not blinking. He had no doubt the feline was saying, *"Keep your shit together, man, so that Josie won't get so mad she forgets to feed me."*

He was sure Josie never forgot to feed her cat. *Me? I may have just had the last meal she'll want to share.* He only pondered where to sleep for a moment, deciding to take her up on her offer. Going out to his vehicle, he grabbed his bag from the back seat and scanned the area. There was no activity on her street, nothing suspicious. Once inside, he bolted her door, checked the windows and other doors, then flipped out the lights in the kitchen and living room. One of the bedrooms was used for extra storage, several boxes piled up, a few pieces of disassembled furniture next to the wall, and a treadmill. The room closest to hers held a queen-size bed, chest of drawers, and comfortable chair with a reading lamp next to it.

He set his bag on the bed, then walked across the hall to the guest bathroom. While he'd gone out to his car, she had laid clean towels on the vanity. *Even angry, she's polite.* He showered quickly, pulled on a pair of loose-fitting running shorts, and headed back to the bedroom. He left the door open, placed his weapon onto the nightstand, and crawled into bed. He'd slept in a lot of places all over the world, from five-star hotels down to sleeping on dirt and rocks out in the cold. But right now, he found sleep was hard to come by with images of the beautiful woman in the next room running through his mind. *She might not like me, but I'll keep her safe.*

Sleep finally claimed him, and when he woke, it was with a cat on his bed, staring at him. Mumbling, "I don't feed you," he climbed out of bed and into the bathroom.

After a quick shower and dressing, he found Josie at the kitchen counter, shoveling in cereal while coffee dripped into a mug. "Hey," she mumbled, then swallowed. "Good morning. I've got some coffee ready, so that's for you. I hope you don't mind cereal for breakfast."

He had meant to rise before her, but the comfortable bed had eventually lulled him into a deep sleep. "No, cereal's good." He turned to the counter to see a box of Loopy Rings. Glancing at the red tint of her milk, it was easy to see she was a sugar-cereal kind of girl. He hadn't had kid's cereal in years but wasn't about to turn it down.

While he ate, she finished and rinsed her bowl before turning toward him. "Listen, Jorge. I owe you an apology."

Her hands twisted as they clasped together, a telling motion he now recognized. He started to object but she kept on talking.

"I'm sorry I was so prickly last night. I overreacted. Chalk it up to being tired, frustrated, a little scared, overwhelmed, out of my element… whatever. You're here to do a job, and I need to let you do it however you think is best. I'd like you to be comfortable while doing that job, but I have no idea what you need."

Again, with her, there was no bullshit. He might not always know what she was thinking, but she didn't play games. "Josie, you don't need to apologize. I know this is all stressful, but you're doing great. Yes, this is my job, but I was glad to volunteer to be here for you."

Jerking her chin back, she parroted, "Volunteered?"

Now it was his turn to jerk slightly. "My boss will assign some duties, but for missions, he gives us a great deal of latitude. We want the right Keeper for the job, and in this case, that was me. I not only know the area, but I understand the political and financial world. But when I realized it was you, I wasn't unhappy about that."

She nibbled on her bottom lip, another telltale sign that she was pondering his comment. Not wanting to give her more time to react negatively, he said, "If you've got travel mugs, I'll pour my coffee into that." Just as he hoped, she moved into action and soon they were out the door.

After stopping at the clinic where she artfully dodged the curious looks everyone was shooting toward them while she gathered the records she would need, they climbed back into his SUV and she directed him to where her first home visit was.

The neighborhood was older and had seen better days. The walk was cracked and the concrete steps leading to the front door listed slightly to the side. The screen door was barely hanging on its hinges.

"Um, if you want to wait, I'll be about thirty minutes."

"Okay," he agreed, still staring out the windshield

toward the front. "I don't need to know anything confidential, but what can you tell me about the resident?"

"We'll visit a couple of new people today that I have to evaluate for services, but this is one of my regulars. He's eighty-four, lives alone. His wife died over ten years ago, but his only son died of cancer about two years ago. His son was the one who came over and helped out, made sure he ate well, and took him to the doctor. His granddaughter helps out when she can, but it's not always easy."

"Do you think he'd be amenable to me fixing his screen door?"

He felt her stare and turned to see a little smile curving her lips. It made the beautiful woman even more beautiful, and he wished he could do more to keep the smile there.

"I'm sure he'd be very pleased, but you don't have to do that."

"I wouldn't have offered if I didn't want to take care of it." They walked up the cracked sidewalk together, and he carefully moved the screen door to the side as she knocked on the wooden door. Cobb could hear shuffling approaching from the other side before the door was swung open. An older man, his skin aged and wrinkled, with bushy white eyebrows and tufts of white hair sticking straight up from his head, greeted them. He smiled as soon his gaze landed on Josie, then looked over her shoulder and up, his eyes narrowing as they landed on Jorge.

"Who's he?"

"Mr. Velez. This is my friend, Jorge. He's helping me

out today. And we wondered if perhaps he could take a look at your screen door."

"My Rob would've fixed it if he was still here, God rest his soul."

"I know, and Jorge would like to see if he can get it to work right. Is that okay?"

Mr. Velez shuffled backward, allowing them to step inside the house. "I'd be a damn fool if I turned down free work." He stopped suddenly and looked back at them. "It is free, isn't it?"

"Absolutely," Cobb said. He stuck his hand out and waited for the old man to balance one hand on his cane and shake with his other. "It's nice to meet you, sir."

Josie and Mr. Velez settled into seats in the living room after he told Cobb where to find the tools. Retrieving them from the laundry room, he went to work. Just as he suspected, the screws were simply loose. Once tightened, he oiled the hinges, making sure the door opened and closed easily. Next, he checked the latch to ensure that it could lock when necessary. All the while, he listened as Josie chatted with the older man.

She found out when he'd last been to the doctor and listened patiently as Mr. Velez complained about the young doctor always being in a hurry. She checked his prescription bottles lined up on the kitchen counter with his most recent list of medications. She double-checked to make sure he had food in the pantry and that the delivery meal service that came three times a week with both breakfast and dinner included was still coming on schedule. And all the while, she smiled, patted Mr. Velez's arm, and listened as he talked of days gone by.

As they were leaving, Mr. Velez cackled with glee as he opened the screen door with ease. Shaking Cobb's hand, the older man held his gaze and said, "You done good here, boy."

Back in the car, Josie turned toward him and said, "You did, you know? Good, I mean. What you did for him may have seemed little to you, but it was a big deal to him."

"Hell, that was nothing. I was listening to the two of you talk, and all I could think of was how much better his life is to have someone looking after him who cares."

"Well, there's one thing about social work," she said, sighing heavily. "There's not enough of us to go around. It's not just here. Every state, every city, every county. Some people need services, counseling, sometimes just someone to make sure they're getting what they need. There's abuse, neglect, and making sure the elderly and the young are taken care of. And that only scratches the surface of social work."

He nodded but remained silent as they drove to the next client. Arriving at the apartment building that had seen better days, Cobb turned toward Josie, his jaw tight. "Please, for the love of God, tell me that you would not have gone in here by yourself."

"When going to visit a new client at their residence, we go in pairs. I'll often bring Mario with me. He's big enough that he would give someone pause. Plus, he grew up on the streets before becoming a nursing aide. Believe me, he can handle himself."

"Thank fuck for that!" Seeing a few unsavory characters hanging around the parking lot, he said, "Looks like you're stuck with me again. I hope that's okay."

"Of course, it is. If it wasn't, I would have brought somebody else. I have to get permission from the client to let you be in with us."

He nodded and they walked to one of the first-floor apartments. Knocking on the door, it was opened by a middle-aged woman, her head covered by a large bandana and an apron wrapped around her waist.

"We're here to meet with Mrs. Carson. I'm the social worker, Josie Rector. This is a friend who is with me but only if Mrs. Carson agrees."

"Friend!" the woman barked out. "More like a body-guard, if you ask me!"

"Huh?" Josie sputtered.

"Honey, this neighborhood? Believe me, someone like you would need a bodyguard around here." She opened the door further and waved them inside. "Come on in. I'm Julienne. My aunt said you'd be coming around."

Cobb reached out to place his hand on Josie's back as they entered, twisting around to glare at the young men hanging out in the parking lot.

"Aunt Maude? The social worker is here." Turning to them, she said, "You'll have to talk loud. Maude is deaf as a post."

"I can hear well enough, girl, if someone's saying something worth listening to."

Josie bit back a laugh as she twisted her head around to look up at Cobb. He grinned in return. Mrs. Carson easily gave permission for Cobb to stay. They sat on the sofa where he could keep an eye out the front window on his vehicle while allowing Josie to sit closer to the older woman. Julienne sat with them, taking notes since she was the person who would drive Maude back and forth to the clinic.

For the next hour, Josie pleasantly interviewed Maude, finding out about her family, her living arrangements, her meal situation, her medications and doctor visits, and insurance and financial information. By the time they left, Josie had assured Maude that the clinic would be able to assist with her medical needs and that she would work with Julienne to make sure that meals were covered for the week.

Cobb stayed focused on their surroundings but saw no evidence of a threat—at least, not to Josie. For him, spending the day with a woman who was as beautiful on the inside as she was on the outside and whose career was based on helping others, the threat to him was losing his heart to someone who'd made it clear that he wasn't her type.

8

Cobb ordered the security items he needed and made arrangements for them to be delivered to Josie's house the next day. He'd asked her to dinner again, but this time she offered to cook. He still wondered why she didn't want to go out, but a home-cooked meal sounded perfect, so he wasn't about to turn it down.

She didn't work over the weekend, so he planned to install the security Saturday at her house and then at the clinic on Sunday. Taking a few minutes while she cooked, he called LSI, not surprised when Josh answered. "Man, don't you ever leave?"

"You got me when I was just heading out," Josh replied. "Rick's taking over for me in a few minutes, but he's already here so you get us both."

"Good. What have you been able to find out?"

"Levi's working with the FBI on Caesar's disappearance, and he'll talk to you on Monday. The agent's name is Floyd Gomez. He's located in the Albuquerque office, but his specialty is fraud."

"Can't he talk today?"

"According to Levi, he's on an assignment that's taken him to Ciudad Juarez, Mexico. Something to do with the casinos there. But don't worry, he's being brought up to speed on this case and will get with you on Monday.

"As far as the bookkeeping, it's a fucking labyrinth. It looks like some of the newer donations have truly come from local businesses that were represented at your father's charity event. I'm still looking at those because I want to make sure, but nothing right now is standing out with them. There are three of the others that were listed as making donations within the past two months, and they're dummy corporations. Some dummy corps are buried so deep under legalese and more dummy corps that the typical person wouldn't be able to find anything. But two of these have fake presences. Of course, that's how Josephine was able to get hold of someone, which turned out to be a mistake. Or good, I guess, depending on how you look at it."

He hated that she was being threatened, but Josh's words made him more determined to not let her out of his sight.

"We're still digging, but I can report that one of them buried under a couple of other dummy corporations is tied back to an attorney in El Paso. Carson Wright. Who, with digging, looks like he's tied into at least one business in Ciudad Juarez, Mexico, right over the border."

"You thinking cartels?"

"Too early to say, but it's a real possibility."

Cobb paced back and forth in the guest room, nervous energy pouring out as he thought of Josie being in the crosshairs of a cartel. "Is there anything you can send to me to start looking at? I thought I'd take some time tonight and dig through what I can on this end."

"Hell, man, it's a Friday night," Josh said, then laughed. "Of course, I'm here working on a Friday night, so I'm hardly one to talk, right?"

Chuckling, Cobb shook his head. "Don't worry about me. Josie's put me up in her guestroom, so I'm close. She's also gone over the reports so I thought we'd look at things together."

"I'll send you what we've got, secure, over your phone."

"Thanks, Josh. Rick. Talk to you soon." Disconnecting, he shoved his phone into his pocket then stood looking out the window with his hands on his hips. Dropping his head back, he closed his eyes and slowed his thoughts as he calmed his heart rate. The best way for him to keep Josie safe was for him to not let anger and emotions cloud his judgment. Hearing the soft pad of footsteps coming down the hall, he walked toward the door, opening it as she approached.

"Hey, I didn't know if you were off the phone. Dinner is ready, and I'm just putting it on the table."

Smiling, he followed her down the hall, trying to keep his eyes off her perfect ass showcased in her leggings. The delicate scent of orange blossoms wafted past, re-igniting memories of her dancing in his arms, and his cock twitched.

Once in the kitchen, needing a task to occupy his mind, he asked, "What would you like to drink?"

She looked over her shoulder and smiled. "There's beer or wine. I think I'd like wine, please."

He found the wine opener and removed the cork. "I'll have the same." Pouring it into two goblets, he carried them to the table. She followed soon with plates piled with spaghetti topped with homemade sauce and grated cheese.

Sitting at the table, the atmosphere seemed to be much more comfortable than the previous evening. The scent of tomatoes and Italian spices filled the air. "Damn, that smells good. My Grandmother Cobb's kitchen used to smell like this."

"Your grandmother?"

"She was born in Italy, and her family moved here when she was just a tiny girl. She always said she learned to cook at her mom's knee, and I believe it."

Eyes wide, Josie stared. "Your grandmother is from Italy?"

His fork halted on its way to his mouth. "Uh… yeah. Is there something wrong with that?"

"Only that I've just served spaghetti to someone with a native Italian grandmother who is probably a phenomenal cook!" She stared down at her plate. "Now I feel bad. I should have grilled a hamburger."

Relaxing, he took another bite and grinned. Swallowing, he said, "This is fantastic, Josie. Seriously, my grandmother has nothing on this, but just don't tell her I said that!"

Her nose scrunched as she took a bite. "My grandmother was from the south. She taught me how to bake, which I love to do on my days off. Maybe tomorrow I'll whip up some of her chocolate pecan cookies."

Their conversation flowed, and after rinsing the dishes, they settled onto the living room sofa again. She tucked her legs under her and faced him, much the same as she had the night before.

"So… Jorge the bodyguard at the gala with the smooth lines. Now Jorge the governor's son and an investigator who can fix an old man's screen door. I'm curious. Who are you really?"

He wanted her to know but felt a trickle of unease at her possible rejection. Always proud of his heritage, he wondered what she would think of his family. "Growing up, it was sometimes hard to have the same last name as my grandfather, the governor. Or my father, the State Department employee, and then the governor. At least when my father became governor, I had already left home, and Cobb became a nickname… at least the part of a nickname I didn't mind."

Seeing her tilt her head in silent question, he chuckled. "The first Recruit Division Commander I ever had called me Corny Cobb."

She laughed, then tried to cover it up. "I'm sorry. I shouldn't laugh at you, but *Corny Cobb*?"

"You know how we like our corn served here… spicy with peppers. In the Navy, it was boiled and boring as hell. He overheard me complain one day and started calling me Corny Cobb. But hey, it was better than some of the other names people got stuck with."

She continued to smile, and he relaxed into the

comfortable cushions. "It wasn't until I finally got out of boot camp that I got to get rid of the Corny part of the moniker. And now that I live in Maine, going by Cobb feels right. But whenever I come back to New Mexico, it's just easier to go by Jorge. That's what my family calls me, of course. And if I'm out somewhere, it keeps me from having any notoriety."

"I can understand that. I imagine as a younger man, wanting some separation from your family's name was important." She hefted her shoulders in a slight shrug. "After all, I didn't give my last name at the gala, either."

He held her gaze, which was impressive considering he sighed heavily. He nodded. "Yeah... the gala. You can imagine my surprise when the mission came in. My boss thought I was the best because of my connections, but then I saw your photograph."

She covered her face, shaking her head. "Oh, that must have been an unpleasant shock."

He leaned over and gently pulled her hands from her face, holding her gaze. "Shock, yes. Unpleasant? Not at all."

Josie continued to stare, and her pale blue eyes pulled him in, keeping him mesmerized.

Finally, she cleared her throat and looked back down at her hands. "So, um... you joined the military. Was that to run away from what was here at home?" As soon as the words left her mouth, she grimaced. "I'm sorry, that didn't sound right."

He chuckled, loving the blush that crossed her face, making her freckles stand out more. "No, no, it's all right. It's a perfectly valid question since we're getting to know each other. But no, I wasn't running away from anything that was here. It was more like I was running toward something. My family had given me a wonderful upbringing. Strong and loving, with a chance to travel all over the world. With my diverse cultural heritage, it was sometimes hard to figure out where I fit in. When we lived overseas, it seemed easier. High school for me wasn't great."

"For someone who looks like you, that's hard to imagine."

Her words hit him in the gut. *What does she think about someone who looks like me?* "Uh… yeah. I was in ninth grade in a private prep school near Washington, D.C. when Dad was with the State Department. My Native American, Hispanic, Italian, and German heritage is worn on my face… and while our nation's capital is diverse, that prep school was not. I wanted to fit in but felt as though I didn't belong anywhere."

"That must have been hard."

He started to shrug and then stopped, holding her gaze. Her eyes held understanding, not condemnation. Hesitating for a long moment, he finally nodded. "Yeah… at that age it was."

She shifted on the sofa, drawing her left leg up and wrapping her arms around her shin, propping her chin on her knee. "When did it get easier?"

"I'd always been big… well, not so much tall as wide. Then, at fifteen, the beginning of my sophomore year, I hit a growth spurt in height but kept the size proportion. So, while the jokes turned to calling me the Hulk, at least I could put the fear of God in them. I'd glare and take a step toward anyone who taunted me, then laugh as they ran away."

Her lips curved. "I can imagine a younger you in school trying to find your way. I swear, I think that adolescence is the worst age."

They sat in silence, each to their own thoughts for a few minutes, and he wondered what high school had been like for her. *Cheerleader? Prom Queen? Most popular?*

"So, the military was next?"

The way she quickly asked the question, he wondered if it was to keep him from asking about her. Not wanting to interrupt the flow of easy conversation they were having, he nodded.

"Yeah. Much to my parents' chagrin, I joined when I was eighteen. I wasn't ready for college, even though I'd earned a year's worth of college credits from my AP classes. I needed to find my place in the world and college just seemed like it would be more of prep school. Joined the Navy. Finished my degree in finance while traveling the world on ship assignments. Got accepted into BUD/S—training to become a SEAL. Made it through, did that for years. Took an assignment with CIA Special Ops and met Mason Hanover. He got out, started a security and investigation company, and hired me when I left the military."

"Wow, you say it all so succinctly, like boom, boom, boom... there's my life."

He barked out laughter and shook his head. "I forget you're used to people analyzing their life for hours."

She reached and play-slapped his arm. "Can I help it if I like to listen?"

"Hey, you haven't shared about you," he fired back, grinning. "Well, other than you rent because you're not sure where you want to live, you have a cat with a weird name, and you like to eat."

Blinking, she reared back. "You shouldn't mention to a lady that she likes to eat!"

He grinned and wiggled his eyebrows.

Rolling her eyes, she glared. "Humph. Maybe I won't share."

"Tell you what. You tell me more about you, about high school, and I'll share more as well."

Shifting her gaze, she stared toward the fireplace. For a long moment, she didn't say anything, seemingly lost in thought as she nibbled on her lip.

He reached out and touched his finger to her forehead and she jumped. Her head jerked around, and she stared, wide-eyed.

"You were thinking so hard over there, I wondered if you even remembered where you were," he said, concerned.

"I was... I... well, to be truthful, I wondered what we were doing. You're here for an investigation. I suppose I'm no longer sure why we're getting to know each other."

He shifted his position on the sofa as well, getting a little closer. His arm rested on the back of the cushion. "Maybe if we'd never met before, this would be different. But we did. I fucked up and insulted you when I asked to go get drinks—"

"You did?"

Her pale blue eyes were wide. As a SEAL, he'd been

in water all over the world reflecting every color of blue imaginable. Deep blue, sky blue, grey and stormy, blue-green. But he'd never seen any blue the color of her eyes. And staring into their depths, he knew he could drown in them and be happy. Sighing, he nodded slowly. "Yeah, Josie. I fucked up. I pushed when I should have let you set the parameters. I thought I was being suave... a rescuer relieving your untouched drink and taking your hand to dance, but I really just wanted to talk to you." Her tongue darted out to wet her bottom lip and he stared, wishing things were different. "I'm truly sorry for coming across so pushy. I promise I can do my job and protect you. One thing I've learned about you is there's no bullshit. No playing games. It might have struck me as wrong, but you told me upfront that I'm not your type, so we'll keep it professional."

"Oh, Cobb, you have to know your type isn't for me," she said, her voice soft as her shoulders hunched.

His brow furrowed, and he leaned back. "Josie, what type am I, and what the hell do you think I can do about it?"

She pursed her lips as a deep blush rose over her cheeks. Letting out a ragged breath, she shook her head and said, "You really want me to say it? You need to hear me?"

"Yeah. Yeah, I do," he growled. "Tell me what the fuck is wrong with my type."

"Jesus, just look into the mirror, Cobb. It's staring right back at you every day. But I get it. There's nothing you can do about it, unless... I don't know... wear a bag over your head. Stop eating and get skinny. Don't shower and start stinking." She leaned back, her breath ragged as she snorted. "There's nothing wrong with your type, Cobb. I've just never had any luck with guys that are... you know... really good-looking."

He jerked his head back as air rushed from his lungs, uncertain he heard her correctly. "What?"

Throwing her hands up she repeated, "Good looking. You know... hot. Gorgeous. You look like a bodybuilder and a model all rolled into one. You're the kind of man who walks into a room and every woman stares as though they are starving and you're their next meal. Every man stares because you're the competition they don't have a prayer of winning against. The kind of man who expects women to fall at their feet because that's what usually happens. Want me to go on, or have I stroked your ego enough?"

Her words stumbled around in his brain, but her irritation was coming through loud and clear. "You think I'm hot, and that's why you think I'm not your type."

"My previous experience would prove me right."

"Well, Josie, I'm here to tell you that your previous experience is shit if any guy made you feel less. And I'm fucking glad to find out what you were thinking because I can work with that."

9

Josie's face burned with blush and she wished she could turn back the clock to where they were just talking about Cobb and not her mixed-up thoughts. *Jesus, I just admitted I think he's gorgeous, and I'm a loser.* But his words made no sense. *He can work with that? He can work with what?* Licking her lips slowly, her gaze stayed riveted on his face, uncertain of his meaning.

She uncrossed her legs, ready to stand.

"What are you doing?"

"I…" she croaked, then cleared her throat. "I think at this point perhaps I should head to bed. Let's pretend that we stopped the conversation earlier. Tomorrow we can focus on what you want to do with my house security."

His hand jerked out and landed on her arm, gently holding her in place. "No… no pretending, Josie. We're a classic example of two people not understanding the other and making assumptions."

"I don't understand."

"I thought you were... well... a racist... that the *type* you referred to was my heritage."

Gasping, her eyes shot open wide. "Oh, my God! No! I... I would never... that's not... oh, my God!" She bolted to her feet, jerking her arm from his hand as her mouth opened and closed rapidly. He reached out again, but she skirted around the coffee table, not having a particular destination but needing to move. She stalked to the window, her gaze staring out into the deep blue night sky. Her chest tightened. "I can't believe you thought that," she whispered, shaking her head slowly. Turning, she forced her gaze to his, surprised to see him smiling. "I'm so sorry, Jorge. So sorry that's what you thought. I can only imagine how difficult this job must have been for you, considering that you... well, you know."

He stood and with two steps made it to her, taking her hands in his and holding tight. "Shhh, Josie. Stop apologizing for something you didn't do. This was on me as much as you. It's my fault for making assumptions when you've been nothing but kind and honest."

She swallowed deeply, still feeling her face heat with blush but unable to take her eyes off him. Everything about him called to her. Broad, muscular shoulders and chest. Hair as inky as the darkest night. Deep brown eyes so dark it was hard to distinguish the pupil from the iris. Tanned skin with a dark beard shadow. Full lips that she was sure would offer a taste as addictive as any drug. *You're so beautiful to look at it almost hurts.*

"Funny, but I was just thinking the same thing about you."

She gasped, realizing she'd spoken out loud. "Uh…"

"Oh, no. No backing away. No more excuses or either of us making assumptions." He squeezed her hands still held by his. "But what I really want to talk about is your previous experience. I want to know who made you feel like you aren't gorgeous."

She tried to tug her hands back but he held tight, leading her back to the sofa. He sat first, and when she would have moved to the other side of the sofa, he pulled her gently down next to him. "It's not interesting—"

"It is to me. And anyway, I confessed my adolescent tribulations. Come on, Josie. Share."

She sucked in her lips as she thought for a moment. *Share? What have I got to lose? What could be worse than him thinking I was bothered by his heritage?*

"You talked about not fitting in while in high school. I felt that way long before. I was shy. Quiet. I was always the smallest in my class. I preferred reading instead of running around. I mean, I love being outdoors, but I wasn't athletic. Even in elementary school, I was the last one to get picked for a team. It always felt so horrible to be the last person standing on the side of the field, watching the team captains decide who was going to have to take me.

"I was called Skinny Minnie. My hair was a bit redder, and my front teeth were too big so I was called Snaggletooth. You know, by the time we get out of elementary school and into middle school, cliques have already been formed, and I definitely wasn't one of the popular ones. And starting high school was even worse.

By then, I was used to the taunts. Geek. Nerd. Bookworm. Loser."

His hand flexed, squeezing hers, and she once again looked down at their connection. Large against small. Tanned against pale. Strong against... strong. If there was one thing she'd learned over the years, she was not weak.

"You know teenagers can be assholes, right?"

She laughed and nodded. "Yes, they can be. I suppose you know that better than anyone."

"It was easier when I was in school overseas. So many different nationalities of students were in the schools that I didn't stand out. But yeah, it was different in high school. You know what's weird? My paternal grandmother was born in Italy and immigrated as a small child. But both my maternal grandparents were born and raised in this country. So were their parents, and their parents before them. And yet it was the Native American and Hispanic part of my heritage that caused the most insults toward me."

Now, it was her turn to squeeze his hands, her heart aching for the young man who'd felt the sting of word darts flung toward him. "I am so sorry, Cobb. My petty high school drama pales in comparison."

He dipped his head to stare into her eyes, and she couldn't have looked away even if she'd wanted to. "Nobody's feelings are petty, Josie. And your pain is every bit as valid as mine was. Tell me more. I want to know when the Josie that was made fun of became the strong Josie that is sitting in front of me now."

She sighed and relaxed into the cushions next to

him. "You don't look like the kind of man who watches chick flicks, but the Cinderella theme is pretty heavy in those movies. The geeky girl gets asked out by the gorgeous guy, usually because it was a bet that he wanted to win. But in the movies, they become friends, and by the end, she's had a makeover and is gorgeous. Very cliché and not a particularly good message for young women. But I can tell you, that didn't happen to me.

"The only time guys wanted to be around me was when they needed a study partner that would give them the answers. I was asked to the prom when I was a junior by a popular guy. I thought it was special. I was finally starting to get a few curves. My hair was thick and wavy, and my mom showed me how to wear light makeup. I went to the prom feeling good about myself, then found out it was because of a dare to ask the geeky girl to prom, and that was me. I was pissed, refused to kiss him, and called my cousin to come to take me home early. I'm afraid that pretty much summed up my high school experience."

"Is that why you went far away for college?"

Her brow scrunched, and she nodded. "Looking back, yes. At the time, I just felt the desire to see new things. I'd been on a few trips and knew there was a world outside of New Mexico that I was longing to see. I got a scholarship to a college in Boston and loved it. In college, there were lots of geeks. Bookworms. I didn't feel like the shy girl that nobody wanted to talk to. I had friends, studied hard, and came out of my shell. I suppose I finally gained confidence."

His top teeth landed on his bottom lip, snagging and holding her attention. Her fingers itched to reach up and trace the flesh, but the evening had brought up a lot of emotions, and she didn't want to make a move that could be misinterpreted.

"Did you ever think about staying on the East Coast?" he asked, jerking her attention away from his lips back to his words.

"Absolutely. I looked at a lot of graduate programs, but I think I felt a pull to come back home. My dad's brother and his wife were killed in a plane crash, and my cousin moved in with my parents as he finished college in Albuquerque. He'd always been good to me, and I wanted to be available to him. So, I came back to the university in Albuquerque for my graduate program. I could have looked elsewhere for a job but pretty much took the first one that came along."

They sat in silence for a moment, hands still clasped, his thumb gently rubbing over her knuckles. The motion was soothing, and she reveled in the ease she found in talking with him. A comfort that she didn't find with most people.

"Tell me about the night we met."

Her chin jerked back before her head tilted to the side. "The night we met? The gala?"

"Yeah. I want to hear from your perspective."

"I don't understand what you're asking, Cobb."

"I know what I thought when I saw you. I want to know what you thought."

"Um…"

He shifted slightly on the sofa, maintaining their

distance while facing her more fully. She chuckled and shook her head slightly. "You know, if you want me to talk to you... about you... you probably should be on the other side of the room. This close, you're a distraction."

"Good." He grinned. "I like knowing I'm a distraction."

Rolling her eyes, she said, "Are you sure you don't want me to just stroke your ego some more?"

His smile dropped slowly as he held her gaze, pulling her in. "No. No ego-stroking. Just honesty."

She bit the corner of her lip, knowing that she was exposing more of herself. *The same thing I ask of clients all the time. Talk to me. Tell me about your life. Let me in.* Swallowing deeply, she lifted her shoulders in a shrug.

"I really hate events where I don't know anyone. I knew my parents, of course, but that was all. Sometimes Bert comes with us, and at least then I have someone to talk to. But he was busy, and my parents were making the rounds, and I felt like a bump on a log. At least at that venue filled with dark corners and dinosaurs, I could find a place to feel less conspicuous. And you were right about the champagne. I wasn't in the mood to drink but having something in my hand felt better than twiddling my thumbs."

"When I saw you standing there, it was your dress that first caught my attention because you weren't facing me. But as you moved slightly, the material changed from silver to blue. I was mesmerized."

She laughed and said, "I love that dress. It reminds me of a mermaid."

"Yes! I'm afraid I didn't think of mermaid, but I was thinking of fish scales in the way they can shimmer in different light."

She snorted, then slapped her hand over her face. "I'm not sure most women would be flattered knowing they look like a fish."

Now he was the one who blushed, and she couldn't take her eyes off the way his tanned cheeks turned rosy.

"God, you're right. But I've spent a lot of time in the water, so trust me when I say it's a beautiful compliment."

"I'll have to take your word for that. I just wanted to get to the end of the night where I could thank people for their donations before going home. And then you showed up. At first, I wondered if you were simply a figment of my imagination. You were bigger, broader, more handsome than any man in that room." She dropped her chin and moaned, "I can't believe I asked if you were a bodyguard, but you looked just like the ones in movies."

"Don't apologize for that."

Her head jerked up.

"Seriously. I've never been a bodyguard like that, although protection details have been part of our missions."

"You just didn't look like the typical man there, flaunting wealth, wanting everyone to see you. Then you recognized that I didn't want the champagne. Taking it from me seemed presumptuous at first, but you were right."

"And dancing?" he prompted.

His dark eyes held hers, and desire pooled through her. Dragging her focus onto his question, she admitted, "I liked that you didn't pull me out where everyone could see us. Being in your arms in our own little corner was nice. But I couldn't figure out why. I'm no longer the confidence-lacking young girl but neither am I hogging for public attention. When you suggested we leave, I wondered if I was just a convenient, easy girl to proposition."

"Shit," he breathed, shaking his head. "I was an ass. Honest to God, I never thought that. You intrigued me... the most beautiful woman in the room, off by herself. Dancing, you seemed confident, and all I could think about was how much I wanted to get away from the party."

"And the dinosaurs?" she asked, trying to keep from giggling.

"Yeah, especially the dinosaurs." His smile widened, showing white teeth. "I wanted to be away from all the people so I could spend more time getting to know you."

As a memory slammed into her, she gasped. "That's when I said you weren't my type. I meant that I wasn't the socialite you probably thought I was. I never meant it to be negative about you."

"And to think that if this mission hadn't come along, we'd have never had a chance to correct our misconceptions."

Her lips curved at the same time his did, and she knew their smiles were mirrored. "Then I'm glad. Well, not glad someone is using the clinic to misuse a charity for their own gain—"

"Hell, Josie, I'm not glad someone is threatening you!"

Sucking in her lips, her chest depressed in a huge sigh. "Yeah, that too." With him so close, it was a struggle to keep her mind from becoming foggy with the thought of leaning closer to see if his lips were as soft and strong as she imagined. Clearing her throat, she asked, "So, tomorrow? Cameras?"

As though his thoughts had to be brought back to the mission, he gave his head a little shake. "Yes. I'll get something on your windows and doors. It'll be able to be monitored by LSI in Maine as well as from my phone. Then, on Sunday, we'll do the same with the clinic."

Suddenly, every limb felt weighed down. She lifted her hand and rubbed her temple, a headache blooming.

"You're exhausted, Josie. Go on to bed, and I'll lock up the house."

She couldn't think of a reason to not do as he suggested, so she nodded. Standing, she walked to the entrance of the hall and stopped to look over her shoulder. "You'll be here in the morning?"

"Right here."

"Okay." With nothing else to say, she headed to bed, the changes in her life over the past few weeks, much less the last twenty-four hours, filling her mind. But as she fell asleep, it was with the calm peace of knowing she felt safe with him.

10

The next morning, Cobb woke early, having slept fitfully. As comfortable as the bed was, the knowledge that the beautiful woman, who he realized was only hesitant around him because she considered him to be handsome, was in the room right next to his. It wasn't easy to go to sleep when his cock was rock hard. The idea of jerking off ran through his mind in the middle of the night, but he refused to give in to the urge. *I was a fuckin' SEAL. I can control my body... at least, I could before Josie was around.*

By the time he was dressed, the scent of bacon and coffee drew him down the hall. Turning the corner, his feet stumbled to a halt at the sight of her in tight yoga pants, bending over with her ass in the air as she pulled something out of the oven. She placed it on the stovetop and then bent again to close the door. If he thought he'd managed to get his cock under control the previous night, it stirred to life once again. He wondered if he was going to have a perpetual hard-on during the entire mission. Hoping his voice didn't croak, he cleared his throat. "Good morning."

She looked over her shoulder and smiled. "Good morning."

Her thick hair was held away from her face with a wide band, her skin glowing and her lips tinged a light pink. Suddenly unable to think of anything to say, he asked, "Are you always up this early?"

Her eyes widened. "Oh, I'm so sorry if I woke you! I was trying to be quiet."

Feeling like an ass, he shook his head, hating that her smile had dropped from her face. "No, no. You're fine. I just wondered if you ever slept in." Her smile returned, and it speared straight through him.

"Melon likes to be fed at the same time every day. If I'm not up, she jumps on the bed and stares at me, batting at my face. Anyway, I had decided to make biscuits for you this morning, just the way my grandmother made."

He glanced past her and spied what she'd lifted from the oven. A cast-iron pan filled with fluffy biscuits. The bacon had already been cooked, sitting by the side of the stove. Using another pan, she cracked several eggs and quickly scrambled them, adding cheese right before dividing them onto two plates.

"I've already got juice on the table, but you'll need to fix your coffee." Her nose scrunched, and she added, "I need to see how you take it."

"There's no need for you to do that. I can fix my own coffee."

She shrugged and grinned. "Yes, but if we're going to

pretend to be dating, I should probably know those kinds of things."

He felt foolish having not thought of that himself. Being around Josie was a distraction even when he thought she didn't like him. Ever since last evening's revelations, he now found his mind settled firmly on the beautiful woman instead of the mission. Walking over to the counter to pour a mug of coffee, he scrubbed his hand over his face. *I have got to get my fuckin' act together!*

While she finished plating the food, he thought about his fellow Keepers. Every one of them had found love while on a mission. His closest friend, Clay, had fought the idea of having to deal with drama while working, but even Christina had landed in the middle of Clay's case. Cobb wasn't opposed to the idea of falling for someone he was protecting, but now, he couldn't imagine how they kept their focus.

"Are you just going to stare at that mug of coffee or are you going to come to eat breakfast?"

He jerked around to see Josie sitting at the table, a wide smile on her face. *Christ, this is ridiculous!* "Sorry," he mumbled. "Guess I need to get caffeinated."

As he sat down at the table, she leaned over and peered into his mug. "Black?"

"Black," he confirmed. Having already looked at her cup the previous day, he inclined his head toward her mug. "Two sweeteners, heavy on the flavored cream. And from looking in your refrigerator, you're partial to caramel, mocha, or hazelnut."

Laughing, she nodded. "I do have a sweet tooth!"

Digging into breakfast, he moaned in delight over

the fluffy biscuits coated in butter and strawberry jam. "Your grandmother taught you well."

"Thanks, but I can only imagine the culinary delights that have come from your family."

He chewed, enjoying every bite, then swallowed as he nodded. "More like food wars. My dad grew up with his mom's Italian cooking, and then my grandfather would insist on Vanillekipferl cookies every Christmas because he remembered his German grandmother making them."

"Wow, what a name. I've never heard of them."

He chuckled and shook his head. "They're vanilla crescent-shaped cookies. Granddad would say they were from Germany originally, then my grandmother would argue that they came from Italy. I just know I like them."

"What about your mother's side of the family?"

Grinning, he said, "That's where I got my love of Tex-Mex, from my grandfather. He was born and raised outside of El Paso, in a little Texas town called Canutillo. My grandmother was born on the Mescalero Reservation but left to attend college. She's an artist and met my grandfather who owns a small art gallery. Her artwork is beautiful, but she also makes the best fry bread I've ever eaten."

Josie had stopped eating while her gaze stayed pinned on him, her elbow on the table and her chin resting on her hand. A smile played across her lips. He reached over and brushed a non-existent biscuit crumb from her mouth just to have an excuse to touch her lips. They were as soft as he had imagined.

"Eat up," he said as an idea popped into his mind. "It shouldn't take me long to get the security up and running here. How would you like to take a trip this afternoon?"

"Sure," she enthused. "Where?"

"We can drive to the reservation. I haven't been in a while, but there's a lot to see. There's even a casino and resort, but I'd like to show you the land."

Eyes wide, her smile brightened. "I'd love to!" She glanced between their plates. "It won't take long to clean up from breakfast and then I can help you. I might as well know what security is on my home anyway."

By lunchtime, he had installed the cameras on the outside of her home, including the garage. Many of her windows had decorative bars over them and considering they had been embedded into the concrete of the walls, he determined they were safe. For the picture windows with no bars, he wired them with alarms. Josie had followed him around, handing him tools and asking questions about the equipment. While he checked the systems with LSI, she showered, then he cleaned up while she fixed sandwiches and chips for lunch.

Soon, they were in his SUV on the way to the Mescalero Reservation. Las Cruces was flat with snow-topped mountains looming majestically in the background. While he loved Maine, the state of his birth had a breathtaking appeal. "It'll take about two hours to get there, but we can walk around and then have dinner there if you'd like."

She smiled her agreement, and he jerked his attention back toward the windshield. He'd never had such a visceral reaction to a woman before, from the moment he spied her at the gala to now, sitting beside him. Once he became a SEAL, women had not been shy about what they thought of his looks, his muscular physique, or his job. But it had been years since he felt any real desire. Scratch an itch occasionally? Sure. But true interest? Not so much.

As he'd met the women his fellow Keepers fell for, he recognized a spirit amongst them. Strength. Character. Beauty. Brains. And for himself, he'd never found that... until Josie.

"Tell me about your grandmother."

Her question jerked him from his musings. Grinning, he said, "She tells of a difficult life there, although with the casino and resort now on the reservation, it brings in money and jobs, two things that are often missing. As an Apache girl, when she turned fourteen, she had a ceremony that lasted for four days. A Sunrise Ceremony. There she was given the name Leosanni. She uses that as her professional artist name."

"She didn't stay on the reservation?"

"No, she was offered a college scholarship. Art was her passion, and she wanted to learn as much as she could, keeping with the old traditions as well as learning new. She's full-blooded, and since my blood quantum is one-fourth, I'm also considered a Mescalero Apache."

He glanced over, seeing her lips pinch tight. "What are you thinking?"

She sucked in a deep breath and shook her head slowly. "I know there are reasons... I can't begin to understand everything historically, as well as now, but to need to have your ancestry proved by blood..." She sighed, her voice trailing off.

"My grandmother tells that it was hard to decide if she should leave or stay. But ultimately, it was her mother that pushed her out the door. There was an independent spirit about my great-grandmother, and for a woman in the 1970s to be able to leave for a college scholarship... well, her mother said it was too great an offer to turn down. But then she met my grandfather, a non-Native, and her life became having one foot in two camps, belonging to both and neither."

"And your mother?"

"She is half-Apache, accepted as part of the tribe, but her life has been completely outside other than visits to her grandparents when they were still living. Now, she never goes back. Me? I go sometimes because I need to remember my heritage, but I know the reservation today is very different from the one my grandmother grew up on."

"Because of the resort and casino?"

"Yeah, in some ways. More jobs. More money. And yet more thefts and crimes."

By now, they were driving through the White Sands National Park and the road was covered with a layer of constantly blowing sand. Mountains still rose in the background but all around were dunes of gypsum sand, the scene appearing almost as driving through snow. There were areas of flat where vehicles parked, their occupants walking up the dunes.

"This is so amazing. I've been here before but not

since I was a teen," Josie admitted. "I swear, it seems like, in recent years, all I've done is work."

"No recent travels?"

She sighed and shook her head. "No, and I really miss seeing new places." Her voice was wistful.

Taking a chance, he said, "You should check out Maine sometime. See the beauty of the northeast again." His breath held in his lungs as he waited to see her reaction. She was quiet but a smile graced her lips. He counted that as a win.

Once they passed the dunes, they neared the reservation and the topography changed again. Scrub brush gave way to trees and grass. In the distance, a blue lake nestled at the bottom of a green hill. After driving around and looking at some of the untouched areas of the reservation, they made their way along a winding road until a massive building rose in the background. "That's the Inn of the Mountains Gods, the resort and casino. I thought we could have dinner there."

Alighting from the SUV, they walked along a path until they came to the patio that gave a panoramic view of the lush, tree-covered hills.

Both sucked in deep breaths at the same time, then looked at each other and laughed. "Is this what you think of when you're in Maine?" As soon as she spoke, she quickly shook her head. "I know the forests are thicker there, so it's not the same. But, I mean, just being able to feel like you can breathe?"

"Yeah." It surprised him how succinctly she was able to put his feelings into words. "I could never feel at home in a big city… or even a house in a suburb. I need space. Trees. Greenery. Water."

She remained quiet, but he could feel unasked questions rolling off her. He reached down and linked his hand with hers, hoping she wouldn't pull away. She glanced down at their connection before lifting her gaze and offering a blinding smile. "Come on." He tugged her around to a place where they could sit alone on the grass and stare at the vista without others crowding around. They sat in silence, still connected by their fingers with his thigh resting alongside hers for several long moments, allowing the breeze to move over them, whispering deep inside. Collecting his thoughts, he loved how she gave him that, seeming to know the quiet was what he needed.

"I come here rarely, wondering what I'll feel," he began. "I do feel a connection to the land. I've studied the culture and taken it in as much as I can, still knowing that I will never understand what it was like to grow up here as my grandmother did. I'm not alone, though. Almost eighty percent of Native Americans don't live on reservations. But sometimes, I do think of all the heritages that have blended together to create me. I've already told you that it was difficult as a teenager to be so different, but I think that helped make me who I am. The military gave me the chance to proudly serve with others who didn't care what my grandparents' heritage had been. My SEAL team, in particular, gave me a brotherhood I'd never had before. And now, the LSI Keepers continue that tradition. So, I can come here and love the view, respect the culture, and hope to one day teach my children inclusivity along with their diverse heritage."

She leaned closer, her shoulder now touching his. "I think that's lovely, Jorge."

He turned his head, her face so close to his. Her pale blue eyes reflected the blue of the sky, and his breath caught in his throat. Her gaze dropped to his lips and the slight inhalation sounded like a clap of thunder to his ears. With no hesitation, he closed the scant distance, sealing his mouth over hers.

He had no plan after giving in to the urge to kiss her, but the instant they connected, all other thoughts flew from his mind. The scent of orange blossoms mixed with the taste of her that exploded on his tongue as he sought and received entrance. Sweeping the inside of her mouth, he groaned... or maybe swallowed the sound from her, but either way, he angled his head for greater access. Her body shifted toward him, and he easily lifted her onto his lap. She plastered her front to his, arms wrapped around his neck.

To him, this was not the gentle first kiss of two people just getting to know each other but the all-encompassing kiss of two halves fitting together. With what little blood was left in his head, he hoped she felt the same, but as most of it rushed to his cock, he wished they were somewhere private instead of on a grassy hillside overlooking the beauty of the land with a massive resort just behind them.

His hands slid around, skimming the sides of her breasts and upward to cup her face. Tongues danced the way lovers had kissed for centuries. Just as he started to lean back, pulling her down on top of him, a door opened from somewhere in the distance and the chatter of others met his ears. He pulled back just an inch, hearing her gasping as he dragged oxygen into his lungs, their foreheads still touching.

After a moment of willing his cock to come under control while not wanting to let go of the beautiful woman in his arms, he finally inhaled deeply through his nose before pulling back enough to peer into her eyes.

"Wow," she breathed, her smile pinning him to the earth as his heart soared into the sky.

"Yeah… wow." He wished he could come up with something profound to say, but words fled. Finally, he said, "Are you hungry?"

She laughed and nodded. "Actually, I am. Although what we were doing could trump eating any day."

Chuckling, he nodded. Lifting her off him, he stood and then carefully pulled her to her feet. Tucking a wayward strand of hair behind her ear, he bent and kissed her lightly. "We'll skip the buffet that most of the families and casino players hit and go to the steak restaurant inside."

She smiled up at him, and this time, she linked hands with him.

Josie looked over at Cobb, her mind in a whirl. After a delicious steak, complete with a baked potato loaded with butter just the way she liked it, broccoli, rolls, wine, and dessert, she would normally be in a food coma. But tonight, all she could think of was the man sitting across from her.

While she had certainly met many accomplished men, Jorge was by far the most interesting. Intelligent, educated, well-traveled, and worldly. Drop-dead gorgeous with the body that could easily grace the cover of a magazine… or a romance novel. And yet so humble. He was self-assured without conceit.

She'd seen the way women's eyes had followed him as they walked through the restaurant, and yet his fingers stayed on her back and his gaze never strayed away from hers. It was as though he wasn't even aware of his own appeal.

"What are you thinking about?"

She startled, then felt her cheeks heat with blush.

"I'm afraid you caught me lost in thought." Wincing, she rushed, "It's not you. To be honest, I was thinking about how much I enjoyed this day with you."

His white teeth gleamed as his smile widened. "I'm glad to hear it because I was thinking the same thing."

As they walked into the lobby, she glanced around, spying the ladies' room door. Turning to him, she whispered, "If we have a two-hour ride home, I'd better run to the restroom."

He nodded and agreed. "I'll do the same and meet you back here in the lobby."

For once, there was no line in the ladies' room, and she soon finished her business and stepped out. Not seeing Jorge, she walked over to one of the many storefronts and perused the items in the window.

"Josie?"

Turning, she spied a group of men, then recognized the one hustling toward her. "Bert!" She opened her arms and they hugged.

When they separated, he glanced around and then looked at her, his head cocked to the side. "What are you doing here?"

"I just had dinner with a... um..."

Bert's eyes focused just behind her, and she turned in time to see Jorge as he slipped his arm around her, giving her a squeeze. Thrusting his right hand toward Bert, he said, "I'm Josie's date, Jorge Cobb."

Bert slowly lifted his hand in response, his eyes narrowed until he blinked, his head jerking back. "Governor Cobb's son?"

Suddenly, Bert was pumping Jorge's hand up and

down, his smile huge, and Josie noticed a group of men that had been standing near Bert moved in behind him, their eyes alight with interest. Seeing her cousin and his friends' reactions, it struck Josie that she was no longer surprised that Jorge had not given his name at his father's gala when they met.

She loved her cousin but now felt self-conscious as she witnessed how Bert's demeanor changed from a suspicious glare to suddenly shaking Jorge's hand with great enthusiasm. She watched him smile politely and wondered if this was something he was used to.

Suddenly, they were surrounded by Bert's friends, pressing forward to be introduced. None too soon, the friends drifted away toward the casino, and Bert turned his attention back to her. He grinned as he inclined his head toward the casino door and said, "We were just heading in for an evening of fun. Would you two like to join us?"

"No, thank you. We're going to head home." She loved the feel of Jorge's hand on her back, his fingers flexing. She instantly knew that he was glad of her answer.

Bert leaned down and kissed her cheek, whispering, "We need to talk, Josie cuz. You've been holding out on me."

She hoped Jorge had not heard her cousin's comment but offered a heartfelt hug. "Things have been crazy lately. We'll try to have lunch soon."

"Sooner than later." Bert tapped her nose and winked before following his friends into the casino.

She and Cobb walked out of the resort, his fingers

finding hers, and she avoided his gaze. They'd made it halfway to the parking lot when suddenly, he stopped and placed his hands on her shoulders, angling her body so that she faced him. Repeating the action Bert had made, he used his knuckle to lift her chin so that her eyes were on his, but unlike her cousin, he was gentle.

"I can't tell what's going on in your mind, Josie."

"I don't know. I mean, I do, but it's embarrassing." Her shoulders hefted slightly in a shrug, and she sighed.

"Embarrassing?"

"Yes. I love my cousin dearly. He's been like a brother to me. But that in there was embarrassing. I felt like he was barely looking at you until he realized who you were. And all I could think of was it's no wonder you didn't give me your last name when we first met."

"Josie, you have nothing to be embarrassed about. Honestly, if that wasn't your cousin, people would've been just as impressed with your last name as mine. We both know what it's like to have parents in politics."

She nodded slowly. "It can be exciting, and it can be so intrusive. I don't share all of my father's views, and yet people expect that I am nothing more than an extension of him."

"And sometimes people want to be around us because they wonder what we can do for them."

Her eyes widened as she nodded. "Yes, exactly." She hadn't realized it but her hands had found their way to his waist, her fingers gripping his shirt. "I understand the appeal you talked about of the military and then your job and home in Maine. You can be proud of your father, remember your heritage, but want to carve out your own place in the world."

His smile widened, pushing out the embarrassment and filling her with warm acceptance. He leaned in to kiss her, this time keeping it soft and light. As he pulled her in for a hug, his arms tightening around her, he said, "Don't be embarrassed by the actions of others. All you're in control of is you."

They walked to the parking lot and climbed into his SUV. The sun had moved behind the mountains, casting the land in shadows. She was quiet, her thoughts in turmoil even as she enjoyed the view. She loved traveling and seeing new places but had always come back to New Mexico. As they left the reservation and drove back through the white sands, she said, "I'm so glad we came here today. I saw an area I've never seen before and it was beautiful."

"It's been a long time since I've been back," he said, "but I've never enjoyed being here as much as I have with you today." He reached across the console and linked fingers again, lifting her hand and kissing her knuckles.

The temperature rose in the SUV, and Josie wondered how the vehicle would survive the inferno with their two-hour trip back to her home. They weren't silent; she managed to answer his questions and find things to talk about, but the feel of his fingers on hers whenever he was able to spare his right hand from the wheel kept her thoughts continually on the feel of his lips and the desire pooling in her sex. Never one to act without caution, the internal war raged with her body's needs.

How would this work? Can he have a relationship with a client? Does he want to? But he goes back to Maine. Relationship... or sex? I've never had a fling... do I want to? Christ, why not? Maybe all he wants is sex. Does he want sex? She spared a glance toward his groin, the bulge evident. *Is he erect? Interested?*

"You're doing a lot of thinking over there," he said.

She looked around, realizing they were on her street, and remained silent until he pulled into her driveway. Licking her dry lips, she blurted, "I don't know what's happening. Or what you want. Or if it's the same thing I want. Or if I'm out in left field, and right now you think I'm crazy."

He blinked slowly, his face lit by the security light shining from her front door and garage. Wondering how she could take back the words that had just blasted from her mind, she watched as his dark eyes darkened even more, not knowing how that was possible, and his lips, made for kissing, curved upward into a smile that threatened to steal her breath, if not her very soul.

Cobb didn't say a word but turned and hopped down from the driver's seat and then jogged around to her side, throwing open the door. She barely had time to unbuckle before he'd taken her hand and assisted her to the ground. Linking fingers, he walked with a purpose to her front door, used a key she had no idea he had, and gained entrance. He turned to the panel and hit the keypad to set the alarm again before planting himself right in front of her.

"Now... I can show you what I want," he said, leaning forward, nuzzling her nose.

With her back against the door, she felt surrounded by his large body as he pressed into hers. His hands cupped her face as though she were precious china and his nose slid along hers. Heat flared throughout when his mouth found its mark, landing on her lips. She opened for him, and he wasted no time as his tongue swept along hers. Her knees threatened to give out on her but his body kept her upright as it pressed her back against the door. She was glad for the slight pressure, and her fingers grasped his shirt, keeping her grounded; otherwise, she would float away, boneless underneath his talented tongue and lips.

This was no light kiss. No polite precursor to sex. No uncertain fumbling from a hesitant date. She had imagined his full lips to kiss amazingly, and the proof was evident as she gave in to the onslaught.

Her senses fired messages to every part of her body. She angled her head, wanting his tongue to have even more access even as she fought him for dominance over the kiss. Her breasts felt heavy, and she arched her back to press them more firmly against his chest. Her arms came alive, her hands feeling the tight muscles of his waist before her fingers splayed over his back. She lifted a leg, wrapping her foot around his calf, his thigh now pressing against her aching core, feeling his thick erection pressing against her stomach.

Just when she thought she would burst into flames, their mouths separated as he rested his forehead against hers, his breathing ragged, matching her own. She wanted to protest, but her lungs were crying for oxygen, and for a moment they simply remained still, gasping. Awareness crept over her, and she realized she was the one holding him to her with her fingers digging in and her legs still wrapped around his.

She forced her fingers to relax, sliding her hands around his waist and uncurling her leg, placing her foot back on the floor.

"Damn," he groaned, his body still pressed against hers.

Uncertain of his meaning behind the one curse, she remained silent.

He stood, and taking her hand, led her away from the door and over to the sofa. Sitting, he gently tugged on her hand. She hesitated just long enough to slide off her shoes before allowing him to pull her onto his lap. With her back against the arm of the sofa, he held her close and she wrapped her arms around his neck.

"So..." she said, licking her lips, feeling the tender, kiss-swollen flesh. "Here's where you tell me how we went from kissing to *damn*."

He lifted his hand, cupping her jaw before sweeping his fingers through her hair, a smile playing about his lips.

"I've never done this," he confessed.

Her brows lifted to her forehead as she fought—and lost—the battle to smile. "Um, you're a talented kisser to have not done this before."

"Smartass." His grumble didn't match the smile on his face. His eyes held her as he glided his thumb over her cheek again. "I've never become involved while on a mission. Ever."

His dark eyes gave away nothing, but their intensity held her entranced. She knew he was trying to convey a serious message but was uncertain what he wanted her to understand. She nodded slowly. "Okay, Jorge. But I'm going to need you to be very clear so that I know exactly what you're feeling."

He hesitated, and for a moment she wasn't sure he was going to explain. Finally, he said, "Many of my coworkers have met their significant other on a mission. I've never become emotionally involved with anyone that I was investigating, providing a security detail for, or assisting in any way. I guess I don't want you to think that you're just one of many women who've needed my help that has ended up with my lips on theirs while their back was against the door. And I sure as fuck don't want you to feel that I'm taking advantage of your vulnerability. Nor do I want you to think that I'm simply out for a good time at your expense."

She shook her head slowly, mimicking his behavior as her small hand cupped his jaw, her thumb sweeping over his cheek, feeling the coarse stubble. "I never thought you were taking advantage of me."

"Good, that's important. But it's also important that you know that this is not usual for me. It's also important for you to know that when we met at my father's gala, my behavior wasn't usual for me either. I don't typically walk up to women and pull them onto the dance floor." He shook his head and snorted. "Well, maybe in my early SEAL days. I've got plenty of friends that have that personality, and it works for them, but it's been a while since I was so forward. But there was something about you that drew me in."

Laughter erupted, her heart lighter at hearing his confessions. "I'll admit it was a bit forward, but flattering, nonetheless." Their smiles remained for a moment, then slowly melted away, their gazes continuing to hold. "So, what happens now?"

"Honestly? I'm not sure. Not only for my mission but for me, I want to make sure you're safe. I want to find out who's threatening you. And when I do, it'll be hard not to make them pay for the fear you've felt. But one of the things I respect about you is that you don't play games. I don't either, and I think that works well for us. So, I'll let you know, Josie, I want to get to know you better without taking advantage of you, and as long as you want that too, that's what we'll do."

"And tonight?"

A heavy sigh left his lips, and his arms tightened around her. "Tonight, I'm going to force myself to walk away from you. We'll go to sleep in our separate beds because I don't ever want you to regret anything that happens. If we have sex, I want you to be sure."

She opened her mouth, the words ready to fling outward that she was sure right now. But as his dark gaze penetrated, she sighed, nodding slowly. It would be so easy to give in to lust, letting this gorgeous man rock her body long into the night with no doubt it would be the best she'd ever had. But he was right. She'd never given in to a fling before, and to do so now would not be true to herself. Especially since she knew her heart would be involved. "Damn," she mumbled.

His brows lifted. "Now, it's time for you to explain how we went from confessing truths to *damn*."

Another bubble of laughter erupted, and she leaned forward, kissing him lightly. "You're right. You're right about everything. As hard as it is to not give in to whatever we're feeling now, we'll make sure we're on the same page." She blew out a breath and added, "Although, if you had just crooked your finger, I have no doubt I'd have dropped my panties."

"Fucking hell, Josie. Christ... you shouldn't say that to me. Now, trying to be noble is taking a back seat to wanting to crook my finger at you." He dropped his head back as he groaned.

Unable to resist, she grabbed his jaws and pulled his head forward, kissing him again, wanting one more taste before they separated. He must've felt the same because he angled his head, his tongue dancing along her lips.

"Meow."

Eyes wide, she jerked backward, twisting her head to see Melon sitting on the floor looking up at her, reproach in her gaze. Turning back to Cobb, she shrugged. "Looks like my cat has decided it's time for bed."

Laughing, he stood and gently placed her feet onto the floor. She watched as he moved around to the various doors and windows, then they walked down the hall and stood outside their respective doors. With his hand on her waist, he leaned down and kissed just to the side of her lips. "Good night, Josie."

Her fingers squeezed lightly on his arm, and she smiled, suddenly shy again. "Sweet dreams, Jorge."

He turned and stepped into his room, and she did the same. From behind, she heard him say, "If I dream about you, they will be." She grabbed her door frame to hold her up as she heard the click of his door behind her. Catching her breath, she glanced down at Melon and walked into her bedroom, mumbling, "Damn."

1 2

After another night of little sleep where he seriously wondered about his sanity at not taking Josie up on her suggestion of *panty-dropping*, Cobb woke with a hard-on that wasn't going away. It was early, and when he crossed the hall to the bathroom, he heard no evidence that she was already awake. Taking advantage, he climbed into the shower and gave in to the urge to encircle his cock with his hand, rubbing out an orgasm as he imagined Josie underneath him. Swallowing the groan, he hoped she was asleep and not aware of his activity. While his release didn't wash away the thought of her, it eased his aching cock for now.

Toweling off, he wrapped it around his waist and shaved after running his fingers through his short hair. Stepping into the hall, he glanced back to flip off the light, slamming into something in the hall that squeaked loudly. His arms snapped out, grabbing Josie by the shoulders to keep her from stumbling into the wall. The towel wrapped around his waist loosened, and he let her go to grab the towel. "Fuck!"

"Sorry," she gushed, her gaze on the towel held precariously over his hips before her eyes darted back to his face.

Red infused her cheeks but he had no doubt his were the same color. "No, I'm sorry. I forgot to take my clothes with me and then wasn't paying attention to where I was going."

"Are you okay?" Her wide-eyed, unblinking gaze stayed glued to his face.

Yep... just horny and distracted. Keeping those thoughts to himself, he smiled. "Absolutely. I'll be out in a moment, and we can head to the clinic after breakfast. I'll get the security up there as well."

She nodded and scurried down the hall, Melon trotting after her mistress. Walking into his room, he understood what the cat was doing. *I'd stay right with her if I could, too.* He was almost dressed when his phone vibrated. "Cobb."

"Hey, man, it's Josh. Any chance you can get to El Paso today?"

"Yeah. I've got to get the security on Josie's clinic, but that won't take long. I need a camera on the perimeter. Other than that, I'm clear. What's up?"

"The attorney who's got a trace back to some of the companies that were donors is in the wind. Not sure if he's a real person or not, but I can't get an eye on the guy's building... he's got no security to hack. You're close so I thought you could scope it out."

He nodded, rubbing his chin. "Sure. El Paso is only

about thirty minutes away. I'll get there right after lunch."

"Good. Let me know what you find."

"I've got something for you to check on."

Just as he knew he would, Josh immediately said, "Go ahead."

"Bert Rector. He's Josie's cousin. Parents died years ago, and he's very close to Josie's family. I saw him at a casino last night, and the friends he was with... let's just say that I'd like you to check him out."

"You got it."

Disconnecting, he walked into the kitchen, the scent of biscuits, bacon, eggs, and coffee once again filling the air. Uncertain of Josie's thoughts this morning, he breathed a sigh of relief as she approached with a smile and a mug. Lifting on her toes, she offered her mouth to him, a bonus he wasn't about to refuse.

They sat at the counter to eat, and he looked over at the dirty pans on the stovetop. "Josie, I never meant for you to cook for me. This isn't part of a security detail. I should be taking care of my own meals."

"I have to eat, and it's no fun cooking for one. You're giving me the excuse to not eat cereal every morning."

"Loopy Rings?"

She blushed, and rosy cheeks looked beautiful on her. "Breakfast of champions."

"I think that's Wheat O's."

"Wheat O's might be for your brand of champion, but Loopy Rings are mine."

He barked out a laugh. "Well, you be a champion and sit and enjoy your coffee while I clean up." He rinsed the dishes before placing them into the dishwasher, then scrubbed the frying pan. Wiping the counters afterward, he leaned his hip against the counter near the sink, mug in hand, and looked at her.

"Why do I get the feeling there's something you want to ask?" she said, her head cocked to the side.

He chuckled. "Okay, there is. I need to go to the clinic to install cameras on the outside, and if you want to stay here, that's fine—"

"I'd like to go if that's okay with you. I can help as I did here unless you think I'll get in the way."

A smile crept over his face, and he shoved off the back counter and stepped forward, leaning on his forearms. Her eyes held hope, and he wanted to acquiesce to her every desire. Setting his mug down, he leaned closer and kissed her lightly. "Can't think of a more beautiful helper."

She held his gaze, then nibbled on her bottom lip. "And... I can tell there's more."

"You can read me, that's for sure," he said, shaking his head. "Okay, I need to go to El Paso this afternoon to take a look at an attorney's office. It might have something to do with the mysterious donors."

She shrugged and nodded. "Okay."

Brows lifted, he repeated, "Okay?"

"Sure, why not? It only takes about forty-five minutes to drive there, so that's easy."

Easy. That word described Josie as well. Honest. Forthcoming. Easy. Grinning, he said, "Okay, then let's get started."

Time at the clinic gave him a chance to check the

building inside and out, satisfied that while she was there, she should be safe since she was never there alone. Once again, with her assistance on the ground while he handled working on the ladder, they installed the cameras efficiently and had them checked by LSI. Receiving the all-clear, they grabbed burgers at a drive-through and headed toward El Paso.

Once on the highway, she turned to him and asked, "Can you tell me what we're looking for?"

"One of the ways that charities get used for fraud is very organized and this makes it difficult to be discovered. Individuals or businesses make large donations, count this off on their taxes or use the donation to hide illegally gotten money, and then someone returns the money through different channels. That someone is on the inside—"

She gasped and turned her head toward him. "Caesar!"

"That would be my guess. Either him or someone he knew. The individuals or businesses get the money back but also get the tax break or never report the money as income to begin with."

She looked out the windshield, quiet for another moment, and he had no doubt her intellect was turning over possibilities in her head.

Sure enough, she twisted her head toward him again. "For more than one company to do this, there has to be a connection. It's too big a coincidence to assume that it's different people who just happened to come up with the same plan with the same charity."

He nodded slowly, not surprised she was coming to these conclusions.

"And," she continued, "that means that it was concocted by someone who is connected to these businesses, or if they are phony businesses, then someone who created them just for this purpose."

He nodded slowly again. "That's what LSI is looking into."

"And the attorney's office we're going to?"

"It's a name that LSI has attached to these donor companies. The person may be real but not able to be located, so my people want me to get eyes on the building. There are no cameras or street security that LSI can tap into to see for sure."

After a few minutes of continued silence other than the radio, he chanced a glance her way. "So, Bert's friends seemed anxious to get to the casino last night."

He watched the road but shot his gaze toward her to catch her expression. Her nose wrinkled as she nodded.

"Yeah, I know. Bert and I are close, or we used to be. Truthfully, with our work schedules and me living in Las Cruces, I don't get to see him as much. I admit that I found his friends to be a bit crass last night. They smiled at me but seemed to be standoffish with you until they realized who you were." She shifted in her seat, still buckled but facing him more. "Does that happen a lot?"

"What? People only wanting to suck up when they realize I'm the governor's son? Sure. I'm pretty used to that."

"No, I mean the overt prejudice that fills some people's eyes."

He reached over and took her hand in his, squeezing it before linking fingers. "Not as much as you might think. I confess that my mixed heritage is all combined onto my face, and I know some people don't care for those who look different from them. But honestly, here in New Mexico, it's so prevalent that it's never really been a problem." He was silent for another moment before continuing to prod. "Does Bert visit casinos often?"

She shrugged and shook her head. "I really don't know. It's not anything he's ever talked about, and I confess I was surprised to see him there last night. But then, as I said, we're seldom around each other anymore."

"I wonder if his friends are true friends or just wondering what the nephew of a state senator can do for them." As soon as the words left his mouth he hesitated, wondering what her reaction would be. She gasped slightly, and his fingers flexed involuntarily.

"That's exactly what I thought!" she exclaimed.

He breathed a sigh of relief. "I hated to say that because it sounds bad. But, well, you know that casinos are designed to take your money. I'd hate to see him get taken advantage of by people who aren't truly his friends."

"Well, I love him, but he's a grown man who should know how to choose his friends."

Cobb nodded, glad to hear her practical assessment, knowing if her cousin was into something he shouldn't be, it would make it easier on her to accept. *But, fuck, if her cousin is using her charity...*

"We're here," she exclaimed as El Paso loomed large on the horizon. It didn't take long to drive to the area where the attorney supposedly had an office. Driving past, Cobb felt sure the office space was empty but wanted to be sure. Parking, he scanned the area. "Stay here and stay locked in. I'm going to take a look around."

She nodded, then leaned over and said, "How about a kiss for luck?"

Surprised, he nonetheless jumped at the opportunity for a kiss that was way too short but oh, so sweet. "Damn, girl," he groaned. Climbing from behind the wheel, he shot her a stern look. "Remember, stay here and stay locked in."

She saluted, and he rolled his eyes. Assuring the door was locked, he walked to the front of the building and snapped several pictures. The area was sparsely populated, and he walked to the door, cupping his hands around his face to peer inside. Wanting to check out the back, he jogged to the end of the street and down to the alley that ran behind the building. A small store was on one corner, a laundromat on the other, but most of the other buildings were uninhabited. Making it to the back of the office where the lawyer was supposed to be housed, he pulled out a pair of gloves from his pocket and snapped them onto his hands. Reaching back into his pocket, he retrieved a set of tools, and quickly entered the back door. There were a few rooms including a small bathroom and kitchenette, all empty. As he made his way toward the front, he could see the building had been deserted for a long time. A thick coat of dust was on the floor, having not been disturbed in recent years from the placement of furniture.

Retreating the way he came, he quickly entered each office and workroom, scanning the area and looking into the closets. The bathroom contained nothing more than a toilet and sink. The kitchenette included a counter with upper and lower cabinets. Bending, he opened the lower cabinets, finding them empty. Glad for his height, he opened the upper cabinets, carefully checking them as well. Nothing. *Whoever Carson Wright is, he certainly doesn't use this building.*

Not wanting to leave Josie sitting outside any longer, he went out the back and locked the door, pulling off his gloves and shoving them into his pants pocket. Hustling around to the front of the building, he clicked the lock on his SUV and climbed into the driver's seat.

Josie's eyes were bright, and her voice was full of interest. "Did you find anything?"

"I think you like the idea of investigating," he laughed.

"I used to love reading mysteries and whodunits when I was younger. I hadn't thought about it, but this is just like those books!"

"Well, the building is abandoned and has been for a long time. At least most of it. There's dust everywhere, no footprints or signs that furniture has been moved. So, I'd say that the building has been empty for a while."

He sneezed from the dust and she unzipped her bag,

searching for a tissue. Pulling out a bottle of water, she handed it to him. "Here, this will help, but I know I have some tissues in here."

She began pulling items from her bag as Cobb looked on after taking a swig of water to wash the dust from his throat. With raised brows, he watched in fascination as she continued to dig through the bag. A small, clear bag filled with cosmetics, a comb, and elastic headbands were placed on the dashboard. This was followed by a spiral notebook and a tablet.

"You write in a notebook and on a tablet?"

Her hand halted as her head swung around to hold his gaze. "Yes. Some of my clients are very tech-savvy and don't mind the tablet. But others are nervous when I use it and they seem more at ease with pen and paper."

He smiled and leaned over, granting her a kiss. "Should have known you'd have a care for all their needs."

He meant to keep the kiss light, but it was the heat of the electricity between them that seared straight through him. He said nothing, not trusting his voice. Her pupils dilated, as lust flared between them. Both moved at the same time, leaning toward each other, his hand cupping the back of her head as her hands clutched his jaws. Lips met, tongues tangled, and teeth clashed in a messy kiss, one that stole his breath as he angled her head to plunge his tongue deeper.

Laughter from outside cut through the haze and they jerked apart, his chest heaving as he dragged oxygen into his lungs, glad to see she was just as affected. A glance to the side gave evidence that the pedestrians had passed on by. Giving her another kiss, this one open-mouthed but fast, he leaned back. He had considered checking out El Paso a little more, but after that kiss, he wanted nothing more than to be alone with her.

She swallowed deeply and her hand shook slightly as she re-buckled her seatbelt. "Wow."

Chuckling, he agreed as he started the vehicle, then turned back to her. "You ready to head home?"

"Yeah," she breathed, a smile still playing about her lips. "I'd like that." He tilted his head in question, and she elaborated, "You, me, alone at my place… that's what I'd like."

Grinning, he pulled out onto the street. "No bullshit with you, Josie. No games, no pretense. Absolutely perfect." As the words had left his mouth, he knew they were true. *Absolutely perfect.*

13

The forty-five minutes trip back to her house seemed to last forever as far as she was concerned. Josie and Jorge attempted to converse, but their responses were more mumbles as she struggled to think of things to say when all she wanted to do was scream for him to pull to the side of the road so she could climb onto his lap.

The sexual tension in the cab of his SUV sent the temperature soaring so that even the air conditioner could barely cool off her heated body. As he drove, she stared out the windshield while darting glances to the side. *How can a man's profile be as sexy as facing him?* Everything about him called to her. The curve of his nose. His full lips. His jaw. His muscular arm was stretched out, and his hand rested on the steering wheel. The way the seat belt crossed his broad chest.

His gaze slid her way, and she knew he'd caught her staring. Finally, unable to take the tension any longer, she blurted, "So, what do you want for dinner?"

Now his whole head turned, and his gaze raked over

her before he faced the front again. He grinned, his white teeth gleaming, and all she could concentrate on was his mouth.

"Whatever you want, I'll take care of it," he answered.

She listened to his reply but could no longer remember the question she'd asked. *Whatever I want? He'll take care of it? What if what I want is him?*

When they finally turned onto her street, she heaved a sigh of relief, the desire to get out of the confines of the vehicle overwhelming. She jumped down and hustled, but his long legs ate up the distance and he met her at the door. Her hands shook as she tried to jam the key into the keyhole. Her fingers felt the jolt when he reached out to take the keys from her. They entered and he locked the door behind her.

Tonight, there was no backing against the door. No rushing of bodies colliding. Instead, they stood, feet apart, staring into each other's eyes.

"What do you want, Josie?" His voice was deep, caramel smooth.

She licked her lips, realizing he was handing complete control over to her. The truth was she had wanted this man since he first approached her at the gala. She'd wanted to give in to a night of no-names, no-promises, no-regrets pleasure. But buried deep inside, she must have known he was the kind of man who would burn her. Not intentionally. Not to hurt her. But just because she could never allow herself to give in to no-regrets pleasure. A night with him would surely bring regrets if there was only sex.

He stepped closer while still keeping a respectable distance, his head ducking slightly so he could hold her gaze. "I see your mind whirling."

She dragged in a ragged breath, wondering if the oxygen had suddenly become thinner in the last few minutes. His dark eyes stared with intensity, the black pupils melding with the irises. His jaw was tight and a muscle ticked at the edge of his cheek. His nostrils flared slightly as he appeared to struggle with his own breathing. His arms hung by his side, his fingers flexing, the only movement she could witness. And behind his jeans, there was no mistaking the erection.

"You asked what I wanted." She licked her lips as she forced her gaze to stay on his eyes. "The truth is I want you. I wanted you the first time I saw you, but I'm just not a one-night-with-a-stranger sort of woman." Her shoulders lifted in a little shrug as her lips barely curved. "You're not a stranger anymore."

She stepped forward and lifted her arms, placing her hands on his shoulders, repeating, "I want you."

As though the dam that held him back had burst, his arms snapped around her and he lifted her feet off the ground, his mouth slamming over hers. Entwining her arms around his neck and her legs around his waist, she clung to him.

Her mouth opened immediately under his welcome onslaught. His tongue invaded her warmth, gliding over hers, eliciting tingles from her toes all the way up to her scalp. Desperate for his taste, her tongue battled his until it swept through his mouth. She was thankful he was holding her upright or she would have slumped into a puddle on the floor. As one muscular arm continued to band around her waist, his other hand moved upward, fingers diving through her hair until they were cupping the back of her head.

She had come to recognize he was a man of many talents, and walking around furniture, down the hall, turning into her bedroom, and stalking straight to her bed with her clinging to him like a monkey and their lips never separating had to be one of his greatest skills. She couldn't wait to see what else he had mastery over.

He sat her gently onto the bed, their lips finally parting as he knelt onto the floor between her legs, his large hands resting on her knees. His gaze roamed over her face, landing on her lips. She didn't need to feel them to know they were swollen. *Please, don't let him stop now.*

"Tell me again, Josie. I need the words. I need you to be sure. You said you weren't a one-night-with-a-stranger kind of woman, and what you need to understand is that even though we're no longer strangers, this isn't a one-night-only. Not with what I'm feeling for you."

She sucked in a quick breath, his words gliding over, around, and through her, landing at her heart. In an effort to keep her lips from curving into a wide smile, her top teeth landed on her bottom lip. But it was ineffective as her smile spread, nonetheless. "I do want you, Cobb. I want this tonight. Tomorrow. And for as long as it works for us."

"Then be forewarned, Josie. I plan on making this work for a long time."

Her hands moved up to cup his jaws, the feel of thick stubble underneath her fingers. Leaning forward, she whispered against his lips. "I'm ready. Let's do this."

A growl erupted from deep inside his chest as he lunged. His hands moved to her waist and he lifted her easily, settling her deeper into the bed. Crawling over her, his fingers danced at the bottom of her shirt, slipping underneath and lightly gliding up her sides, dragging the material until it snagged underneath her breasts. He hesitated for a few seconds, and she lifted her hands over her head, giving him permission and access to strip the shirt away, which he did with ease.

His dark eyes settled on her breasts, and as his nostrils flared, she watched the magnetic pull of pure lust move over his face. She quickly unhooked the front, pulling open the material so her breasts were now exposed, her nipples hard in the cool air. He placed his palms over her breasts, covering them completely, then gently swirled his thumbs around her nipples. The electricity zapped between her breasts and core, and she shifted her hips, wishing for a way to ease the need building inside.

With his legs straddling hers, he bent and pulled her nipple deeply into his mouth, continuing to palm the other. Moving between her breasts, giving equal attention to both, a smile spread over his face as she cried out with longing. Her fingers ran through his black hair, her short nails dragging slightly along his scalp. He continued kissing down her stomach while his fingers unzipped her jeans. Scooting backward off the bed, his booted feet landed on the floor with a thump. He reached into his back pocket and pulled out his wallet, removing several condom packets, tossing them onto the bed next to her before placing his wallet onto her nightstand.

Grinning, he reached a hand to his back and dragged his shirt over his head. The air left her lungs in a rush as she stared at his broad, naked chest. Smooth, tanned skin that had her licking her lips in anticipation of dragging her tongue around his darker, flat nipples. His abs were defined, and her fingers itched to move along the dips and ridges of muscles. He bent, and she lost sight of his hands but could hear his boots being unlaced. He stood to toe them off and bent once again to jerk off his socks.

Now they were both naked from the waist up, and she had no idea what she should do. *Jerk my pants off and spread my legs or keep laying here and fantasize about what the rest of him looks like?*

He chuckled as though her words had been shouted. "Just keep laying there, babe. Once I get you completely naked, it's going to be hard to hold back." His belt unbuckled with a click and the sound of his zipper lowering seemed amplified in the room where the only other sound was her breathing. He shucked his jeans and boxers down his legs, kicking them off his feet before standing erect in front of her, fully naked, legs apart, looking like a god. *And speaking of erect!* His cock was as perfect as the rest of him. Long, thick, and as he palmed the shaft, a pearl drop on the end had her lick her lips again.

He bent forward once again, this time unbuttoning

her jeans, and with a deftness she didn't think possible, he pulled her jeans and panties completely off, throwing them over his shoulder. He placed a knee onto the bed, and with his hands under her thighs, he lifted her legs, exposing her to his perusal. He closed his eyes and inhaled deeply. For a few seconds, she was mortified, but then she saw the expression of ecstasy on his face as his lips curved and he breathed deeply again. *Christ.* The heat in the room skyrocketed.

Her brain was still focused on him sniffing her sex when his head dropped and his tongue licked her slick folds. Surprised, her hips jerked, and he shifted so that his shoulders kept her legs apart and one large hand on her stomach held her in place. He began to feast as a starving man, licking, tonguing, and sucking until she thought she would spontaneously burst into flames. Her fingers dragged through his hair again, and every muscle in her body began to tighten in anticipation. He inserted a finger deep into her channel, quirking it in just the right way to hit the spot. As he sucked on her clit at the same time, the explosion shook her entire body and she cried out his name. His finger and tongue rode out her release as her legs and arms fell gracelessly to the side.

Barely noticing that his lips were now moving back up over her body, she became acutely aware as he danced his tongue and lips over her breasts before moving up to kiss her. With one thrust of his tongue she tasted her essence on his lips, something she'd never experienced before.

Arching up, she wrapped her arms around him, their

kiss not breaking. Mumbling against his mouth, she said, "Want top."

He flipped over, and now she lay on top of his broad body. Scooting upward, she straddled his legs and grinned, shimmying downward to encircle his cock with her hands. Another groan was dragged from his lips as she gently spread the pad of her thumb over the tip, smearing the drop of pre-cum before bending to lick from root to end.

"Christ Almighty, Josie," he growled, his fingers spearing through her hair.

Filled with a sense of power, she lowered her breasts to his thighs and took his cock into her mouth. He continued to make noises rumbling from deep inside his chest as her lips glided up and down, alternating between sucking and long, slow licks. His hips jumped, and she grinned around his cock. Her hands were on his thick thighs, the muscles taut beneath her fingertips.

He had lifted his head and their gazes were as connected as their bodies. His eyes were dark and unfathomable, and she would have had no idea the emotion he was feeling other than the moans he continued to rumble between clenched teeth.

Cobb was by far the most well-endowed of any partner she'd had. There was no way her mouth could take in all of him, so she used her fist at the base to pump along with her sucking. His hands reached out, fisting in her hair, stinging slightly but not enough to cause pain.

It was powerful to feel the strong man underneath her, knowing she was the one in charge. And yet she never doubted the strength in him. He was giving as much as taking.

Finally, through gritted teeth, he said, "That's enough, babe. Sit on me." She hesitated for only a few seconds, then he growled, "Seriously, Josie. If you want me to come in your mouth another time, I'm game. But the first time I come with you, I want to be buried deep inside."

His words, spoken in a voice gravelly with need, had the effect he must have wanted. She withdrew her lips from around him and sat back on her heels as he reached out with one hand and grabbed a condom. He ripped open the foil, and once sheathed, he lifted his hands toward her and she shimmied up his thighs, rising on her knees until his cock was at her entrance.

"I know I'm big, babe, and I want this comfortable for you. You're in charge."

As soon as she began to settle down over his cock, she was acutely aware of what he meant. Long, thick, hard, covered by silk. Easing down slowly, she lifted and settled, each time moving him deeper. His teeth were gritted once again, his jaw tight. She didn't want to tease him so each time she moved further down onto his cock. Soon, she settled all the way to where he was fully seated in her.

With her hands leaning forward and balancing on his shoulders and his gripping her hips with his fingers digging into her ass, she rose and fell over and over, each time plunging. They moved faster until they were both covered in sweat and panting. The coil was tightening deep inside, but she felt her legs begin to quiver with fatigue.

Without saying anything, he must've known as his hands dug in tighter, and he lifted her slightly so that he had room to move. He pistoned his hips up and down, his cock dragging deep inside. Her breasts bounced, and he growled, "Lean down."

Bending at the elbows, she dipped her breasts to his lips and was rewarded as he sucked a nipple deeply into his mouth. The changed angle also gave his plunging cock a chance to rub against her clit and sparks began to fan out through every nerve of her body. Her fingers dug in tightly to his shoulders, and she was now gritting her teeth as well.

"You close?" he asked.

She nodded, unable to speak. A few seconds later, she cried out as her orgasm rushed over her, feeling every inch of his cock as white lights exploded behind her eyelids. Struggling to hold herself up, she locked her arms so that he could find his own release. After several more thrusts with his feet planted on the bed and his knees bent, he thrust up, another groan being dragged from deep inside his chest. His neck muscles tightened and corded, the blood vessels standing out in stark relief against his reddened skin.

Finally, as every drop was wrung from him, she fell forward, forcing out another grunt from his chest. His arms banded around her back, and he held her tightly as she lay completely on him. Both sweaty and panting, their heartbeats tapping out a rhythm as old as time, she tucked her head underneath his chin and rested her cheek on his chest. Several long minutes passed, and she was uncertain if she could move. And she knew for a fact she didn't want to.

His spent cock finally slid out of her body, and he rolled them to the side, still facing each other. Her head now rested on his arm and she looked into his eyes. He angled his head to take her lips in another kiss, this one sweet and gentle. A kiss of lovers.

Untangling his legs from her, he said, "Be right back." He climbed from the bed and walked into her bathroom. She heard the toilet flush and the water in the sink run. He walked back into the room and a wide grin spread across her face. She hadn't dated anyone since she'd moved into the house, so there hadn't been a naked man gracing her bedroom or bathroom. And after the sight of Jorge in all his naked glory, she knew no other man could compare.

He stalked straight over, and she shifted as he pulled the covers back. He climbed under the sheets, wrapping her into his arms again. Legs tangled, her cheek rested on his arm as her hand splayed over his chest, the feel of his heartbeat underneath her fingertips.

"I don't know that I can move, babe," he said, his breath brushing over her cheek.

She remained quiet for a moment, then whispered, "I don't want you to."

His father and grandfather had emphasized watching everything he did when he was growing up, knowing the media and constituency would be looking for fault. He knew many people's opinions of politicians were that they were all unscrupulous. But his father and grandfather, plus many he'd had the distinct pleasure of knowing, were hard-working, concerned civil servants. As far as he knew, Josie's father was the same.

But regardless of his previous ideas of mixing pleasure and business, the change in his relationship with Josie had blown his doubts right out of his mind. He'd handed the choice to Josie, she chose him, and he was going to go forward with the relationship.

Thinking of her brought a smile to his face. The same smile that had stayed on his face all during the day. He'd had plenty of sexual partners over the years, but not as many recently. When he was young, stupid, newly in the military, and then as a SEAL, women had been easy to get when he was not on a mission. Sex was usually a physical release, emotions not factoring in at all. He had dated a few women over the years, but those relationships ended quickly as soon as he realized nothing was holding them together. Cobb had never wanted to be with a woman once he determined that there was nothing more permanent in their future.

But sex with Josie had been by far the best he'd ever had. She was an unselfish lover, wanting to give as much as she took. Quiet and soft-spoken worked for him. She wasn't a pushover, but she also wasn't in his face, and he found himself wanting her in a way he'd never wanted with another woman.

The moonlight filtered through the blinds, casting a soft glow over the bed. His breath halted as he stared at her sleeping face devoid of signs of worry and wanted this for her each night. Pulling her in tighter, he finally found sleep, resting in the comfort of her body tucked into his.

The next morning over breakfast, her brow was furrowed as she nibbled on toast.

"What's on your mind, babe?"

She blinked, so lost in thought that the words appeared to have startled her, so he continued. "For someone who should have a smile on their face after last night, I may need to rethink my technique."

She threw her head back and laughed, then reached out with her free hand and laid it on his arm. With a squeeze and her smile still on her face, she said, "Believe me, there's nothing wrong with your technique."

He smoothed his finger over her brow. "Then what's got your forehead crinkled with thoughts?"

"I was just thinking about going into the office today. I know we've been riding together, but I have a dilemma this morning. I've got a home visit to make with an elderly woman who had been abused for years by her husband. He's gone now, but she's very skittish around men. When she comes into the clinic, she won't even let Mark take a look at her. I have to have Laurie do everything."

Shrugging, he took another sip of coffee. "That's okay. I'll just stay in the car."

"I'm not sure that will work with her. She always stands at the window and watches as I drive in. If she sees you driving and me getting out of your vehicle, I'm not sure she'll trust that."

"What do you suggest? Because I don't want to leave you without eyes on you."

"I know it seems a bit ridiculous, but can we drive separately? Separately to the clinic and then separately to her house. I'll pull into her driveway as usual, and you can just park on the street. I know it's two cars all day when we really only need one, but I can't think of another way."

He hefted his shoulders in a shrug. "Sure."

She grinned and stepped closer. "You're always telling me that I'm easy, but you are, too. You didn't go all alpha-male, not-gonna-do-it-your-way."

Chuckling, he shook his head. "I might be in charge of your security and want you safe, but I'm not going to be unreasonable. You know your clients and their needs. My job is to keep you safe while making sure you can keep doing your job." With that, he leaned forward and kissed her the way he'd been wanting to since he first walked into the kitchen.

Later, sitting in her office, he tried to force his mind to the financial reports in front of him as well as the information Josh had sent to him. But the task, common enough for Cobb, was proving to be almost impossible. Josie filled his mind.

His phone rang and he glanced at the ID. Recognizing Levi's code, he answered, "Cobb."

"This is Floyd Gomez. FBI. Is this a good time?"

"Give me a minute." He walked out the back door and away from the building, then replied, "Go ahead."

"I've been brought up to speed on the case involving Caesar Castiel by my supervisor and your coworker, Levi. I have also spoken to Senator Rector. My specialty is fraud, and I'll tell you, this mess stinks of it."

"Agreed." Cobb liked the way the agent got right to the point. "I'm working through more of the finances left by Caesar right now. It appears he hid a mini drive in Ms. Rector's purse that we just found. There is a reference to Carson Wright on the drive, but I checked out the last known office and it was empty."

"Carson Wright. There's a name I haven't heard in a while," Floyd said.

"What have you got on him?"

"The name is tied into organized crime in New Mexico, Texas, and Mexico. Slippery as fuck. Has store-front addresses, but by the time he's tracked down, he's in the wind. I can't even prove he's a real person. It's even been surmised that it's a name used by more than one person. But you say he was mentioned in the records left by Caesar?"

Cobb heard the interest in Floyd's voice and grinned. He recognized the investigator's rising scent for blood. "Yeah. Sent it to my people, but I've got a copy I can send to you. I have the understanding of the financial records but I don't have time or the resources here to work on them fully."

"Send me what you've got. How is Ms. Rector?"

"Good. She's steady under normal circumstances and is still holding everything together, but she's burying a lot of her nerves. Don't worry about her... I've got her."

"Good to know. Okay, let me have a chance to look at the drive's records, and you focus on her safety. We'll be in touch."

He disconnected and stalked back inside the clinic, re-settling into Josie's office. He'd barely sat down when Mark stuck his head in and smiled as he inclined his head toward the papers in front of Cobb. "Hey. You're here a lot more than Caesar used to be. Maybe now things will run more smoothly for Josie."

"That's the idea," he said noncommittally.

"So, how's it going?"

"Not bad. Just getting used to the way the former bookkeeper handled things," he said, still keeping his comments vague.

Mark sauntered into the room and nodded, sipping from a water bottle. "Man, I hated the finance class that med students had to take. Give me anatomy and physiology any day, but save me from rows and columns of numbers."

Cobb leaned back in his chair, glad to have the chance to scope out Mark on his own. Josh had let him know the young doctor had a lot of medical school debt; not unusual, but it also made him susceptible to a quick money-making scheme. "So, you work at the hospital, also?" Gaining Mark's nod, he continued, "I guess young doctors don't get much free time, do you?"

Mark snorted. "You'd be right. Although, it's not like I do emergency medicine. I thought of that at one time, then knew it was a calling that I didn't have. Geriatric and internal medicine. I like the patients and getting to know them. And I like the pace." He continually glanced down at the files on the desk. "So... uh... any idea why Caesar left his job so suddenly?"

Brows lifted, Cobb plastered a surprised expression onto his face. "Nah, I never knew him. Josie just knew that I had the skills to take care of the books, so it works for me. I get to spend more time with my girlfriend." They were quiet for a moment, then Cobb decided to push for a little more information. "You put in the long haul for medical school. Your education must have set you back."

Mark scrubbed his hand over his face and sighed heavily. "Yeah, I worked every chance I got and took out loans for the rest of it. My family didn't have any money for medical school, so it was all on me. But working here helps. I get part of my debt paid off by working at this clinic. Not that it's the only reason I do it, because I really like the clinic and the patients, but, well... I'll be honest, having the debt forgiveness is a good thing."

"Did you know Caesar very well?"

Mark's gaze shifted down and to the side, his fingers digging into the label on the water bottle in his hand. "I saw him around. He wasn't in here all that often, but I knew who he was."

"Oh, I thought maybe you were friends."

"No, no. We barely spoke when we were here. Our paths just really didn't cross." Mark stood and tossed a wave. "Well, my break is over. I'd better get back to work."

Cobb watched Mark walk out of Josie's office, Mark's mannerisms moving through his mind. Josh had informed him that the young doctor's bank account was fairly steady but his student loans occasionally had a large payment go in. Cobb wondered if that was the money that came from working in the clinic or if there was something else. Shooting Josh another note, he told him to dig for more.

Hearing Mario and Charlene talking in the hall, he leaned to the side, looked out the door, and watched as they walked into the workroom. Standing, he followed, and once inside, offered a chin lift as he went to get water out of the refrigerator. Charlene's eyes flared with interest as they roved over him, something Cobb noted but made sure not to encourage.

She grinned widely and said, "Jorge, you are so much better looking than our last bookkeeper!"

"Well, I never met Caesar."

She was seated at the table but leaned forward, her tongue rubbing over her lips. "Oh, that's a compliment." She winked, then laughed. "Josie is so lucky."

Laurie walked in and nodded toward everybody, then looked at Charlene. Shaking her head, she said, "Girl, I don't know how you do it. I saw you come in with that new Coach bag this morning as well as that Gucci jacket you had on. How the hell you dress like that on your salary, I'll never know."

Charlene's smile was tight-lipped, but she offered a one-shoulder shrug. "It just comes from dating the right kind of guy. One who's got money and doesn't mind showing me how important I am to him."

Laurie plopped her hands on her hips and shook her head. "Whatever happened to good, kind, smart, hard-working—"

Charlene threw her head back and laughed. "Honey, that's all fine, but unless he's got the money to spend, all those other qualities don't mean anything. My mom knew how to keep her eye out for the next man to take care of her and she lived well."

Just then, Josie walked in, glanced around the room at the others, and as her gaze landed on Cobb, she smiled widely. Walking directly to him, she grabbed a water bottle as well and leaned against the counter next to him, mimicking his posture.

Laura piped up and asked, "Did you guys do anything special this weekend?"

"We went to the Mescalero Reservation and had dinner."

"I love their casino!" Charlene blurted, her eyes bright. "Did you win a lot?"

Josie replied, "We didn't go to the casino, just dinner."

Cobb watched with interest as Charlene's smile fell. "I haven't been there in a while. I need to see if my boyfriend will take me. The last time I went, I did pretty good."

Mark stuck his head into the workroom and called for Laurie, who hustled out to see a patient.

Mario had been quiet, munching on his sandwich, but looked over at Charlene. "You'd do a lot better for yourself if you got a boyfriend that was serious about putting a ring on your finger. The way you keep going through them, you'll end up alone."

"I'm not ready to settle down! House in the suburbs. Minivan. PTA." Charlene offered an exaggerated shudder. "I'm all about having a boyfriend who spends money and isn't afraid to shower me with gifts."

"How long did you and Cesar go out?" Mario asked. "I can't imagine him having much money to spend on you."

Cobb felt Josie stiffen next to him and moved his elbow slightly, hoping she took his nonverbal hint to stay cool.

Charlene huffed, tossing her ponytail over her shoulder. "I never dated Caesar! He was so not my type. He asked me to dinner once, and I accepted. That was all. Believe me, that was all!" She stood and swept out of the room, huffing as she left.

Mario held his expression for a moment, then burst out laughing. He stood and looked over at Cobb and Josie. "Sorry, I knew she hadn't dated him, but I like getting my digs in every once in a while when she gets too full of herself." He threw away his trash and headed back out, the workroom now empty except for Josie and Cobb.

"I wonder what you have found when investigating the people at my clinic."

It was a statement, her tone full of curiosity, not outrage. He wrapped his arm around her shoulder, pulling her front into his side. Peering down, he smiled as she tilted her head back to hold his gaze. "I told you I don't trust anybody, and I don't. Plus I didn't have to ask a lot of questions. Your crew here talks a lot. I just listen and nudge them on occasion."

She seemed to ponder this, then cocked her head to the side. "Well, did you find out anything?"

He glanced at the clock on the wall and said, "Isn't it about time we headed out to your last appointment?"

She startled, then nodded. "Yeah, that's right."

"Then let's take care of that, stop at the grocery store on the way home, and then we can talk about everything over dinner."

They walked back into her office where he gathered all the papers and files, and she grabbed her laptop and bag. Waving to the others, they walked out at the same time. As she drove to the small neighborhood, he followed, noting the older houses were decently maintained but not extravagant. As Josie flipped on her blinker and turned into a driveway, he drove to the end of the street, turned around, then came back and parked where he could watch the front door but stayed out of the line of vision of the resident.

Half an hour later, Josie left the house and climbed into her car. She sat there for a moment, and just as he was about to call her, his phone vibrated. "Hey, babe."

"Was that too long?" she asked.

"Not at all. Was it long enough to do what you needed to do?"

"Oh, yes, she just needed me to go over some of her information, and then I've got some referrals to make for her to receive community services. So, are you ready to head to the grocery?"

"Yep, you lead, and I'll follow."

"Oh, I like the sound of that," she laughed.

"Then let's get the shopping done and get back home. Then I'll let you show me what you've got!"

Her laughter continued to ring out, a sound he hoped to hear a lot more of for a long time.

15

Josie couldn't help but smile as Jorge leaned his weight on the shopping cart, moving through the aisles of the grocery store. Looking over her shoulder, she lifted her brow. "Bored?"

"I thought you just had to pick up a couple of things for dinner."

"I did, but once you get into a grocery store, you always find things you need, and you might as well get them so you don't have to come back. I always need milk, cat food, and cat litter. Plus, I want to get the kind of beer you like. And the cookies were BOGO."

His eyes narrowed. "BOGO?"

"You know... buy one, get one. So, I bought four and got two of them for free. It's a deal I couldn't pass up."

His gaze dropped to the half-full cart, and she sucked in her lips, pressing them together to keep from laughing aloud. "Come on, Mr. Grumpy Grocery Shopper. We've made it to the frozen food, so we're almost finished. We've got something for dinner, something for breakfast, and some things to fix for the rest of the week. Now, all that's left is ice cream." She leaned closer and whispered, "We can't live off sex, you know."

At that, he stood up straight, his eyes now full of interest. "Ice cream is absolutely something I can get into. But throw in whipped cream, chocolate sauce, and a jar of cherries."

"Are we going to make sundaes?"

"Yes. Only I plan on making a full-body sundae out of you."

Her brows lifted as her eyes widened, and her smile grew. She quickly grabbed the items he mentioned. Moving to the front of the store, she was grateful there were plenty of checkout lines and they didn't have to wait. With his plans firmly lodged in her imagination, she couldn't wait to get home.

He walked behind her, his hand lingering on her back as he leaned over and whispered, "Now who's in a hurry?" His fingers dragged over the top of her ass as he moved to the end of the line and began bagging groceries.

In the parking lot, her focus was on the evening's plans as he continued to push the cart toward her car, parked just in front of his. He halted, his angry growl meeting her ears, and she jerked her head around to see him staring, anger vibrating off his body. Following his line of sight, she wasn't sure what he'd seen to bring on such immediate rage.

"Stay here," he ordered, stalking forward.

His warning didn't register, and she rushed along

after him as her phone vibrated in her purse. Trying to pull her phone out, she looked down to see her two front tires were completely flat. Jorge circled around the back, drawing her attention to the two back tires, equally flat. Abandoning the cart, she ran around her car, stunned that all four tires had been slashed.

Her fingers landed on her still-vibrating phone, and she pulled it out, glancing at the screen, a gasp leaving her lungs. **Tell ur new bookkeeper to stay out of it.**

Suddenly Jorge was at her side, taking the phone from her hand and stared down at the threat.

"Goddammit!"

She barely heard a beep over his growled curse, but it wasn't until he wrapped his hand around her arm and barked out another order that her gaze flew up to him. His touch was gentle but his words were not.

"Get in my vehicle."

"But—"

"Please, not now, Josie. Get in the fuckin' vehicle, so I can know you're safe."

Staring at him, the vision of an ancient dragon coming to life and breathing fire hit her, and she threw open the passenger door of his SUV and climbed in quickly. He threw the groceries into the back and slammed the door, pulling his phone out of his pocket. She watched as he paced around her car, one hand holding the phone to his ear and the other hand in a fist propped on his hip. His face was set in stone other than his mouth moving and his eyes glittering. For a second, she forgot about the slashed tires as she had the ridiculous notion that almost black eyes could glitter.

"And I want to know now!"

Those words from him ended on a near-shout, and her attention slammed back to her poor car sitting on the completely flattened tires.

He stalked over to the driver's side and threw open the door, climbing inside. She swallowed, not afraid of him but afraid to speak until she knew the dragon's fire was lessened.

He let out a ragged breath and finally turned toward her. His gaze moved over her face and she watched in fascination as his expression gentled.

"What happens now?" she asked, her voice soft.

He said nothing for a moment, and she thought it was prudent to wait and give him the space he needed. Finally, he said, "Let's get you home, babe. I've got to coordinate things with LSI and the FBI agent, and then we'll talk."

She preferred it when he called her *babe* in the soft way he had that made the word curl warmly inside, but hearing it now, rumbling from deep inside his chest in a way that made her feel less alone, was just as good. Nodding, she trusted that he would take care of her vehicle, the threat, and her. Buckling her seatbelt, she leaned back, her mind swirling as they drove home.

Once there, he hustled her inside, his large body close to her back. He had her wait while he did another walkthrough. She stayed by the front door, knowing that was where he wanted her. Her eyes stayed pinned on the hall where Jorge disappeared as he checked the bedrooms. She hadn't realized she'd been holding her breath until he reappeared, stalking toward her like a dark avenging angel. Amid the craziness that was her life, she could not help but admire the gorgeous man… the protector, the lover. He did not stop until he was straight in front of her, looking down, his gaze roving over her face. She knew he was looking for clues as to how she felt. Reaching up, she placed her palms on his broad chest. "I'm okay. I was shaken, but I'm okay now."

He continued to search her face for a moment as though ascertaining the veracity of her statement. Seemingly satisfied, he leaned forward and placed his lips on her forehead, holding on to the kiss for a moment. Stepping back, he linked fingers with her. "I know we need to get the groceries in and get something to eat. First, I need to check in with my people. Why don't you rest and then I'll—"

"Honey, it's okay. You go talk to your people, and I'll get the groceries and feed Melon. We bought plenty of things that will be simple to fix, so I'll throw something together for us. Then, please, let me know what our plan is."

His hands lifted and cupped her jaws, tilting her head back. She saw his intent and lifted on her toes. The kiss was hard and fast, an air of desperation as her fingers clung to his shoulders, and he swept his tongue inside her mouth. Pulling back, he kissed her forehead again and said, "I promise we'll talk as soon as I know what the deal is."

He helped her bring the groceries into the house then walked back to the guest room and shut the door. She was tempted to sneak down the hall and press her ear against the door to listen but knew that was childish. He would handle the security, and she needed to do her part by letting him do his job. Looking down, Melon was weaving back and forth between her feet, meowing.

"Okay, let's get you fed. Then I can take care of Jorge." As she opened up the cat food, she tried to pretend that it was a normal activity on a normal day and not one where someone was threatening her.

"Please, tell me you got something on this fucker," Cobb said, standing in the guest room staring out the window once again with one hand holding the phone to his ear and the other one in a fist on his hips.

"The slasher must have known where the security cameras were at the front of the grocery store and in the parking lot. We can see someone with black pants, black jacket, and a cap pulled down low moving from the side, but they kept their head down," Josh reported.

Mace interjected, "Most of us are here, and we're all working on it, Cobb. Keeping you and Ms. Rector safe is our top priority right now."

Cobb squeezed his eyes shut for a moment, trying to erase the sight of Josie's pale, frightened expression when she realized what had happened to her car. "What about coming and going from the parking lot?"

"They didn't park in the lot or the cameras would've picked it up. They weaved in and out of cars, keeping their face away from all the camera views. The jacket was baggy, but my guess would be it was a male based on the way they were walking."

"And when they left?"

"They ran off to the side where no cameras are, so there's no way to see what kind of vehicle they were in."

"Fuckin' hell," Cobb cursed. "What are you getting on the trace from her phone?"

"Text from a burner, but we pinged the tower, and it came in from your area. Not surprising, but I'm still digging to see if I can find anything," Walker said. "They mentioned bookkeeper. Who else knows that she's got someone taking Caesar's place?"

"Everybody at her office, and I've got a few more people I want you to check out. Dr. Mark Forbes. He works there part-time and has a lot of debt. Charlene Porter. She's a receptionist who dresses like she makes a fuck-ton of money. Says her boyfriend buys the shit, but I don't know. Those two don't add up for me. But while you're at it, check on the other two there. Laurie Mitchell, a nurse, and Mario Rodriguez, nurse's aide. Right now, I don't fuckin' trust anybody."

"How's Josie," Tate asked, his voice soft and full of concern.

Cobb knew his friend was trying to diffuse his anger, and he focused on breathing. "Concerned. Upset. Hiding it behind getting really quiet. It doesn't help that I lost my shit. I wanted to talk to you all first, and then I'll sit down and see how she is and let her know what's happening. She's smart and doesn't fall apart. She wants to know what the plan is."

"Somebody out there is nervous," Mace said. "Somebody's got money tied up into this and thinks Josie can blow everything."

Cobb turned away from the window and sat on the edge of the bed. "We're working with the local police on the side. I'm getting her car picked up and the detectives can send somebody around to the shop. Whoever did this is following her, but they don't know she's called in reinforcements. All they know is that I'm her boyfriend and bookkeeper. We're not dealing with someone who's got intel at their fingertips… it's pettier than that."

"Have you talked to her father?" Mace asked.

"No, not in the past couple of days. I need to. There's something I need to tell him, but I don't want any ears around. I'm going to make a trip to his home, and Josie will come with me. I don't want it at his office. Do you have anything on Carmen Martinez or Tahoma Starr? Or for that matter, those asshole friends of Bert?"

"Yeah, Rick and I have started digging. I'll send you what we've got," Josh replied.

"Right now, I want to see to Josie. Make sure the solid I'm getting from her is really solid and not just an act."

With good lucks ringing in his ear, he disconnected. He stood for another moment as he walked back over to the window and peered out. He wanted to get to Josie but needed a chance to pull his tangled thoughts together. Glancing back at the closed bedroom door, he punched a few buttons on his phone, let it ring twice, then disconnected. A moment later, Tate returned his call. He knew when Tate received a call on his personal phone he would have excused himself from the group and gone somewhere private to answer.

"How the fuck do you do this?" he asked.

Tate chuckled. "Hell, man, I don't even have to ask what you're talking about. So, you've fallen for the mission?"

"I was in the fuckin' grocery store talking about cookies and learning what the hell BOGO is when somebody was outside slashing her tires."

"Yeah, and if you'd sat outside and stared at her car, how do you know someone wouldn't have followed her inside?"

Sighing, he scrubbed his hand over his face.

Tate continued, "I repeat. You've fallen for the mission?"

"Yeah. I just… I didn't expect… she's not like what I thought she'd be. We… she… oh, hell, she's special."

Now, Tate's chuckle turned into a bark of laughter. "Are you okay with that? If so, then I don't see the problem. It's not like it hasn't happened with everybody else."

"Yeah, but each one of you fell for someone who was in a place in their life to make the move to Maine. Her life is here. Which means when the mission is over, we won't be together. But honestly? I'll deal with that when it comes. My main concern right now is keeping her safe while playing house."

"Look, Cobb, we've all done dozens of security details for people and kept things strictly professional. Just because it's become personal doesn't mean you're any less competent. You just have to stay vigilant and keep your mind on her safety. Falling for her doesn't negate your ability to do that. You're the most thorough of all of us. If we can do it, you can, too."

Sucking in a deep breath, he let it out slowly, his friend's words moving through him. "Thanks, man. I think I just needed to hear that." Disconnecting, he slid his phone back into his pocket and walked toward the door, halting as his hand rested on the doorknob.

He'd seen many of the Keepers fall in love, manage to complete their missions, and figure out ways for the relationship to move forward when the mission was over. Having witnessed wonderful relationships in his family, he knew he could handle the emotions. And Tate was right, he was focused and methodical and would work the mission to keep her safe. The last part? *I have no fuckin' clue what happens when the mission is over.* With that thought in his mind, he threw open the door and headed to the kitchen, the desire to see Josie overcoming all doubts.

Just as he made it to the end of the hall, there was a knock on her front door. She squeaked, her eyes wide, and he hated to see her fear.

She blushed and shook her head. "I guess someone threatening me would hardly knock, would they?"

He stalked to the door, looking at the security camera screen on his phone. As though the visitor knew he was being watched, an FBI ID badge was held up to the camera. Opening the door, Cobb kept his body in the way until he ascertained who he was talking to. Stepping back, he said, "Come on in."

Agent Floyd Gomez was not quite six feet tall, black

hair, and piercing black eyes that didn't appear to miss much. The two men shook hands, and Floyd looked past him toward the kitchen. Cobb felt Josie approach, and he reached out to take her hand, drawing her nearer.

"Ms. Rector," Floyd greeted, his gaze moving between her and Cobb. "I'm FBI Agent Floyd Gomez."

Cobb had no doubt Floyd was taking in his hand linked with Josie's but didn't care. She smiled at the agent and asked if he wanted something to drink. Floyd declined, and Cobb was grateful. He wanted the agent to stick to business.

The three moved to the living room, where Cobb settled Josie next to him on the sofa and Floyd took one of the chairs.

"I've arranged for your vehicle to be taken to a garage that's trusted by our local office. It'll be processed for fingerprints, although I doubt we'll find any. Once we're finished, we have a reliable mechanic who'll replace your tires. He'll come to you directly for his fee." His eyes moved to Cobb. "I'll send you his info. He's the brother of an agent and we use him for incidents when we need to keep something off the radar of the public."

Cobb felt her gaze on him and turned to see the wrinkle in her brow. "It's best to keep this out of the public knowledge. Agent Gomez will be handling things officially for you."

She nodded, offering a slight smile. "I know and that's fine."

"I've looked at the records you provided. I've got

codebreakers working on the parts that aren't just financial, but I'd definitely say it was tied into laundering money and illegal betting. I've been working on local casino fraud, and Carson Wright, among many aliases, is right in the middle of things. He represents company CEOs who like to gamble and hide their winnings by shuffling them through various businesses or nonprofits."

Josie's hand flexed against Cobb's and he glanced to the side, not surprised to observe the flash of anger that moved over her face. He offered what he hoped was a reassuring smile before turning back to Floyd.

"The good news, Ms. Rector, is that you're the first person to rattle their cages. That means they're more likely to make an error, show their hand, and we can finally get close. The bad news is that you're in their sights. I can offer—"

"I've got her," Cobb growled, his gaze holding Floyd's, waiting to see if the agent would argue. They stared at each other for a moment, then Floyd nodded.

"Okay. Then we'll process her vehicle and have it back to her as soon as possible." Standing, Floyd extended his hand toward Cobb.

Getting to his feet, Cobb shook the other man's hand and offered, "Thanks for coming by. I appreciate the insight and assistance."

For the first time since meeting, Floyd's lips twitched upward. "I'll be in touch." With that, he walked out after a chin lift toward Josie, and Cobb locked the door behind him. Turning, he held her gaze.

She stood, her hands clasped tightly in front of her.

Sucking in a breath, she let it out slowly, then said, "Let's eat. If we're going to be solving crimes tonight, we need our strength."

Turning, she headed into the kitchen, leaving him smiling in her wake.

16

"Please, sit, Josie. You fixed dinner while I was on the phone, the least I can do is clean up."

It seemed to be important to him, so she simply nodded, watching as Jorge rinsed the dishes, placed them into the dishwasher, and threw the refuse into the garbage. He opened a bottle of wine and poured two glasses. As he sat back down at the table and handed one to her, she smiled. "Is this going to be a *wine* kind of conversation?"

A chuckle rumbled from deep inside his chest. "It might be. I thought about coffee, but we both want to be able to sleep tonight. I figured wine was the way to go."

Her lips curved, and she lifted the glass, taking a sip before murmuring in appreciation. "This is really good. I should have known with your many talents, picking a good wine would be one of them."

Pulling out his phone, he began scrolling through the information Josh had sent to him. His gaze lifted to hers, and she read indecision in his eyes.

"Keeping me in the dark does no good. I can't protect myself if I don't know what possible threats are out there," she said.

"I know you're right, but I don't know how happy you're going to be with where some of the investigation is going."

Huffing, she leaned back in her chair. "I'm smart enough to know that you're having to investigate everybody who has anything to do with the clinic. I know that includes my coworkers, and even though I like them and trust them, I know you have to look at them through a different perspective."

"I like your candor, babe." Pulling out his tablet, he tapped through several screens and then scooted his chair so that he was next to her. "First off, I did talk to my fellow Keepers at LSI. Then I called Tate for a more private conversation between friends."

She pondered the information, her gaze never wavering. "You always manage to offer so much information with just a few sentences. I'm so curious as to why your coworkers are called Keepers, but that can be a conversation for another time. I do want to know what they're working on, and while I'm curious about your private conversation with your friend, I understand it's just that... private."

"I'll tell you all about LSI some time, but you're right, let's start with the information that you need to know. Let me just say that I'm having everyone in your orbit investigated. What I mean by that is everyone at the clinic because they know what Caesar did for you and that he's missing. I'm letting my boss fill in your father as necessary, but when I first met him, there were two of his aides that were present. Your father trusts them, but I'd rather they not know. It's his call, but as far as I'm concerned, they're persons of interest."

"Dad's aides?"

"Josie, you have to know that just because someone is in politics or an attorney doesn't mean they are above reproach."

She snorted. "Believe me, I know. I'm really glad that my father was just an attorney when I was young. It was hard enough to be the teenage daughter of a man running for office. He loves the life. He loves being in the public eye, but it's just not my thing. I've certainly met enough to know that politicians are no different than anyone else... some wonderful and some not so good. A few, absolutely rotten."

"For full disclosure, I'll tell you that the two in the room were Carmen Martinez and Tahoma Starr."

"Carmen? Tahoma? I don't know them well enough to imagine either of them being involved."

"Mr. Starr seemed very suspicious of me with your father. I don't know if he was just curious why I was there. Maybe he looks at everyone that way."

"I've only met him a couple of times, and he's hard to get a read on because he seems rather closed off. I know he was originally from the Jicarilla Apache Reservation and left to go to college and law school. The times I've been around him, my dad seems to have a lot of respect for him, but Tahoma rarely smiles, always seemed suspicious of everyone around him. I just figured that was his personality. "

Cobb nodded, jotting down a few notes as she spoke. Looking up, he continued. "Ms. Martinez struck me as a woman who knew what she wanted and didn't mind going after it. She approached me with a speculative look in her eye—"

"I'm not surprised." Josie rolled her eyes. "I might not know her well, but I've certainly seen her at a few functions. She's a smart woman, navigates a room to find the most attractive or wealthy men in the room. I have no doubt she would've taken one look at you and licked her chops!" As soon as the words left her mouth, she winced at the snarky tone. Jealousy was snaking through her, an emotion she wasn't comfortable feeling. *It's not like I have any claim on Cobb.*

"Are you okay?"

She jerked her gaze up to his, and her cheeks felt the heat of blush. "Yes, I'm fine. I just had a… well, a not very charitable thought."

"About Carmen?"

Wrinkling her nose, she nodded. "It's embarrassing to admit, but I have no trouble seeing her wanting you. She sees men as a challenge and from what I can tell isn't used to being told no. Honestly, this just comes from the few times I've been at social events with her, so it's not fair for me to make that judgment." Shrugging, she added, "Dad says she's brilliant, and I have no reason to doubt her professionalism. Although I can see her wanting to climb to the top, so I don't think she'd do anything to jeopardize that."

"This is good, Josie. I was afraid you were going to

be upset about having people around your father investigated."

She nodded slowly. He was right, it did feel strange to have people that she worked with, were friends with, or had known for several years be investigated. It almost felt like a breach of trust, and for a social worker that was difficult to stomach. She closed her eyes and her mind filled with the sight of her car's slashed tires and the message on her phone. Sucking in a quick breath, she let it out slowly, finding his gaze on her. Lifting her shoulders in a slight shrug, she said, "If anyone was aware of Caesar and what was going on with him, then I agree, they should be looked at."

His finger scrolled slowly over his tablet, and she leaned closer so that she could read along with him. Carmen Martinez's family, education, phone records, bank statement, and speeding tickets. Tahoma Starr's childhood home where his single mother raised him and his four siblings in a ramshackle house. Charlene Porter's multiple maxed-out credit card statements and bank overdraft notices. Mark Forbes' end-of-month bank statements where his expenses have almost exceeded his income, but deposits were made from unknown sources. Mario Rodriguez's small house that included his wife, their children, his brother, and his elderly, infirm mother. Laurie Mitchell's credit card statement that gave evidence of how expensive her wedding planning was turning out to be.

She grimaced once again, her gaze shifting to her clenched hands. She should have known she couldn't hide her reaction from Jorge.

"Josie, are you sure you're okay?"

"Yeah, but it just seems wrong for me to know this information about these people. I know you have to because you're investigating, but it doesn't seem right for me to be looking at this private information."

"If you prefer, I'll go through this myself. The only thing I'll ask is that you keep an open mind when you think about people you and your father have dealt with. Sometimes, you may have noticed things that didn't strike you at the time but now make you suspicious. If so, you need to tell me."

She rubbed her forehead with her hand. "You're right. Let me keep going through this, and I'll just treat it like anything in my profession. With my clients, I separate professional and personal, and I can do that now. I'm used to keeping confidentiality, so I should be able to handle this."

They continued to go through the records, and Cobb made notes. Scrolling to the next screen, she gasped. "Bert? You can't be serious!"

"Josie, no one is outside of the investigation."

She fell back against her chair, irritation warring with exhaustion. "Then you might as well investigate my parents also!"

"Your father is the one that hired us, and your parents want you safe."

Her eyes nearly bugged out of her head. "Bert may be my cousin, but he's as close as a brother to me. We're family. He would never do anything to hurt me. This is ridiculous!"

"He gambles."

"So what?" she bit out, throwing her hands up. "Lots of people do. That's how the casinos are successful… people gamble."

"Josie, listen to yourself. You know as well as I do that gambling can just be for fun or can be an addiction. You also know that casinos are used to hide and launder money. We're trying to tie up loose ends between Caesar possibly running dirty money through your clinic, and there's a very good chance that some of it came from or went through one of these casinos."

"Fine, but Bert? He would have nothing to do with this."

"What if he didn't know?"

Her brows narrowed as she stared at him, irritated at his calm acceptance of the situation. "What do you mean?"

"Maybe it's not him. Maybe it's somebody near him. Somebody could be using him."

"And maybe it's got nothing to do with him at all!" Her lips were pinched together so tightly her face hurt. She finally pushed the papers back and shook her head slowly. "I can't do this. I thought I could. But I'm too close to these people to even think about doubting them. I can't help you, Jorge. It will cloud my relationships."

He remained quiet for a moment, then slowly nodded. She pushed her chair back and stood. "I know you have to do this. I think I'll go take a shower and get ready for bed."

His dark eyes roamed over her face, and then he nodded slowly. She turned and walked down the hall, the weight of the world feeling heavy on her shoulders.

Several minutes later, she let the hot water pound out the tension in her back. Her mind was in turmoil, and she wished she could wash away the negative thoughts as easily as the suds ran down the drain. She regretted walking away from Jorge but was desperate for a few minutes alone. Her mother said that she'd always been that way, needing privacy to ponder a situation, consider her options, and eventually make a decision.

And he is giving that to me. That thought alone eased the tension in her shoulders. He didn't try to argue. He didn't try to prove that he was right. He simply had her review the facts and then gave her the chance to work through everything in her own time.

As her muscles relaxed, she closed her eyes, dropping her head back so the water could rinse through her hair. Behind her eyelids, she could so clearly see Jorge's face, already so familiar to her even though she hadn't known him long.

He was so calm, not a man given to rash thoughts or actions. He was introspective, confident in himself while not in-your-face with his abilities. His body was strong and handsome, but it was his quiet, inner strength that drew her to him.

The water began to cool and she turned the knobs, then stepped out onto the plush bath mat. Toweling off, she then pulled on knit pajama bottoms and a camisole top. She brushed her teeth and moisturized her body, then ran a comb through her long hair.

Leaving the bathroom, she was surprised to see Cobb sitting on the side of her bed, his body leaning forward and his arms resting on his knees. The sight of him caused her heart to skip a beat as her feet stumbled. So handsome. So capable. So serious. She was beginning to learn how to read his expressions but right now had no idea what was on his mind. As usual, he didn't make her wait long.

"Josie, this is my job. Your safety is a priority."

Her heart squeezed, but she tried to ignore the pain, wishing his words didn't hurt quite so much. Swallowing deeply, she tried to smile. "I know. I know this is your job."

He blinked, his chin jerking back slightly as though surprised. She didn't want him to feel bad, so she rushed, "It's okay. I get it. I'm a... uh... this... well, this is a mission." Even as the words left her mouth, the little fissure in her heart widened.

17

Cobb straightened his back at her words. He'd sat at the table, continuing to pore over the information while she was taking a shower, but the whole time all he could think about was how much he wanted to be with her. And now, she'd twisted things around in her mind to think that he only cared about her as part of his job.

His gaze swept over her, from her bare toes to her camisole that did nothing to hide that she was braless. Her wet hair appeared darker than normal, making her face appear even paler. *So beautiful.* "Josie, you didn't let me finish."

Her mouth snapped shut, and her blue eyes blinked, still staring at him.

He stood and walked directly to her, reaching out to take her hand. "Yes, this is my job. But you're more than a mission to me."

She stared up at him, her eyes wide, her body not moving. In fact, he wasn't sure she was breathing. "I know it seems fast, but what I feel for you is real." The air rushed from her lungs audibly, and her tongue darted out to lick her bottom lip, making it difficult to focus on anything other than her mouth.

She tilted her head slightly to the side, and her fingers flexed against his. "You said you'd never become involved with someone on a mission before."

"It's the truth. Never fallen for a mission before. And never had sex on a mission. I've always been about the job. I've always been about professionalism. I've never experienced anything personal while working until meeting you."

Her hand shifted in his, and at first, he thought she was trying to break the hold. He instantly loosened his fingers, regretting the loss but respecting her wishes. To his surprise and pleasure, she was simply shifting her hand so that she could link fingers with his.

He glanced down as he so often did when they were close together, marveling at the difference between them. His large, tanned hand with callused fingertips holding her pale, soft hands. Different and yet so perfectly balanced together.

Lifting his gaze, he was surprised to see that she was also staring at their linked fingers. "What are you thinking?"

Her lips curved gently, and she replied, "I was just thinking that we seemed to fit so perfectly together."

The iron band that had wrapped around his heart, fearful that she might not feel the same, loosened, allowing his heart to pound with joy.

Still smiling, she said, "I feel the same about you,

Jorge. I wasn't sure if it was the rescuee falling for the hero or if it was all something I felt alone."

He stepped closer, bending to whisper into her ear. "I don't mind being your hero, babe, but this is not a one-sided rescue. As smart and capable as you are, you're right here with me."

She placed her free hand on his arm, gliding it up to his shoulder. "I'm sorry I walked out on you earlier."

"No apologies, Josie. This is a lot on you, and you needed some time to think."

"Thank you for understanding that."

He hesitated, his body desiring nothing more than to pull her flush against him, giving in to his desire. But now, more than ever, he needed her to make the move. What happened between them needed to be on her time, her decision.

Her lips continued to curve until her smile was wide and her blue eyes twinkled. She lifted on her toes, her hand going from his shoulder toward the back of his head where she put a little pressure to bend him closer.

He met her smile with one of his own and closed the distance. Her mouth landed on his, and as her tongue swept inside, gliding over his, he could've sworn sparks darted about the room. Still linking fingers with one hand, he banded his other arm around her waist and lifted, thrilled when she wrapped her legs around his waist. The heat of her core through her thin pajama bottoms seared straight to his cock.

Still not wanting to take anything for granted, his lips left her mouth and kissed along her jaw. Whispering, he said, "I'm not asking for promises for tomorrow that you can't give me, but I'm letting you know that this means something to me. You mean something to me. Before we go any further, I need to know exactly what you want."

She let go of his hand to cup his face, smoothing her palms over his stubble. "I was afraid it was only me. I was afraid that maybe this was nothing special to you, but Jorge, I promise you, I feel the same."

He turned and walked to the bed, then stopped and waited.

"Yes, I want you," she said. "I don't know what tomorrow brings, either. But I know I don't want you just for tonight. What I feel is so much deeper." She leaned forward again and kissed him lightly. "Please, take me to bed."

His heart leaped, knowing that future promises had not been made but also knowing that what they felt was real. Their lips met again, and rational thoughts flew from his head as his blood rushed to his cock.

She dropped her legs, but he held her easily, her feet barely dangling above the floor. With their bodies pressed tightly together, he angled his head, sealing his lips over hers. His tongue swept inside her mouth, tasting wine and the unique flavor that was Josie. Drinking her in, he was barely aware of her hands now grasping at the sides of his t-shirt, attempting to lift it from the waistband of his jeans.

With his last bit of rational thought, he wanted them both naked but didn't want to end the kiss long enough to get their clothes off. By now, she'd managed to push his T-shirt up enough to allow her hands to glide over his abs, each trail of her fingertips sending jolts throughout his body. With his hands on her shoulders, he gently pushed her back just long enough to reach behind him, grab his shirt into his fist, and jerk it over his head and down his arms. Her eyes lit as they roamed over his torso, but like a woman who couldn't get enough, they dropped to his crotch where his erection bulged against his jeans. She reached out to his belt buckle, her hands shaking slightly as she jerked the thick leather from the clasp. She lifted her gaze to his as the sounds of unzipping filled the room. The pressure on his cock eased slightly now that it was free from the confines of the heavy denim.

Her hand flattened on his stomach, then slid to the waistband of his boxers. He wanted her hand around his cock almost more than his next breath but gently grabbed her wrist to still her movements. She looked up in surprise, and he smiled. "Your turn."

His fingers clutched the bottom of her camisole and he lifted it with ease, gliding the material up and over her head, past her fingertips, and tossing the garment to the side. With her breasts now free, her nipples budded from the cool air and excitement. He palmed them, feeling their weight in his hands. He circled the taut buds with his thumbs, grinning at her quick inhalation before she closed her eyes and dropped her head back, exposing her pale neck. With his hand still on her breasts, he bent and kissed along her jaw toward her ear, nibbling on the lobe before his mouth glided down to where he felt her pulse pounding underneath.

His hands left her breasts to caress downward, snagging his thumbs into the waistband of her pajama bottoms. Her hands were still clutching his waist, now more for holding upright than exploration, and he loved that he had her off-balance, wanting to give her pleasure. Squatting, he continued to slide her pants off, conveniently putting his mouth at the level of her breasts. Kissing over her chest, her fingers dug in as he latched onto one nipple, pulling it deep into his mouth.

She groaned, her hands flexing the harder he sucked. Moving between breasts, he licked and nipped until she was squirming, her legs pressed tightly together. Suddenly, she jerked, and he looked up to see her eyes pinned to him, determination written in her expression.

"Now, please. I need you now."

Grinning, he stood and watched her head lean back as she kept her gaze on his face. He'd taken off his boots when they came into her house so it was easy to shuck his jeans and boxers, tossing his socks onto the pile of clothes next to the bed. With them both gloriously naked, he couldn't tamp down the pride he felt as her gaze moved slowly down his body, her tongue darting out to lick her lips as she stared at his erect cock jutting out toward her.

He saw the instant she decided to drop to suck him off, but his hands snapped out and caught her underneath her arms. She looked up, an adorable crinkle between her brows. "Uh-uh, babe. Not now. Maybe later, but for now, this is about you."

He stepped forward, moving her body backward until she sat on the edge of the bed. With her palms on the mattress, she scooted until she was completely on the bed. Laying back, she opened her legs to him and grinned while lifting her arms. "Well, all right, sailor. Show me what you've got. I'm all yours."

He'd placed a few condoms in her nightstand in hopes that he would need them within easy reach. Snagging one, he ripped open the foil and sheathed himself, his cock swelling even more with her hungry eyes staring at him. Leaning forward, he placed his large hands on her knees and kissed along her thighs, the heady scent of her arousal filling his nostrils. Her skin was smooth and pale, soft as silk, and he nuzzled her neatly trimmed mound before lapping her slit. The taste on his tongue was nectar, and he dove in with little finesse, first tonguing her core before sliding his finger inside while he sucked on her clit.

Her body was a drug he'd become addicted to. For a brief second, the idea of leaving her after the mission seemed impossible, but as her fingers clutched his hair, all thoughts left other than giving her pleasure. Her nails slightly dragged over his scalp, the tiny sting shooting straight to his cock. He wanted to bury himself deep inside but knew once he entered it would be hard to hold back, therefore he needed her primed and ready.

Her hips jerked upward, and he placed one palm on her belly, holding her still as he continued to work magic with his mouth and fingers on her sex. Finding just the right spot with his finger crooked, he sucked on her clit and she cried out, her body shaking under his ministrations. The grasp on his hair tightened, but he welcomed the pain, knowing she was overtaken with pleasure.

After she rode out her release on his hand, he lapped her juices before climbing over her, settling his hips between her thighs.

Her eyes were hooded, and her smile was soft, but she lifted her hands to his shoulders. "Please, Jorge."

With his cock at her entrance, he leaned down and kissed her lightly, mumbling against her lips. "You've never got to beg, baby. All I've got is yours." With that, he plunged balls deep with one thrust.

She gasped, eyes wide, but her smile let him know she was right with him. He moved slowly, determined to drag out her pleasure as well as his. Leaning over, he kissed her deeply as his hips pistoned, his tongue mimicking the movements of his cock. She groaned, and he swallowed the sound before a moan left his lips.

Wanting to go deeper, he sat back on his calves, dragging her body with him until her pelvis was lifted slightly over his knees. Continuing to thrust, he watched her breasts bounce and he palmed them, squeezing slightly before pinching her nipples.

"Oh, fuck, Jorge," she groaned, her fingers clutching the sheets next to her.

"That's the plan, babe."

She tried to chuckle, but the sound was more of a grunt as her body was rhythmically pummeled by his.

The fire began building in his lower back, moving to his balls, and he knew he was close. With the last ounce of cognition, he slid his hand to her clit, wanting her to come again. With his thumb circling and then pressing against the engorged bud, her eyes shut tightly, and her body shook as her orgasm gripped her.

He pulled out, and ignoring the cry of protest from her, he grabbed her hips and flipped her over onto her stomach before lifting her perfect, heart-shaped ass. Plunging in from behind, he thrust deeply, the changed angle of friction intensifying the sparks. Her back bowed, and her head twisted to the side, catching his attention as she seemed to be focused on something, a smile on her face.

Following her actions, he watched their reflection in the mirror over the dresser. His heavy body bent over her delicate back, her breasts swinging rhythmically, his slick cock joining with her body. Primal. Ageless. Primitive. Timeless. Ancient. The same dance between men and women throughout the ages, throughout the cultures.

Throwing his head back, an animal roar cried out from deep within his chest as he poured his release into her, continuing to thrust until her legs slid down and he dropped forward, his body covering her back. Their panting was the only sound heard although he felt sure she could hear the pounding of his heart battling in his chest.

He pulled out gently and rolled to the side, relieving her body of his weight. Pulling her toward him, they lay facing each other, her breasts pressed against his sweat-slicked chest and their legs tangled, arms banded around each other. Sweeping the damp tendrils of hair away from her face, he left his hand on her shoulder, his thumb against her pulse point, her heartbeat racing. He pressed his lips to her forehead and left them there until her heart rate slowed against his thumb.

He pulled back just enough for his gaze to roam over her face. Clear blue eyes and a gentle smile greeted him. His heart rate may have finally slowed, but seeing her beautiful smile as she lay in his arms, he felt his heart kick in his chest. *This is not just a mission. But how do I let her know I want more? And if she wants that, too, how would it work?*

His thoughts must have shown on his face as he watched her smile slip and a crease settled in her brow. Not one to mince words, he said, "Baby, we need to talk."

18

Josie realized quickly there was nothing to bring down a sex-endorphin high like the words, *"Baby, we need to talk."* Well, maybe, *"Thanks for the sex, and do you mind catching a cab?"* Or perhaps when she was in college and got the, *"That was great,"* while the guy rushed to get dressed so he could get back to the dorm party. But those words only stung slightly, probably since they helped her avoid the awkward *what do we do afterward* moments.

Her chest deflated as air rushed from her lungs, and her muscles tightened in preparation to hear him try to let her down easily. He may have said she was more than a mission, but with her heart already involved, she steeled herself against whatever he might say.

She shifted so that she faced him completely, determined to not give in to the desire to race into the bathroom and hide. "Okay," she said, hating the way her voice shook.

Her head rested on his arm and his hand curled

around her back, holding her close. Their legs were still intertwined, and his left thumb swept over her cheek as his hand cupped her head. She stared at the strong warrior holding her, trying to discern his thoughts. As much as she was getting to know him, she still could not read all the emotions that moved through his eyes.

"I like you, Josie," he began. "But I don't know how to do this."

Her tongue darted out to moisten her kiss-swollen lips, and as much as his words stung, she also felt a bite of anger. "Do what exactly, Jorge?"

"Us. What's happening between us."

Words and retorts fled her, leaving very little she could think to say. "I see." Her response was inadequate, but considering she had no clue what he expected, it was the best she could do.

His gaze roved over her face before his brows lowered. "No, I don't think you do."

"I'm not a mind reader. Whatever you want to say to me, you just need to speak plainly. That's not usually a problem for you."

"I know, and I'm sorry. I've never done this before, so I'm afraid I'm making a mess of it."

As irritation moved through her, she still reached up with a gentle touch to the side of his face. He seemed almost in pain. "Jorge, if you're trying to tell me that you like me but all we can be is here and now, you don't have to beat around the bush. I get it. I'm not asking for promises you can't give."

"I really am fuckin' this up," he said. "What I feel for you is real. I look at you, Josie, and I don't just see a mission. I see a woman that fascinates me. Intrigues me. One that I respect and care for. And one that I want to take what we have and build on."

Her chin jerked back and she blinked. "Build on?"

"Yes, but that's what I can't figure out. I'm used to analyzing situations and coming up with solutions. Sometimes I have time to plan, but often it's on the fly. As a SEAL, I excelled at that. As a Keeper, my coworkers depend on that. A cool head. Calm rational solutions. But with you, I can't seem to do that."

She licked her lips again, still uncertain what he was getting at. His face remained unreadable, other than his eyes which were warm on her. "I know you're trying to tell me something profound, but Jorge, I still feel like I'm in the dark. Maybe it's because my sex-fatigue brain can't function normally yet, but you're talking in circles. Please, don't make me try to figure out what you're trying to say."

Determination filled his features as he sucked in a deep breath before letting it out slowly. "Right now, we have to focus on your safety and find out how Caesar's disappearance affects you. But something is building between you and me. Something special. Something real. Something that I want to keep going beyond the mission. I can't stand the thought of leaving you when all this is over. But I live and work in Maine, and you're here in New Mexico. I can't figure out how we can make this work beyond the mission, so I tried to think about us just being here and now and we'll figure things out later. And yet that goes against who I am. I want to have all the answers now. Not just for the mission but for us as a couple."

"You want to be with me?"

Now it was his turn to blink as he nodded. "I thought that was obvious."

"No, I thought you were breaking up with me. Or since we weren't officially together, you were letting me down easy. You know, letting me know I was a... um... mission fling."

His arms jerked against her back. "Mission fling? Seriously?"

"I don't know. I guess I thought maybe I was just a fling that you were having now and when the mission was over, so were we."

"Is that what you want?"

Huffing, she shook her head. "No, Jorge. I want you. I'm falling for you. But I thought maybe it was all on my side and not reciprocated."

"Then damn, babe, I'm glad we got that cleared up."

She shook her head slowly, not an easy task as she lay on her side wrapped up in his arms. "I... you..."

He chuckled, pushing her hair gently back from her face, his fingers trailing along her ear. "Now who's not making any sense?" he teased gently, a smile curving his lips. With their bodies still tangled together, they lay quiet for a moment, speaking volumes with their eyes as fingers trailed along their arms and backs.

Her mind raced as fear had turned into hope and hope had turned into joy. And yet their relationship had advanced at the speed of light... or at least faster than any other relationship she'd ever had. *Is it less real because it's so fast?*

"I don't think so, babe."

She blinked, surprised that she'd spoken aloud.

He continued. "Real is real, whether it's fast or slow. I know what I feel for you. I know where I hope we're going. I admit I don't have all the answers as to how we'll make it work for both of us, but I know you're in my heart."

"Is that what you were talking to your friend about?"

He nodded. "I know we have a lot more to discuss about you and me, but maybe it's a good time to talk about the Keepers."

At that, her finger traced over the lighthouse tattoo she'd admired on his shoulder. Nodding, she waited patiently.

"My boss got out of the military after doing a stint with the CIA. Over the years, he met others with the same work ethic and like-mindedness about what they'd like to do when they got out. He moved back to Maine and established the Lighthouse Security Investigations business. Then he proceeded to recruit former military and Special Ops who joined him at LSI. Mace grew up in Maine, close to a lighthouse, and said his grandfather used to tell stories of the lighthouse keepers. He said that it was once his dream as a child to become a keeper."

"Keepers," she whispered, entranced with his story.

Nodding, he said, "Yeah, that's what we call ourselves. The Keepers. The keepers of the light in a dark world. Trying to keep others safe."

"And your tattoo?"

"Each of us has the same tattoo, and there's a tracer buried underneath the skin at the light. Our headquarters can keep track of every Keeper no matter where they are."

"I like that. I like that you're a Keeper. I like that you help others and use your strength to protect."

His fingers glided down her back, landing on her hips where he gave a gentle squeeze. "Josie, you do the same thing with your caring nature and your strength, helping all those you work with."

She took in what he said, turning it over in her mind. Lifting her gaze to his, she asked, "And your friend?"

"I found I needed some advice. You see, over the past several years, a number of the Keepers have fallen in love. While the women come from various walks of life, careers, all with their individual personalities, every one of the women that Keepers fall in love with has certain things in common. The same things I just mentioned about you. Strength. Conviction. Selflessness. It's been said that it takes a very special woman to be with the Keeper."

"Are you the only single one left?"

He chuckled and shook his head. "No, there are several of us that are still single, and our ranks keep growing as new people come on board. My boss was the first when he fell in love with Sylvie and her young son. The interesting thing was he met them when he was investigating a murder her son witnessed."

Eyes wide, she gasped. "The little boy saw a murder?"

"From a distance, but yes. They started out when he was protecting them, but they fell in love. Another Keeper fell in love when he was in the middle of conversing with an informant and a woman literally dropped off a ladder on top of them."

"You're kidding me?"

"No, that's how Rank met Helena."

"So everyone is falling in love with someone they met on a mission?"

"Walker met Julie when he was rescuing her in Mexico. Babs works with us, and she and Drew had a thing for years but only gave into it when he had to fly to the Caribbean to help her out. Blake fell in love with Sara when she was kidnapped in French Guiana. The friend I was talking to, Tate, is with his high school sweetheart, but they were separated for many years. When she was kidnapped, he rescued her and they rekindled their romance. Levi was traveling across the country and picked up a woman who had car trouble. She was on the run from embezzlers, and as they traveled toward Maine, fell for each other."

"Oh, my God, Jorge, this is crazy!"

"The last one to fall was Clay. He found a symphonic violinist who had nothing to do with the mission. But then she ended up in the middle of a drug investigation, so it turned out that every one of us has met someone like that."

She was quiet for another moment, continuing to turn the information over in her mind. Sucking in her lips, she was uncertain what he was telling her was good. Hesitantly, she asked, "Isn't anyone afraid that meeting under such extreme circumstances might not be the best way to start a relationship? Or maybe it's a relationship that won't stand the test of time once the crisis is over?"

"That's the counselor in you, isn't it? I get it, Josie. I used to think the same thing. But all I know is that there's a certain type of woman that a Keeper looks for and a certain type of woman that is right for each Keeper. As I said, they've got to be smart, strong, independent, and trustworthy. Believe me, those are not easy traits to always find. Sweetheart, I found those traits in you, and you're definitely in my heart."

She smiled, still pondering what he was saying. "I guess—maybe—that makes sense. When you meet someone under extreme circumstances then you get to see them for who they really are. Not who they're pretending to be. Not who they'd like you to think they are."

His smile widened just before a chuckle erupted. "Not like a stranger who comes over to you at an event and tries to get you to dance."

She blushed and nodded. "Exactly. The way we met was not really who we are. But this, right here, lying in your arms, is perfect."

He leaned over and kissed her, new emotions flowing between them causing the kiss to flame brighter. His cock thickened against her stomach, and she reached between them to encircle him with her hand. Just as she hoped, he growled and rolled over her, encasing her whole body with his much larger one.

"Damn, woman." His groan was swallowed by her own and she opened her legs, wrapping them around his hips with her heels digging into his back.

The kiss broke only long enough for him to grab another condom, roll it on, and then plant himself deep inside her channel.

She grinned, but he kissed the smile right off her face until she was lost in the euphoria of their combined releases. Later, much later, she drifted off to sleep, naked in his arms. And thinking she'd love to do this every night… not just for the mission, but for the rest of her life.

19

Josie glanced to the side, once again staring at Jorge's profile. He'd insisted she take a day off of work, and they were going into Albuquerque to meet with her father. She hadn't seen her parents since she first told them about the threats. They talked on the phone but had no idea of the latest incident.

"Are you sure we couldn't have just done this by phone?" she asked, thinking of the clients she'd had to move around.

"No, what I want to talk to your dad about needs to be done in person."

A slight snort erupted. "I'm not sure that's going to make him feel any better when he hears about my tires being slashed."

He reached over and took her hand in his, linking their fingers. "It's not just about the case, Josie. I want to let him know about us."

"Us?" she squeaked. "Wait a minute! Let me get this straight. We're going to visit my dad so that you can tell him about us? Don't you think that's something we should have discussed first?"

He glanced to the side, and she was grateful the traffic was light. But then with his super skills, he could probably drive with his eyes closed. "Why? Are you saying there's not an *us*?" he asked.

"Of course, I'm not saying that, Jorge. I'm just saying that this is my dad. This should have been a decision we talked about, not just something that you decided we're going to do."

They had entered the city limits of Albuquerque, and he flipped on the blinker, steering the SUV off the highway and turning into the closest parking lot he came to. Once parked, he shifted around to face her more fully. "You're right. I should have said something. When I came up with the idea to come today, it was initially just to talk to your father to bring him up to speed on the case. But the more I thought about it, I couldn't look your father in the eye with him just thinking that I'm your protection detail and investigator. That feels disingenuous."

She opened her mouth to refute his reasons, but the full force of Jorge's honor slammed into her. She sucked in her lips and nodded slowly.

"I truly am sorry that I didn't bring this up earlier. While the relationship that you and I have is between us, it doesn't feel right to not let your father know."

"How do you know how he's going to react? What if he decides to fire LSI? Or contact your boss and tell him that he wants you taken off the case?"

"He won't."

Her chin jerked back slightly in surprise. "What makes you say that?"

"Because if there's one thing I know about your father, he loves you."

Her lips curved slightly as his words moved through her. He was right, her parents loved her dearly, and she couldn't see them being upset about a relationship that brought her happiness. "You're right about my parents loving me, but it still seems risky."

"Not to me, Josie. There's nothing about being with you that seems risky at all." He gave a little tug on her hand, and she leaned forward, responding to his silent plea as their lips met in the middle. The kiss was soft but heartfelt. She drew from his strength, and as she leaned back, she nodded.

Just when she thought he was going to start the engine, he gave her hand another squeeze and added, "I guess what I said wasn't right. There is a risk. A risk of me losing my heart."

With that, her smile broke free, and she settled back in her seat as he started the engine and pulled back onto the street.

Soon, they came to her father's office. As many times as she had been to her father's office over the years, Josie couldn't believe how nerves were hitting as she walked in with Jorge's hand resting lightly on the small of her back. Her stomach was doing flip-flops, and she could only imagine what it would have been like if he'd reached down to take her hand. As much as she liked that link with him, she was glad for the moment that he was not overtly claiming her for all to see.

"Josephine! We knew to expect Mr. Cobb but had no idea you'd be coming too. It's lovely to see you again, my dear."

"Thank you, Mrs. Murphy. It's lovely to see you, as well." She smiled at her father's longtime secretary. Turning to the other woman sitting nearby who was openly drooling over Jorge, she greeted with much less enthusiasm, "Carla. Nice to see you again, too."

Mrs. Murphy had risen from her desk and walked around, inserting herself between Carla and Jorge, her lips pinched tightly. It was all Josie could do to keep from smiling, knowing that when they left, Mrs. Murphy would have something to say to the younger receptionist.

"You may go on back," Mrs. Murphy said. "I won't announce you. I'll let your father be surprised."

Walking down the hallway, they quickly made it to the end office, and she was glad her father's door was open but no one else was there.

"Josie!" Her father's smile was wide as he hustled around the desk and wrapped his arms around her, pulling her in close. "I was just telling your mother that we needed to see you. Oh, I do hope you'll stay so that she can have a chance to spend some time with you as well."

The feel of her father's arms around her as she rested her cheek on his shoulder always sent comfort through her, and this was no different. She blinked away the tears that threatened to fall, uncertain why they were so close to the surface.

As her father pushed her back gently and stared at

her face, his eyes narrowed. Jerking his head toward Jorge, he reached his hand out for a shake while saying, "What's going on? I thought this was just going to be an update from you, but now, seeing Josie, I'm worried."

"Dad, you can talk to me," she jokingly complained.

"I'm not ignoring you, sweetheart, but I'd rather hear from the investigator what's going on."

"I agree, sir," Jorge said. He nodded his head toward the chairs. "Josie, why don't you have a seat?"

"Yes, yes, I'm sorry. Please, sit," John agreed, waving his hand toward the chairs in front of the desk.

As Josie settled into her seat, she was aware that Jorge had stepped away from her. Glancing over her shoulder, she watched as he closed the door before moving back to shift the empty chair closer to hers. Once seated, his assessing gaze roamed over her face before he smiled.

Her heart was pounding as though she were sixteen years old and introducing her parents to her boyfriend, but his smile eased the butterflies inside.

"Sir—"

"Please, call me John."

"John, it's important for me to start out saying that LSI is making headway in finding out who is threatening your daughter. Another threat came in yesterday, and we are coordinating our efforts with an FBI agent experienced in fraud. I'm not leaving Josie's side, but the last threat was her tires being slashed yesterday evening when we were in the grocery store. While I wasn't able to keep that from happening while being inside with her, the most important thing to me is keeping her safe and out of harm's way."

John nodded emphatically but his brow, creased with worry-lines, gave evidence to his concern. "Josie, I'm so sorry that happened. But I quite agree with Jorge. He should be right with you."

"There's something else I need to tell you, John. Josie felt like it would come better from her on her own time, but I'm not a man to have anyone think I'm taking advantage of them or a situation."

"I don't understand." John's eyes moved between both of them, his head tilted slightly.

Just as Jorge was about to speak, Josie reached over and linked fingers with him, needing his touch as an anchor. "What Jorge wants to tell you, Dad, is that we're seeing each other… um… dating. While it may seem fast to you, please, keep in mind that I'm almost thirty years old, and I know my own mind."

John's eyes widened in shock, then narrowed for a few seconds, almost in disbelief. He glanced down at their linked fingers, then suddenly smiled widely. "Josie? Jorge?"

Wishing her mouth was not so dry, she nodded. Jorge's fingers caressed lightly over her hand, and she let out a calming breath. "Yes, Dad?"

"Praise, God!" John said, throwing his hands into the air. "I couldn't be happier for you."

Josie blinked, surprised at her father's exuberance. "Wow, Dad."

John moved around his desk again and pulled Josie to her feet, hugging her tightly. "Sweet, baby girl, all I've ever wanted is for you to be happy and healthy. But every parent wants to see their child in a loving relationship. Maybe I shouldn't have used the word *loving*. Maybe that's too soon or too old-fashioned, but knowing that you've got someone taking your back, and not just as a job, makes me feel so much better."

He let go of Josie but only to reach his hand out toward Jorge. "I'm not just saying this because you're the governor's son, but I'd be a liar if I didn't say that was exciting. I've known your family a long time and have no doubts about your integrity or abilities. I just ask that you keep my daughter safe regardless of the relationship the two of you have or don't have at some point."

"John, I assure you, that her safety is paramount to me. Not just as an investigator but as a man who cares a great deal for her. But you have my word that if our relationship changes, her safety will remain first and foremost with me."

Josie twisted her head to hold his gaze, her smile matching the lightness of her heart. As her father stepped back, Jorge placed his arm around her shoulders, tucking her next to him.

"I was going to take Josie by my parents' house. I'm sure they'd love to have you and Mrs. Rector come by as well."

At Jorge's words, she blinked before making bug-eyes at him. Her attention was drawn back to her dad as he clapped his hands.

"Oh, I can't wait to call your mother."

Ushered out of his office with vows to see them

later, she glared up at Jorge while he kept his arm around her as they walked down the hall. "You could have mentioned we were meeting your parents!" she whispered.

"Didn't want you to be nervous."

"Well, surprise... I am now!"

Just before turning the corner at the end of the hall, she felt a prickle on the back of her neck. Glancing behind, she caught a glimpse of Carmen's narrowed-eyed stare boring straight at her. It only lasted a second before Jorge propelled her forward, but it was enough to send a trickle of unease slithering over her. Jorge's words from the other day came back to mind. *I told you I don't trust anybody.* At the time, it was hard to understand his statement... now, she was beginning to feel the same.

20

Jorge looked across the room, unable to keep the smile from his face. His parents had reacted with excitement as soon as they arrived at the family home, calling the grandparents to join them. It didn't take long for Josie's parents to pop by, making for a lively gathering. He wanted to shout to everyone that Josie was *it* for him, but knowing that wasn't fair to her, they just let their families know they were dating.

His gaze followed her as she stood to one side, admiring his grandmother Naomi's turquoise jewelry while complimenting his grandmother Maria's canapés. His mom and Betty Rector had their heads inclined together, whispering discreetly, but he felt sure they were trying to figure out a way that he and Josie could marry and begin producing grandchildren immediately. Their fathers looked as though they'd won the lottery and were soon joined by his grandfather, Edward, Sr.

A hand on his shoulder had him turn around, his

heart warming as his grandfather Carlos' wizened smile met his. "Tata," he greeted affectionately.

"You are well, Jorge?"

He chuckled and nodded. "I am."

Carlos nodded toward the women on the other side of the room. "Josephine is a beautiful woman."

"She is. Inside as well as out."

The creases in Carlos' face deepened with his smile. "That is best. Like my Naomi." They were quiet for another moment, but he had no doubt his grandfather had more to say. The older man cast his gaze to the side, his smile still on his face. "So, the women are wondering if you two are just dating while you're here or if there is something more going on between you two."

He let out a long breath, his gaze pinned on Josie's gentle laughter at something Maria said. Swallowing deeply, he said, "I can't say for sure. I know that when the threat against her is over, and I have to return to Maine, I'd like her to come with me. But it seems too early to ask something like that of her. We've just started our relationship."

Carlos nodded. "Tardé una hora en conocerte y solo un día en enamorarme. Pero me llevará toda una vida lograr olvidarte."

His breath caught in his throat as he listened to his grandfather's words, repeating them in English. "It took me an hour to get to know you and just a day to fall in love. But it will take me a whole life to be able to forget you."

His grandfather nodded. "I knew the first day I met your grandmother that she was the one for me. I was in love. We had so many obstacles in our life. My family... her family... traditions. But I knew that if we weren't together, I would regret it my whole life." He twisted his head to look up at Jorge. "If that's what you feel, then how long you've known her doesn't matter. All that's important is what you'll do about it." With another pat on his arm, Carlos walked over to the other men.

Just then, Josie turned and caught his eye, her smile capturing his heart. He walked over and slid his arm around her shoulders, loving the feel of hers around his waist. Bending, he whispered, "You okay?"

She nodded, but before she could answer, the clinking on a glass caught everyone's attention. Turning together, all eyes landed on his father as he held his drink.

"It's always a pleasure when our adult children make a visit, and especially when they bring others into our fold. It's with pride and love that I toast my son, Jorge. To the man he has become, we are so proud of you as you forged your own path of honor and duty in this world. And to the sweet and lovely Josephine, we are so pleased to have you with us as well. My son warned me not to make too much of things, so let me just say that I hope your... uh... *friendship* continues to grow together."

Laughter rang out as they toasted the couple. Hugging her to his side, he kissed her blush-heated cheek.

It took thirty minutes for them to finally make it through goodbyes, each parent and grandparent having to have their moment with each of them. Once ensconced inside the SUV, he turned at the sound of her giggle and spied the gathering on the front portico of his parents' house all waving goodbye.

"Jesus, you'd think they'd never had guests before," he grumbled, looking askance toward Josie, unsure of her reaction to his multiple surprises during the day.

"You know, I should be furious with you."

Her voice was calm, but he understood the gentle censure coming through her tone. Sighing, he nodded. "I know I shouldn't have sprung all this on you. Originally, I thought of coming by myself to speak to your dad. But after yesterday, I didn't want to leave you alone. But I couldn't figure out how to tell you that I wanted to speak to him about us. Not the case, but us."

"I get that, Jorge. I do. But we're new. There's still so much we don't know about each other." She snorted and shook her head. "That's an understatement if there ever was one!"

"Every great relationship starts with two people just getting to know each other. I may not know your favorite color, but I know you as a person. You're the perfect blend of reserved in a large crowd and yet fun with your friends. I know you work tirelessly to help others and yet don't toot your own horn. I know you love your family. Love to travel. Love to see new places. Are smart enough to not buy a house until you know it's where you want to stay. I know you're beautiful straight out of the shower with wet hair and no makeup or first thing in the morning when your eyes are barely open."

The soft inhalation coming from next to him caused

him to jerk his gaze toward her, observing the tears in her eyes and the play of a smile about her lips.

"Why do you always have to say things to me that make me want to jump you when you're driving?" she asked.

Chuckling, he said, "Damned if I know!" He made an exaggerated effort to swing his head around. "Why the hell isn't there a hotel around when you need one?"

She laughed and shook her head. Reaching over, she placed her hand on his leg. "Okay, you're right. We know enough about each other now to be sure of what we feel."

"Damn straight."

The rest of the drive was spent in lively conversation, beginning with a game of twenty questions as they discovered a shared love of music, Thai noodles, homemade bread, long walks, and British comedies.

Parking in her driveway, he scanned the area as his typical precaution. Her security was monitored by LSI and he knew they had not noticed anything untoward.

Entering her house, she slid off her shoes and plopped her purse onto the counter, saying, "I'll feed Melon." As the cat slinked into the kitchen, its tail twitching in anticipation of a midnight snack, her phone vibrated an incoming message.

She reached into her purse and glanced at the screen. Her scream pierced his heart as he stared to see her wide-eyed horror. Racing to her side, he grabbed the phone. There, on the screen was a photograph of Caesar, slumped as he was tied to a chair. Blood covered his bruised face and a bullet hole was in his temple. The message under the picture was clear. **Don't be next.**

"Fuck!" he shouted. The soft moan to his side sliced through the white-hot rage that roared through him. Whirling around, he watched as Josie slumped backward, her hips hitting the counter behind her. Her lips were as white as her complexion, causing the intensity of her blue eyes to stand out even more. She slumped further, and he snapped his hands out to grab hold of her, gently settling her on the floor as he knelt with her.

Softening his voice, he murmured, "It's okay, babe. I've got you. I've got you." Her head fell forward onto his chest as heat poured from her body. Recognizing the adrenaline of fear running through her, he shifted his ass to the floor, easing her into his embrace. The hair along her forehead was soaked with sweat, and he pushed it back, placing his lips against her skin. His fingers found the pulse on her wrist, noting it to be slow but steady.

"Josie, stay with me, baby. I want you to lean forward and put your head between your knees."

"I'm okay," she mumbled in a whisper. "Do... whatever..."

"I need to report this to Floyd and my team, but you're my first concern. Take deep breaths. In through your nose slowly, then out through your mouth slowly. Breathe with me." He mimicked the slow breathing, glad when she followed his lead.

She lifted her head, her eyes still glazed. "I'm okay."

He slid his hand into his pocket and pulled out his phone. Quickly pressing a few buttons, he said, "Got a problem. Josie just got a text. It's a photograph of Caesar. He's dead. I need all hands on deck. Give me a call when you're ready." He disconnected, knowing the Keepers on the other end would know what they needed to do. With another few clicks on his phone, he waited till Floyd answered. "It's Cobb. I need you at Josie's now." Disconnecting from that call, he also knew the agent would be at Josie's soon. Figuring he had about fifteen minutes before Floyd's arrival, he shoved his phone back into his pocket and turned his full attention toward her.

She lifted her head, and while still pale, the deep breathing had the desired effect as her complexion now had a faint tinge of pink instead of pure white.

"I want to get you off the floor, baby." He shifted to a squat, and with his hands under her arms, he gently lifted her to her feet, continuing to hold her, not trusting her legs to support her slight weight. "Floyd is on his way over, and I want to get you into your bedroom."

She lifted her gaze, her eyes searching his face, then slowly shook her head. "Jorge, I don't want to be off by myself."

"Baby, I'll be right here in the house with you. But I don't want you to have to be part of the conversation that I'm going to have with my people and Floyd."

Her tongue darted out and licked her lips as she continued to shake her head. "I'm already involved."

She appeared steadier on her feet, and as much as he wanted to tuck her into bed and hide her away, he knew she was right. "Then let's get you comfortable."

With his arm wrapped around her shoulders and the other arm holding her hand, he escorted her to the sofa, settling her against the deep cushions. Jogging back into the kitchen, he grabbed a bottle of water and a banana from the bowl of fruit. Stalking back over, he unscrewed the lid off the water and handed it to her. "Stay hydrated and eat the banana." Knowing she was perfectly capable of eating and drinking on her own, he could not help but stand watch over her, his hands ready to reach out if she needed any assistance.

Looking up, she said, "I don't need you to stare at me while I'm eating a banana—"

"Give this to me, Josie." He knew his voice was guttural, and her nose crinkled in surprise. Letting out a deep breath, he added, "I need to know that you're okay. And you need to let me." He held his breath for a second, wondering if she was going to argue. She simply nodded, and he breathed a little easier.

His phone vibrated, and he pulled it out, seeing a one-word message from Floyd. **Here**. A few seconds later, there was a knock on the door. He flung it open, stepping back to allow the agent to enter.

With no preamble, he held out Josie's phone and said, "This just came in."

Floyd's calm demeanor fled as his eyes flashed. "Goddammit," he growled. His gaze jerked back up to Cobb's and then over to Josie sitting on the couch. He reiterated," Josie's phone?"

Nodding, Cobb said, "Yeah. She got to it before I did. And the accompanying message."

Floyd's gaze dropped to the phone screen again, his jaw tightening.

"We've run out of time. Whoever this is, they're escalating."

"Have you talked to your people?"

"I should get a call any moment. I told them I was bringing you in." Cobb twisted his head around and looked toward the sofa, seeing Josie's gaze pinned on him. He moved over to her, sitting on the coffee table, his legs spread so that his knees bordered hers. And leaning forward, with her hands now in his, he tried to offer his body as a comforting shelter. "Josie, I know you want to hear what's going on. And I swear, I don't want to keep you in the dark. But I need to know that you're safe. Not just physically, but emotionally. I'm not sure I can do that with you sitting here in the room. I'm going to be watching every word I say, and every word that anyone else is saying."

She held his gaze for a moment, then nodded slowly. "I don't like the idea of hiding out in my bedroom, Jorge. But I don't want to hamper you, either."

"How about we run a tub and you soak in a hot bath for a while. I'll check on you to make sure you're fine—"

"I think I know how to bathe myself," she said, her lips trembling as they curved slightly.

"I know, but you've suffered a shock, and I still want to keep an eye on you. If you try to relax for a little bit and let me, Floyd, and the Keepers see what we can come up with, I promise to bring you up to speed when we're finished."

She held his gaze for another moment, then nodded

slowly. "It feels like it's going against what I want to do, but I agree. I don't want to hinder your investigation. I know you're protecting me."

He stood and gently drew her to her feet. Looking over her shoulder toward Floyd, he offered a chin lift. "I'll be right back. Grab something to drink and make yourself at home."

He escorted her through the main bedroom to the bath and leaned over to turn on the taps. Turning around, he lifted his hands and cupped her face, sweeping his thumbs over her shock-chilled cheeks. "I'm not going to shut the door, but I promise you'll be safe in here. I want to be able to hear you if you need me."

She nodded her acquiescence, and he bent, sealing his lips over hers in a soft, gentle kiss. She stripped quickly and stepped over into the tub, groaning as she eased into the deep water. Bending to kiss the top of her head, he walked out, making sure to leave the door cracked.

Stalking down the hall, he allowed his focus to center, but the warrior inside raged again. *Time to fucking figure out who killed Caesar and is threatening Josie.*

21

Cobb felt Floyd's intense stare but ignored the agent as he settled at the table, his encrypted, secure laptop open in front of him. Jerking his head to the side, he invited Floyd to sit, glad when the man was able to understand head motions considering Cobb wasn't in the mood for social niceties.

A few minutes later, the screen filled with the sight of the other Keepers, and from the looks of things, most had made it into the headquarters from their beds in the middle of the night. He knew there were no regrets, just as he knew he'd be there for any one of them if he'd been at home.

"How's Josie?"

He appreciated their concern and the fact that none of them wasted their time telling him to hold on to his shit or asking him how he was doing. They would know he was holding on, even if it was by the barest edges of his fingernails.

"I've got her soaking in a hot tub filled with some

kind of lavender shit that's supposed to be relaxing and a glass of wine perched on the side."

"Best thing you can do right now." Mace's voice was his usual growl, but Cobb recognized concern.

"What have you got?"

"Is Floyd with you?" Levi asked.

"I'm here," Floyd said.

"Good to have you with us." Again, not wasting time, Mace jumped in. "I know you haven't had a chance to study the photograph. We have and hope we can give you enough information that you can locate where it was taken. That investigation is on you. Same with finding Caesar's killers. But we'll give you everything we can. Our responsibility is the security of Josie."

"Understood." Floyd leaned forward, his gaze pinned on the computer screen where an enlarged, enhanced version of the picture was displayed.

"The Bureau will have its analysis, but with the picture being so close on Caesar, there's little background to ascertain as to exactly where he is. But looking at what we can see of his body, there's bruising on his face, some appearing older than others. This would indicate he's been hit, probably throughout the time he's been missing. This could also indicate that they're looking for something. Why else keep him alive and beaten? And the gunshot to his temple is execution-style. We can only see the entrance wound with its abraded skin, but since there is blood on the floor on the opposite side, we'll assume it came from an exit wound." Cobb wasn't surprised to hear Tate's voice. All Keepers were weapons experts, but Tate's knowledge of weapons was exceptional.

Floyd leaned even closer, nodding. "Got it."

"Looks like a hard-contact wound from the searing. Definitely execution. I'd say twelve-gauge, but your people will make that call," Tate continued. "The orange-red tattooing indicates Caesar was alive when shot."

Cobb shook his head, his gut clenching. "I'd feel better if this was someone in Josie's orbit with just a gambling problem and needing a way to hide takings. This here... fuck... this is indicating organized crime, probably cartel involvement."

"That's our take as well," Mace concurred. "Not going to waste time trying to figure out more 'cause that's Floyd's concern."

"Agree, but with this information, we can look at who might be in her orbit that could have those kinds of connections. What have you got on any of them?" The unfamiliar slither of emotions-over-mission running through him made Cobb hope his voice sounded stronger than it felt coming from his lungs.

"Okay, let's start with Bert. You know he's an attorney, but it took him an extra year to get there because he almost flunked out of college his first year. Honestly, probably not a big surprise considering his parents had not been deceased very long. From all accounts, he's tight with Josie's family, his bank accounts look normal, and he has an investment portfolio that, again, doesn't ring any warning bells. Now, he's still friends with a bunch of guys he was in a fraternity with at the University of New Mexico. No red flags on most of them except two that have finances that show deposits that look suspicious. Timothy Hobson and Roberto Mendez."

"Those are the two that were with Bert at the casino on the rez. Looked down their nose at me until they found out I was the son of the governor. Then they couldn't shake my hand enough. Fuckin' pricks."

"Both have money shifting around. Deposits that don't equal their paychecks, cash going into various accounts with various banks. Could just be gambling winnings but could be other kinds of payoffs. Both work for a textile shipping company that, believe it or not, has accounts in Mexico."

"So, these guys may just be using Bert as a way to move in and out of political circles to hobnob with movers and shakers? Maybe even the way they found out about Josie's clinic?" Floyd scribbled notes on a pad, occasionally tapping the end of his pen on the table.

Josh answered for the Keepers. "It's certainly a possibility. And if they're engaged in illegal activities, laundering money at the least, and possible drug trafficking, then Bert could just be a pawn, or he's involved as well. One of the things we've discovered is that they go across the border to a casino in Ciudad Juarez, Mexico—"

Floyd interrupted. "They don't have to pay any fucking taxes on their winnings."

"Exactly. So, it's not only lucrative for gambling, it makes it lucrative to run your money through the casinos."

Cobb asked, "How is the money laundering through the casinos tied into Josie's charity?"

"I've been looking at this," Tate said. "My guess is that Caesar was working with this lawyer in El Paso, Carson Wright, who has ties to several of the casinos. It would be easy for him to take money from individuals or cartels and flush them through the books of the clinic since he was the only one looking at them. Caesar could move the money in any direction. A cartel running a casino could move money to someone in the states by shuffling it through a charity organization. In and out with no one the wiser other than the book-keeper who was handling everything. It could also be used by somebody in the states who's dealing with the cartel as a way to get money to them through the charity and through the casino. The more shuffling of money, the less someone's going to try to follow the trail."

"Anything on Carson Wright?" Floyd stopped bouncing his pen and made eye contact with Cobb.

"Right now, he's in the wind, too. I got a bad feeling that he may be meeting the same fate as Caesar, or maybe he's just hidden. The drive you found is full of codes that even Josh couldn't crack. We've turned that over to the FBI as well."

"Okay, what about anybody else? Mark Forbes? Charlene Porter? Hell, I don't trust Senator Rector's aides, Carmen Martinez or Tahoma Starr, at all. Anything on them?"

"Nothing that ties anyone into laundering or cartels, but we're still looking."

"I know we've already talked about Mark Forbes and Charlene Porter. We've been able to pull up a little bit more on Charlene's boyfriend that she claims spends money on her. Looks like she's hooked up with a man about fifteen years older than her who runs an investment company that's got a presence in El Paso as well as Albuquerque. Anton Sanchez. Don't know if she's aware, but he's married. There's nothing on her phone that would indicate he's promising to leave his wife."

"Tahoma Starr was born on the Jicarilla Apache Reservation. Parents are dead, no siblings. It doesn't look like he's been back, or at least he has no ties there. Took a scholarship straight outta high school and went to college and then law school. Can't find anything strange about his accounts or money, but at this point, that could just mean that he hides things well."

"You haven't gotten to Carmen," Cobb noted.

Chuckling, Josh said, "Honestly? She looks like a maneater. Sharp. Smart. Plays the field and doesn't date any one person. Makes no bones about having her eye on politics and her dates are movers and shakers."

Floyd looked over at Cobb. "I can't see someone like her risking it all on gambling or money laundering."

"You never know what makes someone take risks. Sometimes it's nothing more than a bad decision then they get trapped in having to continue to do things they wouldn't normally do just to keep it quiet," Mace responded.

Cobb snorted. "Tell me about it. It's the way of politics. And I've got no doubt that the cartels and politicians can have inroads with each other." He sighed and squeezed the back of his neck, willing the tension to ebb. "So, where does this leave us right now? Other than I'm not going to leave Josie's side."

Floyd leaned back in his seat. "I've already sent the photograph of Caesar to my superiors. Right now, he goes from someone missing to a murder victim. The Bureau will kick this into high gear."

Cobb growled, "The big question comes to what is it that someone thinks Josie can do? Caesar gave her the mini drive, so is that what they are after? Is that why they tortured him? If Josh can't figure out the code right away, what makes them think that she can?"

Mace's calm voice cut through Cobb's frustration. "Could just be because she had a copy of the records. Maybe they were beating him up to find out if he gave that information to anyone else. Or if he knows if she did."

"And she did. They know I'm around. They know I'm looking."

"But the message said to keep her bookkeeper out of it. They don't know you're investigating. Just that you're dating," Tate reminded.

"I can't just fuckin' sit here and wait for something else to happen."

"We're working it on this end, but you're right... things are heating up. I'm sending Tate and Bray to you. Drew will fly them in and be there as backup. With you staying with Josie while she works, they can help with keeping an eye on what you can't."

Silently, but surely, the air released from his lungs and some of the tension released from his neck.

Hearing that three more Keepers were coming meant he could stay with Josie twenty-four seven and still have eyes on her house and her clinic. And as far as he was concerned, she wasn't driving separately from him anymore regardless of what a client thought. A flash of concern ran through his mind that she might not like the restrictions, but that was immediately followed by the reminder of her expression when she'd stared at the vision of Caesar's body on her phone screen.

The Keepers, Floyd, and Cobb continued to plan for the next ten minutes before disconnecting with promises to see Drew, Tate, and Bray the next day. After walking Floyd to the door, the two men shook hands. "I figure working with a crew like mine might be out of your element, but I appreciate everything you're doing."

Floyd nodded, his handshake firm. "That's quite a team Mace has assembled. I knew some good people who went into security after they left the military, but I've never experienced anything like the level you work with. I realize you can go your own way, but keep in mind that I'm bound by rules, and I'll follow them."

"I wouldn't expect you to do anything other than follow your rules. We both have our own jobs to do while trying to keep Josie safe. I know you're going to focus on Caesar's murder and hope that anything you discover you let me know if it'll help me eliminate the threat to Josie."

Still nodding, Floyd agreed. "And I'll ask for the same consideration. Whatever you find, send that information my way."

He watched Floyd head to his vehicle before shutting and locking the door and setting the alarm. Glancing at the clock on the stove in the kitchen, he realized that the meeting had taken much longer than he'd anticipated. Flipping off the lights, he hustled down the hall and into the main bedroom. The bathroom door was still cracked open but he could hear water draining from the tub.

Stepping inside, his gaze landed on the empty wine glass and Josie standing at the double-sink vanity. Her hair was haphazardly piled on top of her head, multiple tendrils streaming down, their ends wet. Her skin was rosy from the warmth of the bath, and she'd pulled on her sleep shorts and camisole with a floral, silky robe draped over her shoulders. Her hands were gripping the counter and her gaze was staring into the mirror at herself before drifting to his reflection.

"Josie, baby." His voice was soft, the desire to comfort strong. He stepped behind her, one arm banding around her waist, his hand resting on her stomach, and the other arm wrapped around her upper chest. He tucked her back close to his front, and with his added height rested his chin on the top of her head as they both continued to stare at each other's reflection in the mirror. "I was hoping the bath would make you feel better."

She rolled her lips in for a few seconds. "It did. I was so cold, and it chased the chills away. I drank the wine, closed my eyes, and lost track of time."

"Good. That's exactly what I wanted to happen." When she remained quiet, he gave her a little squeeze, drawing her gaze back to his. "And now?"

"I keep thinking about Caesar. It's hard to wrap my mind around the fact that the man that sat in my office a few weeks ago... a man that I used to see twice a week for the last couple of years... a man that occasionally ate in the workroom with us... is now dead. And not just dead like he was in a car accident or had a heart attack. Or even killed in some random act of violence. But he was murdered."

She swallowed deeply, and he felt her chest heave with the movement but remained quiet, giving her a chance to voice her struggle.

"And not just murdered for a reason that had nothing to do with me. But murdered because he was involved in or found out that someone was moving money through the clinic's finances."

She dragged in a breath that wasn't ragged, but he still felt her chest shudder with the effort. She turned with his arms still encircling her and wrapped hers around him as well. Tilting her head back, she looked up and her blue eyes penetrated straight through him.

"I don't know what to do with that, Jorge. I don't know how to reconcile that in my mind. It's all so horrible, and I don't know how to begin processing all of this."

"For starters, babe, just know that you're not going to process it by yourself. I'm here, and I'm not leaving. You've got nothing to fear because I'm going to stay with you every second. And the Keepers are on this as well as the FBI. In fact, tomorrow, you're going to get to meet some of my crew. Three Keepers are coming in."

Her brow crinkled as though his words were difficult for her to comprehend. "Coming here?"

"Drew, Tate, and Bray are coming. That way we'll have more backup. One of them will be able to keep an eye on your place here while I am with you constantly. The other two are going to be able to help keep an eye on the clinic and we're stepping up the investigation into who's behind the threats."

He was afraid she was going to have more questions, and right now, he didn't have a lot of answers. But in true Josie form, she simply nodded, giving her trust over to him.

"Okay."

He couldn't help the smile that curved his lips. "Okay? Just that easy?"

She lifted her shoulders in a little shrug and nodded. "This is what you know best. This is what you do. I'd be a fool to argue against that."

He kissed the top of her head and muttered, "Easy. Absolutely perfect and easy." Her exhaustion was evident, and he asked, "Have you finished in here?"

She nodded, her head moving against his chest. "Yeah, I was all done when you came in."

"Then I'll tuck you in before taking a quick shower. Ten minutes, and I'll join you."

She acquiesced, and he did exactly what he said he would do. Ten minutes later, he crawled into bed with her, wrapped her back into his embrace, and finally relaxed as her breathing eased and he knew she had found sleep. He hoped her dreams were peaceful but was prepared to slay her nightmares if needed.

22

Josie woke in a warm cocoon, blinking at the early morning dawn peering through the slats of her blinds. She'd slept, although fitfully, waking numerous times during the night. Each time, Jorge's arms had tightened around her, his lips pressed against her forehead, and his hand gently soothed over her shoulders and back until she fell asleep once again.

She heard his steady breathing, glad that he had finally found rest, knowing she'd woken him often. For a few minutes, she stared at the ceiling fan slowly circling, her mind revolving in a similar pattern. Over and over, she thought of Caesar. *Did he know what was going to happen to him? Was he the one running the money through the clinic or was he an innocent pawn? A criminal mind or a bystander? Did I simply stumble into something he was trying to hide?*

Part of her wanted to curse the bad luck of making the decision right then to review the donations, but in truth, she knew it was better to have discovered the subterfuge than for the clinic to blissfully be ignorant of the various uses of its finances. *Or be shut down if it had been discovered by someone else!*

For the millionth time in less than a day, the image of Caesar on her phone screen hit the back of her eyes. She licked her dry lips, battling the nausea that threatened to rise. As a social worker, she'd seen abuse, neglect, fear, need, drug use, poverty, homelessness, and desperation. She thought she'd seen the worst of human depravity, but she'd never seen the aftereffects of possible torture and then murder. The air in her lungs rushed out, but she stilled her movements, not wanting to wake Jorge.

And someone wants me silent.

Jorge stirred, and she knew he was waking. Glad for his presence now in her life, she battled the feeling that her life was no longer her own. His eyes blinked open, their darkness warm as they landed on her. He lifted his hand and brushed her hair away from her face before his palm cupped her cheek. He shifted to his side and drew her close, placing a gentle kiss on her lips. "How's my Josie today?"

My Josie. How was it that in the middle of a nightmare those two words moved through her, swirling about her heart, sending a smile to her lips?

"If I said *okay* or *fine*, I'm not sure that would be correct. But I'm safe and here in your arms. So, I think that's the best it can be right now."

He nodded, his thumb sweeping over her cheek before touching his lips with hers again. "I'd like nothing more than to keep you right here all day—"

"I know, but I missed going to the clinic yesterday, and I don't want to miss again. And for my sanity, I need to keep things as normal as possible."

"That's my Josie. Fuckin' beautiful and resilient. Absolutely perfect." With another touch of their lips, he rolled out of bed and gently pulled her along with him.

As he stalked into the bathroom, she looked down as Melon weaved about her feet. "I know, I know, it's time for you to be fed." Padding into the kitchen, she determined to go about her business as normally as possible. Hearing the water in the shower turn on, her feet stumbled slightly at the thought of Jorge and how fast life was moving for them.

Life's too short for doubts. And for the first time, the possibility of Maine loomed as a beacon in the distance... like a lighthouse guiding the way.

Josie moved through her normal routine in the clinic... at least, she hoped, as far as the others could tell. She completed paperwork, had several counseling meetings in her office, and oversaw new clients as they came in needing medical assistance. She smiled at her coworkers, listened with interest as Laurie talked about buying her wedding dress, joked with Mario as he described the latest antics of his children, and managed to eat lunch with them without choking.

Jorge had decided to be less conspicuous at the clinic and was sitting in his SUV near the back door. He'd texted her to let her know that the other Keepers had arrived and would meet them at her house that evening.

She hated for him to be in the car most of the day but knew he was working securely from whatever super-secret computer he had readily available. Before her situation, she'd had no idea what a security business might look like. Even with her little knowledge of what all Jorge did, she realized that his boss seemed to have spared little expense in preparation for the missions and security details they undertook. Just remembering his quick descriptions of some of the other Keepers meeting their significant others on missions made her realize that her initial comparison of him to a TV bodyguard seemed ridiculous.

After her last client had left the clinic, Josie walked toward the break room on her way to the restroom, slowing as she heard Charlene and Mark conversing. Hearing the word 'casino', her feet stumbled. That word normally wouldn't have hit her radar, and yet, because she was now suspicious of everything and everyone, she stopped just outside the door, glancing around to make sure no one else could see her.

"I love the casinos in Ciudad Juarez," Charlene said. "I only go to the nicer ones, but winning there means the money is all mine."

"Have you ever been to the Sol Ciudad Juarez?" Mark asked.

"A couple of years ago I had a boyfriend take me, but it's not as nice as the Grand King. I think the food and drinks are better at the King."

"Did you say you're going tonight?" Mark asked.

"We try to avoid the crowds on the weekend, so the middle of the week is better." Charlene laughed. "Personally, I think the casinos let you win a little bit more money if you go in the middle of the week. At least, that always happens when I'm with Anton. I call him my good luck charm!"

"What do you do with the money you win besides spend it on clothes?"

"Anton is some kind of investor. I don't know exactly what he does, but I give him my money, and it doesn't take too long before I get more back! It's like having my own little personal money machine!"

"I wouldn't mind having someone like that in my life too."

"Let me talk to him, maybe he'll take you on as a client."

It sounded as though footsteps were getting closer, and Josie quickly backtracked to the end of the hall, then turned around. As Charlene and Mark stepped out of the workroom, she greeted them as though she had just left her office.

Getting ready to leave, she shook her head, wondering about her sanity. *This is getting ridiculous. Two coworkers are just talking about their plans, and I'm worried about it being nefarious.* As she walked out of the clinic heading toward Jorge, a vision of Caesar ran through her mind, causing a shudder to run through her whole body, giving the reminder that she was not being ridiculous.

Seeing Jorge's dark eyes follow her from the back door of the clinic toward him, his smile widened, and her heart lightened. Too old to break into a skip, she hustled over to his SUV, not surprised when he climbed from the driver's seat and met her at her door.

Bending, he kissed her lightly, mumbling, "Christ, I've missed you, babe."

"You didn't have to stay out here all day," she said, placing her hand in his as he assisted her up into the passenger seat.

Instead of closing the door, he leaned his large body into the space, his hand cupping her cheek. "I thought it was best to stay out of the clinic today but close where I can keep an eye on you. It would give you a chance to feel a little bit more normal... less crowded."

She reached up and wrapped her hand around his wrist while leaning her face into his palm. "You may be a big guy, but you never crowd me." She hesitated, then decided to go all out and let him know how she was feeling. "I missed you. In such a short time, I got used to you being around. I like you being around."

He leaned in and kissed her again. She opened her mouth in an invitation, glad when he accepted, and his tongue slid between her lips. The kiss deepened, and he pressed forward a little more, their chests flush. After a moment, he leaned back, his breath ragged as she sucked air into her lungs.

"Damn, babe. All I want to do is take you home, strip you, and not come up for air until we're both sated and can't move."

"That sounds perfect to me," she admitted, tightening her thighs to ease the ache.

"You forget, we're ordering for five tonight. My coworkers' meeting is at your house."

She blinked, her chin jerking back slightly. "I've been nervous about meeting them, and after one kiss, you knocked that fear right out of my mind."

He laughed and stepped backward, closing her door before jogging around and climbing behind the wheel. "They're good guys, good friends, and believe me, they'll love you."

The ride home only took fifteen minutes, barely time for her to get nervous again. Pulling into the driveway, she caught sight of the large, black SUV sitting out front. "They don't worry about being conspicuous, do they?"

Jorge laughed and shook his head. "Nope. As far as we're concerned, we want anyone looking to know you've got protection."

Following their usual protocol, he hustled her inside, then turned to welcome the three Keepers into her home. As each one entered, her eyes bugged a little bigger and her mouth opened a little wider. Tate was tall and muscular, with dark brown hair and a square jaw. He smiled as he shook her hand, greeting her warmly. He was followed by Bray, whose smile was even wider and his greeting just as warm. Bray was not quite as tall as Jorge but appeared to be just as muscular, with wavy dark hair that curled slightly over his ears. Next came Drew, and while she thought Jorge and the other two men were tall, Drew was easily over six and a half feet tall. Feeling completely dwarfed, his huge smile, wink, and ready laugh had her quickly at ease.

"Thank you all for coming," she began but got no further because the men quickly waved her ready concerns away, letting her know they were happy to assist.

Just as she was about to offer them something to drink, Melon made her presence known. "Whoa, gorgeous cat," Bray said, bending to rub Melon's ears.

"Babe, why don't you take care of your cat, and I'll grab some beers for the guys." He turned to the others. "There's an Italian restaurant nearby that delivers, and they are fucking amazing."

"Sounds good to me," Drew said, the others quickly agreeing.

Jorge took care of the ordering while she fed Melon and then disappeared into her bedroom to get comfortable. Normally, she would have thrown on yoga pants and a slouchy sweatshirt, but now stood in her bedroom in indecision. *What does one wear when one is going to have dinner with four huge, gorgeous, protective men, one who holds my heart and three who hold his friendship?* Unable to come up with the correct outfit, she decided comfortable was best. A few minutes later, with a headband holding her hair back and her comfortable yoga pants and slouchy sweatshirt with ballet slippers on her feet, she moved back into the living area.

It only took a few more minutes for their dinner to be delivered, and she grabbed fresh beers for the men and a glass of wine for herself. Uncertain if she should play hostess, it appeared that Jorge didn't want her to be concerned as he placed the food containers on her kitchen counter next to a stack of plates and called out, "Come and get it."

The men insisted that she go first, and she scooped a few spoonfuls onto her plate.

"Babe," Jorge said, leaning in close with his hand on her waist. "You don't have to be afraid about eating in front of these men."

"Oh, it's not that." Her gaze darted around before landing on his. "It's just… I haven't really been that hungry since… um…"

"Shit, Josie. I'm sorry." His fingers dug in slightly, and he kissed the side of her head, nodding.

Soon they were settled at the table. Still nervous at first, she soon found the Keepers to have lively conversations, never excluding her. Her eyes widened as they went back several times to refill their plates.

"Cobb, man, you were right. This food is amazing."

A grin slipped across her face as she listened to Jorge's friends refer to him by his last name. He looked over and caught her smile and responded with one of his own. "Believe it or not, Mace told me that in the late 1800s, there was a lighthouse keeper named George Cobb, no relation to me, who served in a lighthouse near San Francisco. He was awarded a Lifesaving Medal when he saved three young men from drowning. There's a U.S. Coast Guard ship named after him."

"I'm not surprised." As soon as the words left her lips, she blushed slightly but continued to hold his gaze, ignoring the other men at the table. "I just mean that even though he's no relation to you, it doesn't surprise me that your name so resembles another hero."

A movement from across the table drew her attention, and she watched as Tate reached into his pocket and handed a small box to Jorge. Curious, she didn't want to ask what was in the box, but from the smile on Jorge's face, he wasn't surprised.

She soon forgot about the box as the conversation around the table continued, especially when it evolved into a discussion about her situation.

"The attorney whose empty office you checked out in El Paso is still in the wind. With your information, we've determined that that was nothing more than a space to give him a legitimate mailing address. Everything we can find on him points to him operating in Mexico as well as the States. His name is tied into the Grand King Casino in Ciudad Juarez, which we know has cartel backing," Tate reported.

"Have you determined if he is real?"

"The name Carson Wright on paper is real. But if it is one person or just a name that others use? We still can't confirm."

Josie startled, quickly turning toward Jorge. "I can't believe I forgot, but I heard Charlene and Mark talking about the Ciudad Juarez casinos today. It sounded like Mark hasn't been to the Grand King, but Charlene said her boyfriend takes her there. She was bragging about how it was easier to win money during the week and not having to report any winnings. She also mentioned that her boyfriend was the one who handled her winnings, not knowing what he did but saying she got a high return on it."

"That goes along with what we've been finding out."

Cobb reached his arm out and rested it along the back of her chair, his hand gently rubbing her shoulder. "They told me that Anton has a standing table at the Grand King Casino every Wednesday night. His name has come up as a person of interest with the FBI, and he's definitely a person of interest with us as well."

"Are you still going in?" Drew asked.

Her brows lowered as her attention was drawn to Drew. Seeing he was staring at Jorge, she swung her gaze back to him. "Going in where?"

He dug his fingers slightly into her shoulder. "Everything ties this attorney to the suspicious companies that were running money through your clinic with the assistance of Caesar. And everything indicates that he works for a cartel that runs the Grand King."

"But Charlene said it was a really nice casino. She wouldn't go to a dive."

"Babe, that's just the kind of front that a cartel would want. We're talking big money, hundreds of millions of dollars if not more. It serves as a way to get drug money in and out of the country, and the Mexican government is, quite frankly, powerless to do anything about it."

With her elbow propped on the table, she rested her head in her hands and sighed. "I thought I was more worldly than this, but I had no idea how these things work."

"No reason for you to, Josie. What you do is healing... what the cartels do is tear apart, " Bray said, and she shifted her gaze to him. His eyes were kind, and it struck her as odd that he was one of the Keepers that was still single. Jorge had told her that Bray had been a medical officer in the Army Special Forces, having been trained as a physician's assistant.

Suddenly jolting as Jorge's earlier words slammed into her, she jerked her gaze back to him. "What do you mean by *go in*? You're not talking about going into a cartel's casino in Mexico, are you?" Her voice raised with each word until she almost squeaked at the end.

"Josie, I can go in tomorrow, legally crossing into Mexico and legally coming back. I'll just be one of the many people gambling in the casino but can check things out."

"But why you?"

His chin dropped slightly, and his eyes widened then rolled as he stared back at her. "Babe, really? Look at me. I can get in and out with the least threat of anyone suspecting me."

Her eyes narrowed as his meaning became clear. "You've got to be kidding me! You're the Lighthouse Security's heritage-diverse-special-agent-man that they can just send in whenever they want somebody to blend?"

The occupants of the table were silent for a second before all four men burst into laughter, including Jorge. She wasn't sure her eyes could narrow more than they were, but before she was able to become even more indignant, Jorge reached out and placed his hand on her arm. "Chill, sweetheart. I promise that's not what I am."

"I don't know, maybe the special-agent part sounds pretty good," Drew said, still chuckling.

She threw her glare at him before Jorge brought her attention back to his warm eyes.

"Seriously, Josie. That's not what's happening here. I know the investigation, and I know on sight what I might be looking for. The fact that I can blend in easily with a local crowd is just a bonus. No one is using or abusing me."

She sucked in her lips and nodded slowly, fighting the desire to blush for having lost her temper in front of his friends, but as she chanced a glance their way, noticed all three had a look of respect on their face. Unsure what to do with that, she turned back to Jorge and asked, "If you're going to be gone, do you want me to go with you?"

"Fuck, no. You'll be here with Tate. Bray is going with me, Drew is going to be monitoring the situation with LSI, and Tate will hang with you tomorrow. He can sit in the car outside the clinic, and then make sure you get home safe."

It seemed as though everything was planned, so she remained quiet, pondering the way her life had changed in the past month. Soon, the other Keepers said their goodbyes and headed to the motel with promises to see her the next day.

That night, she and Jorge made love, slow and easy, with whispers of affection. When he slipped back into bed after taking care of the condom, he sat with his back to the headboard and reached to the nightstand where the small box Tate had given him had been placed. Curiosity filled her and she pushed to sit up, draping the sheet across her breasts.

He opened the box, exposing a silver chain with a lighthouse pendant dangling from the center. Her gaze fell onto the necklace, and she gasped, staring at the piece of jewelry that held so much meaning.

He draped it over her neck, fastened the clip, and let the lighthouse pendant settle at the top of her breasts.

"Oh, my goodness, Jorge, it's beautiful!"

"It's beautiful on you, babe. But it's more special than you realize. Inside the lighthouse is a tracer. If you are ever separated from me, I can find you wherever you are. And I promise... I will find you."

Tears stung her eyes as she pulled him in for a deep kiss. And with the lighthouse draped about her neck, they made love again.

She fell asleep easily but woke in the middle of the night, a snake of unease slithering through her. Unsure what it meant, she burrowed tighter into his embrace and fell back into a fitful slumber.

23

Cobb sat at the edge of one of the blackjack tables, keeping an eye on the activity all around. The Grand King Casino was a hubbub of activity, lights, movement, and sounds. If he was not so adept at being able to filter out the extraneous from the necessary, it would be overwhelming. Dressed in a dark polo and clean jeans, he blended easily into the afternoon crowd. A grin slipped over his face as he thought of Josie's angry defense when she assumed that he was volunteering for this particular duty because of his ethnicity. He had only been partially truthful when he told her it wasn't. After all, even as a SEAL and then on CIA Special Operation assignments, he used every advantage possible, including his appearance.

This casino was the same as others across the world in the attempts to relieve visitors of their money with the temptation of leaving with greater riches. He watched as people cheered when they won without having considering how much they'd spent in the effort.

Serving girls walked around with trays of drinks, offering patrons cheap libations to keep them happy enough to stay and continue gambling their money away. Coffee stations were offering strong brew in kiosks nearby, encouraging the cycle of losing money while under the influence, then sobriety to start the process over again. But the common practice could be found in any casino, and certainly, here in Mexico, it was no different.

He'd moved around to several tables, having added several hundreds of dollars to his spending card when he first arrived. Nursing the occasional drink, he finally stood and straightened his back as though working the kinks out of his spine while surreptitiously scanning the area. Tossing a tip to the dealer, he walked through the casino toward the coffee station.

Off to the left were the higher stakes tables and toward the back were the tables where the starting limits were in the thousands. Those tables were separated from the general public with roped access, but they were still visible for spectators standing at a polite distance. He knew that private rooms would hold the highest stakes games, the ones where privacy and discretion were guaranteed.

A band had set up on the low stage to the right and their rendition of rock was not only subpar but added to the cacophony of casino sounds. Cobb winced more than once at the auditory assault.

As the late afternoon moved into evening, he planted himself at one of the slot machines near the entrance, and his position paid off as he spotted Charlene enter on the arm of a man in a dark grey suit. She was in a short, tight cocktail dress, smiling for all the world as she clung to Anton's arm.

While Anton was greeted with familiarity by the lower floor casino manager, Charlene grabbed the first drink handed to her by the server. As they weaved their way toward the back, Cobb followed at a discrete distance, not wanting to be recognized by her. The couple settled at a table in the back, and he was grateful they were still in the area where he could keep an eye on them by finding another slot machine on the periphery with a perfect view of Charlene's preening and Anton's determined efforts to make money. It seemed to be working. In only an hour, he had managed to win most of the time.

A boisterous group moved behind him, and he cast a glance to the side, spying Bert along with two of his entourage, Timothy Hobson and Roberto Mendez. Shocked that multiple suspects had turned up at the same place at the same time, he wasn't about to complain. He fired off a quick text to Bray, who was just across the border in El Paso. Keeping his face turned to the side, he watched as they made their way to the back tables as well, but not toward Charlene and Anton.

His suspicions were on high alert, but he still didn't see any evidence of the two groups co-mingling. After three more mind-numbing, ear-assaulting hours, Charlene and Anton walked away from the tables and out of the casino. She beamed as he collected his winnings and they left. Another text was sent to Josh, asking if Anton had his own security. Ciudad Juarez was teeming with thieves, especially at night. Receiving an affirmation from Josh, Cobb moved to the back again, assured that Charlene would be safe as she made her way over the border and back home.

His attention was diverted when the door to the back room opened and a few well-heeled people exited while several others entered. Women in expensive cocktail dresses and men in tailored suits made their way down a back hall to avoid the main entrance where the masses gathered. Firing off another message to Josh, he told him to check the back hall security cameras.

It took two more hours before Bert, Timothy, and Roberto finished winning. By the number of people that stopped to greet him, it appeared Bert had no shortage of acquaintances there. The trio wandered to the bar with skimpily-clad women now hanging onto their arms, and Cobb was ready to get out of there and back to Josie. He hadn't learned anything new, but his suspicions grew that someone close to Josie had probably sent Caesar her way and then became fearful when Josie grew suspicious.

Stepping into the house well after midnight, he was struck with the thought that while Josie's house did not feel like home to him, just knowing she was inside gave him the feeling of coming home. The TV in the living room was on, so low the sound was negligible, a welcome respite from the noise of earlier. He looked to the sofa, Tate offering a chin lift in welcome. Cobb's gaze drifted to the cushion next to Tate where Melon was curled up sleeping, pressing tightly to the new human in her orbit. Not even attempting to suppress a grin, Cobb inclined his head toward the slumbering feline. "I see you've got a friend."

Tate stood, and it didn't escape Cobb's notice that the other Keeper did so gently, barely disturbing Melon.

"Josie asleep?"

"Yeah, I think so. She had trouble finding it, but it's been quiet now for a while."

He thought he detected a tone in Tate's voice but chose to ignore it, walking into the kitchen to grab a bottle of water. Setting one on the counter for Tate, he watched as his friend moved toward him and settled onto one of the stools at the counter.

"I got your message," Tate began. "Seems like all indications are on the Grand King as being the probable place of cleaning the money."

"I've already passed on the information to Floyd. Nothing he can do across the border, but at least he'll know some of the people to watch from here. I hate like fuck if Charlene's involved in any of this because of Josie's relationship with her, but she doesn't strike me as a very discerning young woman."

"Wrong place, wrong time, wrong man?"

Cobb nodded. "Yeah, I think so. Anton's not quite the high roller that I think he or she thinks he is, but he was definitely winning, so I'd say he's got something going on with the casino. If he's bringing in client money, he could be moving a lot every week through them. Didn't help that Bert showed up with his two hangers-on, but I watched them for over two hours and his group never so much as looked over at Anton."

"Josh turned up something."

Cobb's body remained loose but his mind shot to high alert. "Yeah?"

"Carson Wright."

"He's been found?"

Tate shook his head slowly. "Nope, but Josh discovered that's not his name."

Eyes narrowed, Cobb paused. "So, he's not real? Just a complete fake front?"

"No, it's one person, but that's not the real name. The attorney who's connected to Caesar and the dummy contributions to Josie's clinic is still hidden."

"You're shitting me?"

"Nope," Tate repeated. "Right now, Josh is trying to figure out who they are so we can protect Josie better as well as give the info to the FBI. But then that's not our concern. Just as long as we keep your girl safe, the others can have the case."

They were quiet for a moment before Tate finally asked, "She is, isn't she? Your girl? I've got to admit that she was handling tonight well. At first, she paced, and I wondered if she would be able to handle you on a mission. But then I realized as she talked through her anxiety, it wasn't really how it affected her, but how everything affected you."

"Never figured on this when I came down here," Cobb admitted. "But yeah, I can see her fitting into my life easily."

"And you fitting into hers?"

He had wondered when Tate was finally going to ask what was on his mind. "You're going straight to it, are you?"

"We haven't had a Keeper leave the group yet."

Cobb hardly needed Tate to remind him of this, but he remained quiet.

Tate continued, "Not that that won't happen sometime. There will always be a first. Whether it's from a new job offer, something personal, or a woman."

"If that's your way of asking if I'd consider staying in New Mexico for her, I can't say it hasn't crossed my mind." Cobb scrubbed his hand over his face and sighed. "This place doesn't feel like home anymore. It hasn't for a long time. But I've got family here." He dropped his head back and stared at the ceiling for a few seconds, then slowly shook his head as he dropped his chin and held his friend's gaze. "But I can't see leaving Maine. And I sure as fuck can't see leaving LSI."

Tate remained quiet, the silence of the night moving between the friends. Finally, he said, "Then if it's meant to be, she may have to relocate. From what I've seen, she can handle the life like our other women."

Snorting, Cobb shook his head again. "Gone are the days where a woman is expected to pick up and travel wherever the man goes."

"You don't have to tell me that. Nora was a nurse who'd grown up and lived her whole life in Wyoming. I had no clue how it would work and just lucked out that she was ready for a life change." He shrugged. "Maybe Josie will feel the same."

"Yeah, but I don't know if it's even fair to ask her to do that."

"You'll never know if you don't at least ask."

"On that somber note, I think I'll find my bed."

Inclining his head toward the hall, he said, "The spare bedroom is ready for you, I'm sure. I'll see you in the morning. I'll have you on Josie detail again. I'll head to Albuquerque. While Bert is at work, I want to take a look at his apartment. He may be family, but I don't trust him... or at least not his friends." With that, he turned and headed to the main bedroom, desperate for a shower and to curl up around Josie's warm, sleeping body.

Josie woke the minute Jorge slipped underneath the covers, aligning his large body with her much smaller one. Warmth immediately infused her as his front pressed against her back, his knee nudged between her legs, and his arm curved around her waist, his hand tucked just under her breasts.

"Are you okay?" Her words came out in a whisper, and she wanted to turn around to face him, staring into his dark eyes lit only by the light of the moon coming through the window. But the tightness that had been in her chest since he left caused her to lay still, facing away as uncertainty moved through her.

"Yeah, babe, I'm fine." His arm squeezed her waist gently. "You?"

She nodded, feeling his chin pressed against the top of her head. "I probably made Tate crazy, pacing the floor after you left. I admit it was weird to have you out and not know exactly where you were or how you were." He remained quiet, and she stumbled on, words that had crowded her head now all wanting to get out. "I couldn't help but think about the other Keepers' women… the ones that you told me about. They all sound so strong. Capable. And yet I wondered how I would be compared to them."

"Josie, I wouldn't want you to be anything other than yourself—"

"I know, I know, Jorge. That's not it. Please, let me finish." Gathering her bravery, she shifted around so that their fronts were plastered together, her head resting on his bicep as he pulled her in close. "I know people well enough to know that if those women are in love with their man, they are going to worry about that man. But that doesn't bother me. I figure in many ways it's the same as someone who is with a police officer, or a service member, or even someone who works construction on skyscrapers. There are lots of dangerous jobs out there, and so the person with them is going to feel fear."

"When I looked at the apartment building you were going into the other day, knowing that if I wasn't with you that you might go alone or with just Mario, I felt fear." He lifted his hand and gently pushed the hair away from her face. "Depending on the situation, even social work can be considered high risk."

She grinned and nodded. "I don't want you to think that just because I might pace and worry that I wouldn't be good for you."

"There's not a doubt in my mind that you would be good for me. But tell me, was all that pacing just your way to deal when your mind is racing, trying to figure things out?"

Her lips curved and she rolled her eyes, certain that he could see neither in the darkness. "You think you know me, do you?"

A chuckle rumbled from deep in his chest. "I might not have known you long, Josie girl, but I do know you. So give it up."

"I have no idea what you discovered at the casino tonight, but I kept thinking about Caesar. He was always a nice man, at least to me, but if I'm honest, he was also weak. He was an adequate bookkeeper, but he didn't have an accounting degree. He understood enough about a business' finances to help them keep their records, but he just could not have been the mastermind of money laundering. So, someone else was handling everything, and it struck me that that person has to be much smarter than he was. His motives? I have no idea. Maybe he was getting paid well. Maybe somebody was blackmailing him into doing it. He never expected me to look at the books, and when I did, it made him very nervous. He must have known at that point that he was going to be found out. If he knew they were as cutthroat as they are, he must've known they might come after him or me. And that's what I keep coming back to, Jorge. In my gut, I don't think Caesar would have wanted harm to come to me."

Jorge rolled to the side, turning on the small lamp on the nightstand. She blinked at the sudden brightness, her brow knit as she peered at him.

"What have you decided?" he asked. "Now that you've been thinking about it, what's different?"

"I just thought he disappeared. That would fit someone weaker. You know, not go to the authorities and give himself up. Not do the strong thing and take his punishment. But he ran away. At least, that's what I thought, and it fit his weak personality. But when we realized he had been taken and…" She sucked in a deep breath and let it out slowly before continuing. "… killed, then I knew that maybe he wasn't as weak as I thought. Maybe he tried to do the right thing before he died."

"I get you're trying to tell me something, Josie, but I'm not following. What do you think he did?"

"I'm not sure he had time to do anything. But it makes me feel better thinking that he would have tried to warn me."

"But he didn't."

Jorge's statement wasn't posed as a question because they both knew the answer. She had received only the mini drive from Caesar, and considering her office and home hadn't been searched by anyone, no one must have suspected that he'd given her anything. She sighed heavily. "No, he didn't. I tried to wrack my brain while you were gone, but I think the only thing I accomplished was to make Tate nervous."

He chuckled again. "Tate can handle himself." Tucking her hair back again, he added, "I'm more worried about you."

His words burrowed deep inside, and she leaned forward to press a kiss against his collarbone, feeling when his lips met her forehead.

"I get it, Josie. You feel guilt that Caesar met such a horrific ending, but remember, his choices were his own."

She nodded again. "I know. I just can't help but feel that he was just caught up in something that went terribly wrong. Something that took him deeper than he meant to go. And I suppose it makes me feel better to think that he never wanted this to come down on me."

"Babe, if he was any kind of man at all, he would have protected you. Maybe he just didn't have time."

They lay quietly for a few more minutes until she thought about the day. "Will you be with me today?"

"I'm going to Albuquerque with Drew. He'll fly us so it won't take all day. I've got just a couple of trails I want to check out. Tate will be with you at the clinic."

"I've got some home visits."

"He'll be right with you until I get back. I should be finished in the early afternoon at the latest."

She nodded, knowing he was doing everything he could to alleviate the threat against her.

He gently pushed her backward so their gazes met again. "Are you going to be able to sleep?"

"Yeah," she whispered. "Now that you're here and I'm in your arms, I won't have any problem sleeping."

He smiled, rewarding her with another kiss before tucking her in tighter. She was right... in his arms, she quickly fell asleep.

24

Cobb had to admit the view was one of the best in Albuquerque. With LSI disabling the security, he and Drew easily broke into Bert's high-rise condo building, one of the few in the city. Slipping inside unnoticed, he was immediately struck by the hardwood floors throughout the open space which included a living and dining great room just off the open kitchen. The most eye-catching part of the condo was the wall of windows along the entire back of the room that overlooked the city but more spectacularly overlooked the majestic mountains rising in the background. The housing market in Albuquerque was not particularly robust, but Bert had paid a premium for this condo.

He knew Bert had received an insurance policy from his parents, so Cobb wasn't overly suspicious of the housing expenditure. But still, the condo was one of the best in the city. It sported two bedrooms, and he went first to the one used as a home office and guest room. With gloved hands, he fired up Bert's laptop, quickly using a secure external drive to download the contents while simultaneously wiping away any trace of having done so. A quick look didn't show anything overly suspicious, which Josh had already determined, but Cobb still could not get over his distrust.

He searched the small filing cabinet and the desk while waiting but found nothing. Just as he disconnected the drive, he looked up to see that Drew was leaning against the doorframe, a prescription pill bottle between his fingers. Lifting a brow, he waited to see what Drew had to say.

"Looks like our boy is a recreational user. He's got the shit hidden in prescription pill bottles."

"What does he use?"

Still leaning against the doorframe, Drew said, "It's a small amount of coke. Not enough to sell, and not enough to look like a hard user."

"Fuckin' moron," Cobb said, shaking his head. "He's got everything he could want in a state that is mostly poor, and he's snorting his money up his nose."

Drew grinned. "His closet is full of tailored suits. His liquor cabinet has the good stuff. You never did get a good feeling about him."

"No, but I'm not finding anything here that shows he's running money. Mostly, it just shows what I said earlier... he's running through his money on expensive real estate and habits."

The two walked back through the great room, and Cobb looked at the framed photographs on a shelf over the credenza. One with the Rectors, he and Josie standing with her parents at his college graduation. One of a much younger Bert with a couple that he knew must be his parents because the man resembled John.

Drew picked up a photograph and chuckled. "Looks like he has plenty of friends, and seeing his condo and his sort of recreation, they probably sponge off him."

Cobb looked at the photograph in Drew's hand, recognizing Timothy and Roberto amongst the group hanging in a bar. Leaning closer, he recognized the location. "I was just here last night. This is near the back area of the Grand King Casino where the tables are for those playing with higher stakes."

Drew handed the photograph to Cobb, who narrowed his eyes as he scrutinized it carefully. Startling, he said, "Shit, I know one of the other guys in this picture. That's Tahoma Starr. He's one of Senator Rector's aides. I don't know why nothing ever came up about him hanging with Bert."

"Is that all that strange, though? Bert hangs around Josie's dad a lot."

"Maybe. I don't know, it just strikes me as odd." Pulling out his phone, he fired off a quick call to Josh. "Check out any relationship you can between Bert and Tahoma Starr. For that matter, check Tahoma's relationship with Timothy Hobson or Roberto Mendez, as well." Disconnecting, he looked at Drew. "Let's get outta here. I've got another stop I want to make."

Drew turned and glanced out the window. "He's got an amazing view, that's for sure."

"I thought the same thing when I first saw it."

Drew turned around and held Cobb's gaze. "You grew up with this view."

Cobb shrugged. "Part of the time. Remember, my parents traveled with my dad's job for a while, so I was overseas and then in D.C., but yeah, my grandparents were always here and part of my childhood was here as well."

"Miss it?"

"You, too?" Cobb asked.

Drew chuckled. "I take it Tate was wondering if you're thinking of staying."

Shaking his head, Cobb replied, "No. I love the state but I've got no desire to move back here. Visit? Absolutely. Live here? No."

"And what about Josie?"

He sighed heavily, knowing what his friends were asking. "I'll tell you the same thing I told Tate. Right now, I don't know. My main concern is keeping her safe. When that threat is gone, she and I will have to figure out the next step in our relationship."

They slipped out of Bert's apartment, but Cobb's mind was in turmoil. He wanted Josie. He wanted Josie with him. *But what if she wants to stay here?*

Once in the rental SUV, Cobb drove to Senator Rector's office. "I'm gonna run in to talk to him for a few minutes."

"Take your time." Drew leaned back and closed his eyes. "Take your time."

It didn't take long for Cobb to be escorted into John's office. The senator lifted his gaze from his desk, a wide smile crossing his face as he looked at Cobb and then past Cobb's shoulder. His smile faltered as he brought his gaze back to Cobb.

"Isn't Josie with you?"

"No, sir, I had business in town today, and she is at the clinic—"

"But—"

"Don't worry, John, she's well accompanied. I had a friend fly me here, so it's a quick hop back as soon as we're finished."

The senator leaned back in his chair, heaving a sigh. "I'll be so glad when this business is over. My wife and I were just saying that we hated the danger that Caesar put our daughter in. If only I hadn't listened to the advice to recommend him to her."

"Who recommended him, sir?"

"I think it was Carmen… no, maybe it was Tahoma. Oh, now I can't remember. I'm sure it was someone from this office, but I wasn't paying much attention at the time." He looked up, his eyes wide. "Should I ask them? Would that be important?"

"No, sir, let's not do that now. I wanted to warn you before anything comes out in our investigation, but your nephew, Bert, has habits that could be potentially embarrassing to your next campaign or even your current senatorial position."

John's lips tightened as his face hardened. "Gambling. I've warned him to be more careful."

"That and other habits that aren't healthy."

The silence loomed between them and John finally sighed heavily. "I was afraid of that. He's so much more of a follower than a leader, and a few of his friends haven't impressed me."

"I'm looking into him because no one is outside our

investigations, but I'm relying on your discretion to not say anything to him now."

"You don't want Josie to suffer for her cousin's poor choices."

"I'd rather be the one to talk to her when this is over."

John nodded slowly. "You care a great deal for my daughter. I'm glad, Jorge. In the middle of this mess, it gives her mother and I great pleasure that you two are together." He looked down at his clasped hands resting on his desk and hesitated. Finally, sucking in a deep breath, he looked up and held Cobb's gaze. "And when the threat is gone?"

"I'm not sure what will happen, but Josie will be the first person I'll talk to about what I hope for her and me."

A slow smile met Cobb's gaze and the senator nodded. "You're a good man, Jorge. Like your father and your grandfathers… all good men. I couldn't ask for better for my daughter."

Cobb's heart felt lighter as he stood and they shook hands. "Now, if you'll excuse me, John, I've got to get back to her."

John walked him out, and once in the reception area, he turned to his competent receptionist. "Can you have Carmen and Tahoma come into my office, please?"

"They just left for lunch, sir. I'm not sure when to expect them back."

Cobb left the building and hustled to his SUV. Climbing inside, he asked Drew, "Did you see Carmen and Tahoma leave?"

"She did about ten minutes ago, and he left just before you came out."

A tingle of unease moved through him as he pulled onto the road and called Tate. "Josie okay?"

"Of course, man. Why?"

"Keep on her. Stay right with her until I get back."

"You got it. We're on our way to visit a client and will head to her home as soon as we're finished."

"Anyone know where you are?"

Tate replied, "You know the answer to that, man. Everyone at the clinic knows her schedule."

Cobb hated the growing feeling in his gut. "Okay, okay. Just stay right with her. I have no idea why, but I just sense this is coming to a head."

"I won't leave her," Tate promised.

Disconnecting, he felt Drew's eyes on him. Turning to the side, he growled, "I know I sound like a fucking mess, but I swear I just feel like she's in danger."

"Not a mess, bro. Just a man in love who is scared shitless about the woman he cares for." Drew faced the windshield but wasn't finished. "Been there and it sucks, Cobb. So, get us to the airport, and I'll break the sound barrier to get you back to her."

25

As soon as Josie stepped into the bright sunshine from the client's house she had been visiting, Tate was right there waiting on her. She assumed everything must be fine due to the wide grin on his face.

"Since this was your last stop of the day, how do you feel about heading to the airport?"

Now, her smile was as wide as his, and she couldn't help but clap her hands together. "We can meet Jorge?"

"Yep. He and Drew are on their way back, and it's such a short flight from Albuquerque that by the time we drive to the airport, they should just be landing."

"I'd love to!" She climbed into the passenger seat of her car, not even attempting to argue with Tate that she should drive. He had informed her the previous day that while he wasn't sexist about male and female drivers, he had specific training she didn't have.

They soon arrived at the small airport in Las Cruces, and Tate passed by the main terminal and parked outside a fenced area.

"Bray is going to meet us here and drive me and Drew back to your place. We'll pick up dinner so you can let us know what you like to eat."

She nodded her agreement as they walked over to the chain-link fence, standing together, their eyes toward the sky. Glancing over, she looked at his profile. Not for the first time did the thought cross her mind that Jorge's friends were handsome. She knew Tate had finally gotten with his childhood sweetheart, and she wondered how they made everything work.

Suddenly, Tate looked down at her, his expression unreadable. She held his gaze, feeling as though he was coming to some kind of conclusion, and while she had no idea what she was being tested on, she desperately wanted to pass.

"You're good for him."

She blinked, uncertain of his meaning. Cocking her head to the side, she waited to see what else he wanted —*no, needed*—to say.

"Not just any woman can handle the life of a Keeper. You understand him. His need for intellectual stimulation. His need for working out problems in his head, wrapping his brain around a case, and figuring out what someone is thinking and why. You get that. While you two are different, you have that in common, and it works."

While she appreciated his analysis of her and Jorge's intellectual compatibility, it wasn't a resounding endorsement of care, comfort, and companionship. Nodding, she waited.

"I'm screwing this up, aren't I?" he asked, his smile quirked on one side.

She shook her head and smiled in return. "No, Tate. You're looking out for your friend. I confess that I'm not quite sure what you think of me yet, but I know you have his best interests at heart."

His hands landed on his lean hips. "What I think is that you and Cobb are good together. I know he cares for you, and I can tell you feel the same."

"But…" she let the word drag out, hoping he would finally get off his chest what seemed to be pressing him down.

"But nothing. He's one of the best men I've ever known and deserves to be happy. So do you. I think you're both good for each other."

The sound of a small engine plane approached, interrupting more conversation, and they turned in unison to watch a private plane coming in.

"There they are," he said.

After the heaviness of the talk she and Jorge had had in the middle of the night, her heart leaped at the sight of his plane as the wheels touched the runway. Glancing back at Tate, she refused to let his concerns weigh her down. Without waiting, she waved as Jorge and Drew alighted from the plane.

The exit gate was near a small building, but she laughed as Jorge jogged over to the fence, his fingers latching onto hers through the chain links. She stood on her tiptoes, and with her lips pressed between a small opening kissed him lightly. Setting back on her heels, she complained, "That's hardly the welcome home kiss that you see in movies."

He laughed and said, "Babe, any kiss with you is worthy of the movies." He glanced to the side and said, "I'll be right out. Drew's rental SUV is just over there near the building. He and Tate can go back to your house in that, and we'll take your car."

Tate fist-bumped Jorge through the fence. "We'll meet you at your vehicle."

She settled into the passenger side as Tate started her car and they drove toward the rental SUV parked near the gate of the fence. She watched Jorge as he walked, loving the way his body moved with a grace that belied his bulk. Suddenly, he jerked around, his gaze shooting toward the other side of the parking lot.

"Go!" he shouted, waving his arms, but before she could react, she pressed back in the seat as Tate stepped on the accelerator.

Before they had a chance to change direction, the horrific sound of crunching metal hit her ears at the same time her body slammed against her door, her head bouncing off the window. She cried out as pain exploded in her temple. "Tate," she cried out as she spied the crushed driver's door now barricaded with another vehicle and blood running down his head. More sounds of crashing metal against metal sounded but it came from farther away.

Her door was wrenched open, and hands reached in to jerk her out of the seat as Tate tried to hold onto her. She turned to see Jorge scaling the tall chain-link fence, but something hard and cold was pressed against her head and his movements halted.

"Come no further, halfie," the growl sounded next to her.

Rage moved through her but pain and fear edged for dominance in her emotional battle.

Jorge's fierce gaze never wavered. "You're making a huge fucking mistake. I know who yanks your chain. And I will come after you."

From that distance, she could see that her car and Bray's SUV had been rammed into, rendering them both unusable. Afraid to move with the gun still next to her head, she felt the air rush from her lungs at the sight of Jorge atop the fence. An ancient dragon breathing fire had nothing on him at the moment.

"Chill, man. The boss just wants to have a chat with the little lady. And tell your friend over there to back the fuck off."

Josie's feet stumbled as the man whose arm was banded around her waist walked backward. Her head pounded as she slid her eyes sideways to see a black vehicle parked close, the windows all darkened. Another man leaned out, and before she had a chance to react, his hand shot out with a hypodermic needle that he quickly jabbed into her arm.

She cried out before losing control of her body and was hauled inside, her door barely closing before the vehicle took off. Popping sounds fired all around, but they sounded far away as though a thick fog had settled over her.

Swallowing down the nausea that threatened to

overtake her, her fingers gripped the seat as she slid into unconsciousness.

Josie blinked awake, the world fuzzy as she rolled over in bed. She tried to remember what she had been doing. *Was I drinking? Did I take cold medicine?* None of the reasons for her grogginess made sense, but she stretched slowly, wiggling her fingers before rubbing her hand over her face. She winced in pain as a knot was found on the side of her head. *Did I fall?*

With some difficulty, she pushed to a seated position, finally focusing enough to look around, startled when she didn't recognize her surroundings. The room was not large, but it was clean. The bed she was sitting on was a thick, foam mattress on a fold-out cot, the type that hotels would offer for a guest if an extra child's bed was needed. It was also clean. There were no windows but two closed doors.

Memories slowly came back. The crash of metal on Tate's side of her car. Blood trickling down his face and his legs trapped in the crushed door. More sounds of crunching metal as the other vehicle was rammed. Drew racing toward them with a gun in his hand. And the last thing she remembered was Jorge at the top of the fence, a look of barely controlled rage on his face.

Taking a deep breath, she stood with effort, her head still woozy. With her hand gliding along the wall for support, she opened one door, glad to see that it led to a small but clean bathroom. Having no idea if anyone would come in to get her, she quickly used the toilet and washed her hands, then splashed cold water on her face to help chase the cobwebs away. She stared into the mirror over the sink, not surprised by her disheveled appearance. She lifted a shaky hand to run her fingers through her hair in an attempt to tame the thick waves. Her complexion was more pale than usual, and her blue eyes seemed larger on her face.

Turning away from her reflection, she walked gingerly back into the bedroom. Trying the other door, she wasn't surprised to find it locked. *What do they want with me?* She'd hoped that finding the mini drive from Caesar and giving it to Jorge would have ended the threats against her. *But then if they don't know I did that, they'll still consider me a threat.*

Looking around the room, her mind ran wild with scenarios, most from movies or TV shows. Try to break the lock. Look for an escape route. Hide behind the door and hit whoever walked in.

But with nothing in the room to use to break the lock she had no way to escape, and with nothing to knock someone out her imaginations were futile. Tired, she sat down on the small bed and leaned her back against the wall. With no idea how long she might be held captive, or how much time had passed that she had been unconscious, she decided she might as well get comfortable.

The image of Jorge settled front and center in her mind, and a shiver ran down her spine at the memory of his face right before she lost consciousness. Her fingers drifted up, feeling the lighthouse charm on the chain underneath her shirt. *"I can find you wherever you are."*

Somehow, she imagined that he would be able to do that even without the location sensor in the necklace. But knowing it was around her neck, she breathed easier. He will come. Whether an avenging angel, fire-breathing dragon, or ancient warrior... he will come.

A jiggling noise came from just outside the door before it opened. Gasping as she looked up at the sudden sound, she tilted her head to the side in confusion. "What are you doing here?"

"You just couldn't keep your nose out of it, could you?"

"She's in Ciudad Juarez."

While not surprised, hearing the words from Rank shot adrenaline throughout Cobb's body. Blanking his mind as best he could of all extraneous emotion, he barked, "Get me the location."

It only took a few more seconds for his fellow Keeper to add, "The Grand King Casino."

"I fuckin' knew it," he growled, looking across the room as Drew, Tate, and Bray readied for their accelerated rescue mission. Dark pants, dark long-sleeved shirts, dark knit caps, dark boots. Tate's forehead had three stitches but he had no concussion. After the firefighters cut him out of Josie's car, they realized how lucky he had been. The metal had crushed the driver's side, trapping him, but it had not crushed his leg. Once out, the only injury was his head wound, which Bray stitched up after Tate refused to go to the hospital. Now, they were in Josie's living room, preparing for her rescue. And her retribution for anyone who dared touch her.

"Coordinates being sent to you and the others," Josh interjected. "I've got their security up on my screens. Good, but not great. You'll have no problems."

Cobb knew he'd have no problems anyway. *Nothing —and no one—was going to keep him from getting Josie back.*

Mace's voice cut through his thoughts. "This needs to be clean. Shut the emotion down and go in as planned."

It was on the tip of his tongue to bark at his boss, letting him know that he didn't need anyone telling him how to run a mission, but before he could, Drew spoke.

"Got it, boss."

He glared at his friend, but Drew only cocked a brow at him. Turning, he checked his weapons before slinging his backpack over his shoulder. "We're out of here."

Before they had a chance to leave, Josh called out over the line. "The info on the drive Caesar stowed in her purse confirmed the operation as we suspected. Once the code was broken, it listed the money received from the cartel and moved through various charities before being sent on its way. We've got names, dates, companies… he kept meticulous records, and this backup must have been made as his insurance policy. Too bad it didn't work for him."

"Any surprise names?" Cobb asked, wondering if his suspicions were correct.

"Carson Wright. We know their identity."

As Josh called out the name belonging to the fake

attorney's true identity, Cobb's jaw ticked with anger. "Fucking hell."

Floyd met them at their vehicle parked outside. "I'll go as far as El Paso and smooth the way for you to get back if you have any problems. I know you want her... so do I. But I want the person masquerading as Carson Wright. And any other American citizens involved."

"You'll get 'em... after I do."

Floyd looked as though he was going to argue but wisely kept his mouth shut.

An hour later, the dark SUV maneuvered off the highway in El Paso that passed close to the Rio Grande. With papers and IDs that LSI had created and sent to Cobb, he went through the checkpoints at the bridge leading to Ciudad Juarez. Behind the wheel of the old truck filled with boxes of vegetables hiding the other Keepers in the back, he gave his papers to the guard and without a problem drove across the Rio Grande into Mexico. Once there, he drove to the Grand King Casino, pulling into the wide alley at the back where a few other delivery trucks had parked.

While he climbed down, the Keepers slipped unnoticed from the back and crept along the shadows in the alley. With Rank's voice in his ear, he and Bray moved toward the kitchen door, each hauling a crate of vegetables while Tate and Drew made their way further down the alley.

Unlike many of the casinos in the U.S. that never closed, the Grand King Casino and restaurants were closed from one a.m. until seven a.m. This worked in Cobb's favor since the kitchen now had a skeleton crew, mostly cleaning up from the previous day or prepping for the next. Security was so lax that no one in the kitchen even looked up to see who was walking through. Entering a back hall, Cobb and Bray set down the boxes and waited for the all-clear from LSI that the security cameras were on a different loop, allowing them to traverse the halls without any guards noticing a difference.

Following the trail given by Josh, they moved with stealth toward the stairs. Knowing he was getting closer to Josie but having no idea what had been happening with her, his heart pounded. Working to control his emotions, he focused as they slipped through the fire door at the top of the stairwell.

With an angled viewer around the corner, he could see a man at the end of the hall guarding a doorway. A gun was in his holster, but he must've felt no threat considering his back was against the wall, his arms crossed leisurely in front of him, and his eyes closed. Almost laughing at the ludicrous excuse for a guard that either the cartel or the casino employed, he listened for Drew's signal. Once given, he bolted around the corner. The deliberate noise Cobb made brought the guard to an alert, stumbling as he straightened his body while reaching for his weapon. The guard had barely moved before Drew came up behind him, putting him in a chokehold. As the man dropped to his knees, Drew and Tate grabbed him and noiselessly dragged him back to the door where they'd entered. Cobb knew they'd have him subdued and gagged, no longer a threat.

Josie stared in dumbfounded confusion. Carmen had entered her confinement room dressed in a dark red cocktail dress, modest in length but immodest with the slit up the leg from knee to hip. Carmen's hands were on her generous hips, her long fingernails painted to match the dress exactly. She also wore the same color on her lips, which were tangled in a snarl.

"First, that imbecile Caesar let you see the clinic records, and then you had to put your nose where it didn't belong." Carmen's hand darted into the air at her sides. "How moronic can you be? You suspect him of illegally moving money and you don't think that someone with power and position might not want that investigated?"

"But… you?"

With her hands back on her hips, she towered over Josie, still seated on the bed. "Hate to burst your bubble, dearie, but being your father's political lackey isn't my career goal."

With too many thoughts crowding her brain, it took Josie a moment to hit pause and give consideration to just one. "You… my father?" she screeched. "He gave you a chance over so many other candidates."

"Yes, and I would make pennies compared to what I can do now. But the people I work for need his influence, and you've put that at risk."

Josie realized that Carmen had no idea Caesar had kept his own records. She wondered if he did it to eventually use as blackmail or for his protection but never got a chance. Or maybe he knew if everything else went to shit Carmen wouldn't get away with what she was doing. Trying to keep her expression blank, she battled the desire to ask Carmen how the operation worked. *That's what they do in the movies, right before someone gets killed. Then a hero comes in.* Right now, with Carmen looming over her, she was uncertain that Cobb would get to her in time. Swallowing deeply, she said, "Well, since I don't know anything, I don't know why you felt the need to threaten me."

For the first time since she'd entered the room, a flash of fear raced through Carmen's eyes. She sucked in a deep breath through her nose, then let it out slowly. "I can't have any loose ends."

A gasp of nerves flew from Josie's lips. "Loose ends? Do you really think kidnapping a state senator's daughter—one who's dating the governor's son—is going to be swept under the rug?"

"No, but there's nothing to tie you back to me. Nothing to tie any of this back to me."

Before Josie had time to react, the door slammed open, and the air rushed from her lungs again as another familiar person raced in. "Timothy?"

His gaze landed on Josie before shooting over to Carmen. With his face screwed into a grimace, he groaned, "Fuck, Carmen. I heard you brought her here! What the hell are you thinking? Jesus, this is a train wreck!" He walked the length of the room, his hand tearing through his hair. "Christ, Bert can't know you've done this!"

"Bert?" Josie blinked, her voice shook as her body began to quiver. "There's no way he's part of this."

Timothy whirled around and looked at her, opening and closing his mouth several times. Finally, he ignored her and turned toward Carmen. "What the hell are you doing? This is about making money. Only making money. Jesus, what are you doing?"

"I make sure that we keep making money, you idiot. Something of the rest of you don't seem to be able to understand."

Josie's mind was still reeling with the idea that her cousin would have been part of any scheme in any way but especially knowing that it affected her and her clinic. Still shaking her head, she repeated, "There's no way Bert's part of this."

As though remembering she was still in the room, Timothy turned around, his gaze meeting hers. "No, he's not part of this."

"Only because I made sure to keep him in line," Carmen bit out. "Well, keep all of you in line."

"What is she talking about, Timothy? What does this have to do with Bert?"

Timothy sighed, his chest deflating and his chin dropping. His head shook slowly from side to side. "It's not Bert. He would never do anything to you."

"Then what is she talking about?"

"It's his... um... habit." Lifting his chin, he added, "It's just recreational, I swear. But it was enough for her to hold over our heads. She promised a way to make a lot of money. Bert didn't even know what she was talking about but said 'no'. Same with Roberto at first, but then he came along with me. We partied together, gambled together, but Bert was never part of her deal."

Her wariness was still heightened, although fatigue was nipping at her heels. "None of this makes sense." She kept her eye on Carmen, who seemed to swell with vibrating anger as Timothy seemed to deflate.

"It was just supposed to be a way to make money," he said. "That was all. I swear I didn't know we were in bed with a drug cartel. I had no idea that was where the money came from. It was supposed to be just like investing. Put a little in and hope you come out with a lot."

"What's the matter with you? If you're doing that illegally, then it's just wrong. You can't make it sound like it's anything else but just wrong."

He lifted his gaze to her, defeat written on his face, and whispered, "But it felt so right."

"Getting your friend hooked on drugs to keep him complacent? That felt right to you? Kidnapping me? Threatening me? What's next? Killing me?" Josie's voice lifted with each word, her chest hurting with the exertion. Her anger rose to rage burning in her heart, and it focused on the sneering woman standing next to him.

"No!" he shouted. "That's not going to happen!" He shifted his gaze to the side. "Right, Carmen? You're just questioning her?"

A perfectly arched brow lifted as Carmen sneered. "You really are pathetic. A sniveling excuse for a man." Casting a glance toward Josie before pinning him with a glare, she added, "You just might be next after her if you're not careful."

Timothy gasped, but Carmen ignored him as she peered down into her small handbag and pulled out a plastic case, then extracted a hypodermic needle. Smiling at Josie, she said, "Don't worry, sweetie. You've already had this done once today, only this one will be a little bit more permanent."

She barked at Timothy to hold Josie, but he threw up his hands and stepped back. "No, no!"

"You know what will happen if you don't. It will be a lot more unpleasant than this. The people we work with would be much more likely to handle you the same way they handled Caesar." Carmen took a step closer, but Timothy intercepted, swinging out to hit Carmen's hand.

Fury flowed through Josie's veins as much as the drugs still in her system, and she swung wildly, her fist connecting with Carmen's face as the door slammed open, bouncing against the wall. She screamed, "That's for getting my cousin hooked!" Pain rocketed through her hand and radiated up her arm, and she dropped to her knees, ignoring the blood running from Carmen's nose.

The room filled with so much vibrating electricity, she swung her gaze over just in time to see her warrior enter the room.

27

Having stood directly outside the door, Cobb had listened to Josie's scream. His knees nearly buckled at the sound of her voice. Tate's hand landed on his shoulder, the barest touch that let him know his friend knew exactly what he was feeling. The two men lifted booted feet and kicked out in unison, easily popping the door open. With weapons drawn, they rushed in.

His gaze instantly took in the occupants of the room, zeroing in on the threat facing Josie as she punched outward, her small fist making contact. Carmen, blood streaming from her nose, stumbled backward, her arms windmilling to remain upright. Drew rushed forward, his immense height towering over the woman as he grabbed her wrist, exerting the pressure necessary for the hypodermic to drop from her hand. Tate's weapon was trained on Timothy, but the younger man's hands were in the air as his body shook. Bray quickly bagged the hypodermic, placing it in a container before shoving it into his bag.

Cobb dropped to his knees and grabbed Josie, who was staring at him through wide, still-dilated eyes. Swinging her up into his arms, he stalked over to the edge of the bed and sat, holding her tightly. She cradled her injured hand but placed her face directly in front of his and chanted, "I'm okay, I'm okay, I'm okay." A trail of dried blood was on her arm, and as though she anticipated his imminent roar, she rushed, "That's where I got the needle earlier. Honestly, Jorge, I'm fine."

Cobb kept his arms around her, unsure if the shaking was from her or himself. He glanced to the side and watched as Drew pulled out a gag for Carmen.

Timothy was pale, sweating profusely. "What's gonna happen? Christ, we're in Mexico. We're never going to get out. Christ, why did I come here?"

Cobb stood, his arm still around Josie. Bray moved in and bent low, checking her pupils. "You steady on your feet, Josie?"

She offered a wobbly nod, and Bray shot a look toward Cobb before looking back at her. "You did great, Tiger, but we'll all be close as we get out of here."

While their medic checked Josie, Cobb took the opportunity to approach Carmen, who eyed him warily. "We're going back across the border. While I would love nothing more than to leave you to the cartel to carve up at their leisure, we're taking you back with us." His face held no emotion, but rage burned in his veins. "I'm telling you right now we're getting out of here. We'll get you turned over to the FBI. If you don't want that? If you try to alert anyone here to our presence? I will leave your ass to the cartel to deal with."

Tate pulled out a gag, but Timothy shook his head. "I won't say anything. I won't do anything. Just get me the fuck out of here, please." Tate chuckled as he continued to gag Timothy.

Checking with LSI, they received the all-clear that the security was still disabled. Moving quickly into the hall, Drew and Tate hustled Carmen and Timothy along, finding neither giving resistance. He picked up Josie and carried her out despite her soft protests. "Babe, we can travel quicker out of here if you let me carry you. Right now, I don't trust that you have your full abilities with the drug still running through your body." Ready for an argument, he should have known she would offer no fuss. Acquiescing, she wrapped her arms around his neck, and they hustled out of the doorway and down the stairs.

The guard at the top of the stairs that Drew had subdued was just beginning to stir. Grinning, Drew bent, dragging Carmen along with him, and pressed against the artery just long enough to render the man unconscious again. Standing quickly, he jerked his charge along as she fought against the gag.

At the bottom of the stairs, Bray exited first, then signaled for the rest of them to follow. Slipping back through the shadows of the alley, they arrived at their truck. Cobb set Josie's feet onto the concrete carefully, making sure she was steady. Bray stepped over, his arms reaching for her while holding Cobb's gaze. "Go on, I've got her."

Cobb hated to let her go but knew there was no other way. He watched as Bray climbed into the back, then turned and assisted as Josie scrambled up into the bed of the truck. They disappeared underneath the boxes. Drew shoved Carmen into the small space then followed her, sitting close enough to keep her under control. Tate did the same with a wide-eyed Timothy.

Back in the driver's seat, Cobb rumbled out of the alley. Receiving a message from LSI, he answered, "Talk to me."

"Floyd has reported that someone may have alerted the border guards that something is up. They are checking every truck," Mace said. "Follow your backup plan."

Turning away from the border bridge, he left Ciudad Juarez and traveled on a road toward the north. The Rio Grande was not deep at several junctions but the U.S. Border Patrol had the area under close surveillance. Receiving the notice from LSI that Floyd was waiting for them at the backup rendezvous, he turned off the headlights and moved closer to the river.

"Look for an ally," Josh radioed. "He should be close. Someone Floyd set up."

A man stood in the road, a rifle slung over his shoulder. Bringing the truck to a stop, Cobb kept his eye pinned on the man as he walked toward the driver's side. He rolled down the window and peered at the man with suspicion.

The man stuck a cigarette into his mouth and inhaled deeply before letting out a long curl of smoke. "You ever been to Faro El Palmar?"

Shaking his head slowly, Cobb kept his left hand on

the steering wheel while unobtrusively sliding his right hand to his weapon. "No."

"Pity. A beautiful lighthouse is on the point."

Cobb lifted a brow, then slowly raised his right hand to his shirt, pulling up the sleeve, exposing the lower half of his lighthouse tattoo.

The man stared, then nodded. "Yes… a beautiful lighthouse." He inclined his head toward the border. "Cross here. You can make it. Your people are on the other side. I'll get rid of the vehicle."

He held the man's gaze for a few more seconds, then nodded. Still keeping his hand on his weapon as he climbed down, he hustled to the back and called out, "Let's go."

Tate alighted first, quickly followed by Timothy, who anxiously looked around. Tate unlocked his hand-cuffs and removed the gag. "One word and—"

"No, man, I'll be quiet!"

Drew stood at the back of the truck bed and lifted Carmen by her arms only to settle her onto the ground. Tate unlocked her cuffs but before he removed her gag offered her another warning. "You seriously do not want to be left over here. So, keep your fuckin' mouth shut."

Her gaze jerked over to the Mexican with the rifle and licked her gag-swollen lips, nodding.

Anxious to get to Josie, Cobb raised his hands as soon as Bray appeared with her. She smiled, her eyes lighting as soon as her gaze met his. She immediately fell into his arms and kissed his cheek.

"You can let me walk for now."

He agreed but kept her right by his side. The four Keepers shook the man's hand, never knowing or needing to know his name. They knew he would be paid well for his assistance, and he'd get a truck out of the deal, as well.

The crossing area for the Rio Grande was easy to traverse due to the lack of rain. The group hurried through the water that in some places was only knee-deep, led by Cobb with Josie's hand in his. Lights on the other side provided guidance, and they were soon in the U.S., greeted by Floyd standing with several agents wearing jackets emblazoned with FBI on the back. Others were with the Customs and Border Patrol, CBP on the backs of their jackets.

Cobb's body tightened as Tahoma Starr stepped into the light and his gaze landed on the initials IDTF stitched into his jacket.

"International Drug Task Force?" Cobb asked, his gaze not wavering even when Tahoma nodded.

Tahoma's gaze scanned the group, lingering on Josie before pinning Carmen with a hard stare. Stepping forward, he looked at his co-aide to the senator. "Had my eye on you for a while, so I gotta tell you, even though I'm a step behind these guys in getting my hands on you, this feels fuckin' good."

"You want to tell me what the hell is going on?" Cobb growled.

Tahoma turned and walked toward him. Leaning to the side, his gaze scanned Josie. "Are you okay? Your parents are waiting to hear."

Cobb heard the gasp behind him, and Josie popped

out to his side. She looked up at Tahoma, her body still weaving slightly. "Oh, God, I need to tell them that I'm okay—"

"I'll get word—"

Interrupting Tahoma, Cobb snapped, "My people already have." He knew that LSI would be in contact with her parents, and it might be selfish as fuck, but he had no desire to let Tahoma fuckin'-task-force Starr step in at the last minute as though he had saved the day.

Floyd looked at Carmen, then turned to Cobb. "Been wanting to get my hands on *Carson Wright* for several years. Can't thank you enough."

Drew shook his head, saying, "You can have her, man. It's a pain to listen to her."

The agents loaded Carmen and Timothy into two separate vehicles as Timothy began turning on her immediately and her curses and threats rang out in the night.

Josie moved in closer to Cobb, and he breathed easier as his arm wrapped around her again. Giving her weight to him, she squeezed his waist as she looked up at Tahoma. "I don't understand. You don't work for my dad?"

"I was undercover, Josie. My people have been working on the drug trafficking between the Grand King Casino, which is secretly run by the Sinaloa Cartel, and getting drugs and drug money into the U.S. Carmen came across our radar, and I was tasked to get close to see what I could find out. I had no idea she was using an alias of Carson Wright, a person the FBI has been looking for. Until your father mentioned your clinic's financial difficulties, I started to put it all together."

"So, you knew Carmen could be a threat to Josie but let it ride out anyway?" Cobb said, his barely-controlled rage returning.

"Babe... I'm safe. Let the dragon rest."

He jerked his gaze back down to Josie, his brow knit until he saw her twinkling eyes staring up at him, an exhausted smile playing about her lips. Bending, he kissed her lightly, and with the touch of her lips, he calmed.

Ignoring Tahoma, Cobb offered chin-lift thanks to the others and escorted Josie to Floyd's extra-long SUV. Climbing inside, he guided her to the middle seat and wrapped his arm around her, loving the feel of her head on his shoulder. Drew rode shotgun next to Floyd while Bray and Tate filled the back seat.

Closing his eyes, Cobb breathed a sigh of relief. Years of missions, some more successful than others. But there was nothing quite like the feeling of heading home after one where the objective had been met. But now, he knew there was no comparison to the feeling of the woman he loved being in his arms, safe and secure.

28

Josie and the Keepers had made it back to her house by dawn, where Jorge fed Melon as she took a quick shower and fell into bed with him joining her shortly thereafter. Hours later, they woke, and with whispered words of affection, made love.

Tate, Bray, and Drew checked out of the hotel in Las Cruces and came by her house to say goodbye before they flew back to Maine. She stood back and watched the true affection as they shook hands and back-slapped Jorge.

Drew was the first to approach, lifting her off her feet with his hug. "You gotta come to Maine, darlin'. My Babs would love to meet you. Especially after I tell her how you belted Carmen right in the face." She blushed, but he was laughing so she figured his woman had probably *belted* someone, too.

Tate's hug was more gentle, his words whispered for only her to hear. "Remember, you two are good for each other. In this life, that's not easy to find." Tears pricked her eyes, but she nodded and offered a smile.

Last, Bray offered a tentative hug then pulled back and held her gaze, his eyes searching. She wondered if it was his medic background that always had him checking to see if someone was all right. But he surprised her when he said, "I agree with Drew. You need to come to visit us in Maine. You never know... it might just feel like home."

Jorge stepped in, pulling her body close to his as they stood in her doorway and waved goodbye. He turned, his gaze as penetrating as his friends' had been. "Are you okay? I never meant for them to put you on the spot about Maine. It's no secret I hope you'll come, but—"

With her arms wrapped around his waist, she tilted her head back to stare into his gorgeous, dark eyes. "Is that an invitation to visit?"

He grinned and nodded. "Absolutely." He leaned down and kissed her lightly before pulling back, his hands cupping her cheeks. "I've been trying to figure out how to bring this up, but now is as good a time as any. I'm crazy about you, Josephine Rector. And I don't want to walk away at the end of this mission and have us be done. I don't have all the answers as to how we'll work things out, but I definitely want you to come to Maine. I'll take whatever time you can give me, but I hope you plan for a long enough visit to get a feel for the place."

The smile on her face could barely match the lightness in her heart. "I can't think of anything I'd rather do more."

"Well, all right, babe. Now… we've got to get to Albuquerque and see our families before they descend to make sure you're okay."

A few hours later, Josie wasn't sure she could handle another tear-filled hug from her parents, but catching a glimpse of Jorge's smile and wink from across the room made it easier. They were in his parents' home, the room filled to the brim with her parents, his parents, and all four of his grandparents. Bert had made an appearance, his expression full of remorse as he held her tightly, his apologies overflowing.

"I had no idea, Josie. No idea at all what they were doing. I was such a prick, thinking how smart I was hanging with them. Christ, I'm such an idiot."

She shushed him, more interested in getting him clean than any apology. He had moved over to talk to her parents before he left but his promise to meet with them later seemed sincere. John was still reeling over the duplicity of Carmen and the fact that his other aide was undercover for a drug task force. "Dad, I'm sure it won't reflect on you—"

"Oh, Josie," he exclaimed, red-rimmed eyes wide as they peered down at her. "I don't care about the office or politics. I care that someone I trusted tried to harm you! I let you and Bert down."

"No, you didn't. Bert made his own choices, and with help, he'll make better ones. And as for Carmen, you were as duped as the rest of us. She was that good.

And it was important for Tahoma to be believable in his role, so that's not on you, either."

She could tell his confidence was shaken, but with more hugs, she finally felt him relax a bit. Jorge's father had taken him to the side, and with their heads bowed together and more low words spoken, she had no doubt the governor was offering assurances.

Jorge was still on the other side of the room, his mother, Maria, and his two grandfathers engaging him as they spoke with affection in their smiles. She startled as Naomi approached silently and stood close to her. She turned, the older woman's smile and warm, dark eyes holding her gaze. Her beauty shone through with her high cheekbones and her long black hair streaked with grey.

Naomi reached out and gathered Josie's hands in her own. "You've been through a lot."

"I was scared until Cobb came into my life. Your grandson made all the difference."

"He cares for you."

She pressed her lips together, uncertain how Naomi felt. Replying truthfully, she admitted, "I care deeply for him, too."

"You'll have decisions to make."

Josie startled slightly, understanding what Naomi was referring to. She simply nodded, not trusting her voice.

"There is a saying attributed to the Chief White Eagle, Ponca. 'When you are in doubt, be still, and wait; when doubt no longer exists for you, then go forward with courage. So long as mists envelop you, be still; be still until the sunlight pours through and dispels the mists as it surely will. Then act with courage.'"

"That's beautiful," Josie whispered, tears filling her eyes.

Naomi smiled, still holding Josie's hands. "No one can tell you what decisions to make. But do not despair, beautiful Josephine. You'll have courage when the sunlight pours through and chases the mists away." With a squeeze of her fingers, Naomi drifted away and moved toward her husband.

As though sensing her need, Cobb stepped away from his family and stalked directly to her, enveloping her into his embrace. No words were spoken as they stood with their arms about each other. The family looked on but drifted back to their soft conversations, leaving the couple standing alone in the middle of the room, surrounded by loved ones.

One Month Later

Josie slipped from Cobb's bed, having woken early despite their late evening with the other Keepers and middle of the night lovemaking. Restless, unable to go back to sleep, she grabbed one of Cobb's flannel shirts and slipped it on over her pajama bottoms and camisole. Pulling thick socks onto her feet, she padded softly out to the great room area, rolling up the sleeves of the oversized shirt.

It had taken her a month to settle the clinic's finances, hiring an independent auditor to not only protect their money but who would report with the FBI any irregularities found. The social worker who had interned previously was anxious to return and had eagerly accepted a full-time position, allowing Josie the chance to take a week off.

Now, she was halfway through her visit with Cobb, loving every moment of their reunion. She'd met the other Keepers the second day she was in Maine, having been invited to the lighthouse for lunch. Greeted warmly by all, she was especially excited to see Drew and his wife Babs, Tate, and Bray. For several days, she and Cobb had alternated between touring the area, hiking along the forests and water, and time in his house, both in bed and out.

He'd made his wishes known that he wanted her to stay with him, but she hadn't given her agreement yet. A move across the country. Looking for a new job. A major life change. Moving away from my family. *Do I have the courage to take this leap of faith?*

She walked through the great room, the awe of his house still hitting her days later. Two-story vaulted ceilings with a wall of windows that overlooked the water and woods. Exposed wooden beams, hardwood floors, and a stone fireplace. A dream kitchen and dining room big enough to hold family and friends. The living room with oversized, deep-cushioned sofas.

She moved to the coffee machine and made a quick

cup, fixing it just the way she liked. Holding the steaming mug in her hand, she slipped through the sliding glass door out onto the deck. Fog had rolled in during the night, the low clouds clinging to the earth, obscuring her view. The air was fresh and clean, the sweet scent of pine and tangy seawater filling her senses. She closed her eyes and recalled the view of the mountains in the distance from her rental house in Las Cruces. She loved the view of the mountains but had to admit she didn't miss her little house with its gravel yard. A neighbor was taking care of Melon, and it struck her that Melon would love to lounge in Cobb's massive living room where the sun could create numerous cat sunspots to discover.

She opened her eyes and took a sip of the hot coffee, seeing snatches of brighter sunlight as the fog began to lift, the mist now only clinging to the treetops and the water in the distance. Naomi's quote came back to her, and she gasped with enlightenment. *So long as mists envelop you, be still; be still until the sunlight pours through and dispels the mists as it surely will. Then act with courage.*

She was struck with the peace of knowing Jorge's place felt like home.

The sound of the sliding glass door opened behind her, but she didn't need to turn around to know he was approaching. It only took a few seconds for his arms to lean against the rail on either side of her, his front to her back, his chin resting on the top of her head, enveloping her with his presence, his protection, his love. Closing her eyes again, she smiled as she stared out at the beauty of nature in front of her, feeling the beauty of the man behind her.

Setting her mug on the railing, she turned in his arms so that she was facing him, her palms resting on his chest, the feel of his heartbeat under her fingertips. He looked down, his brows lowered in question but quiet as usual to give her a chance to gather her thoughts and speak.

Not making him wait, she said, "If you'll have me, I choose you. I choose this place."

She watched as the smile spread across his handsome face before he threw his head back in laughter, the most beautiful sight she had ever seen.

His arms squeezed tighter as he dipped his mouth to hers. "Oh, yeah, Josie, babe… I'm in love with you."

"Yeah?" she breathed.

He kissed her deeply before holding her gaze again. "Yeah."

"Since when?"

A chuckle erupted from low in his chest. "I think I started falling when I saw you in a shimmery dress standing under a Triceratops."

Now, she threw her head back in laughter, and his arms banded tighter as he lifted her off the deck, twirling her in his arms. As she looked around, she observed the mist had completely lifted and the sun poured down on them.

Two Months later

"Melon, please get out from under my feet. You've been fed!" Josie tried to move around her cat, much to the amusement of Helena and Sara, who were setting out platters of food on the kitchen counter. Josie and Melon had moved to Maine two weeks ago, and her cat was still getting used to the transition. Just as she assumed, the large feline loved the space and sunlight, finding numerous places to sleep.

"Do you want me to set the wine here?" Julie asked as she and Sylvie were pulling wine bottles from the refrigerator and bags.

"Hell, let's be honest. Anywhere is fine for wine!" Babs quipped, walking into the room with Drew trailing behind, carrying more bags. "Flyboy, we'll put the tubs of beer on the deck, and the guys won't need glasses."

Nora, Christina, and Claire walked into the room with more bags. Josie's eyes widened and she shook her head. "How much food do we need?"

Nora laughed and patted her arm. "Don't worry. We've learned that it takes a lot of food to feed our Keepers."

"How's the job hunting going?" Julie asked. "I didn't have any trouble finding a teaching job here, and I can't imagine you will, either."

"You know social work. There's always a need out there, but Jorge is encouraging me to take my time and not rush into anything. I think he really wants me to get used to being here, and maybe there's a part of him

that's terrified I'm going to regret my decision to move."
She saw the immediately raised brows from the other women and shook her head. Laughing, she assured, "Don't worry. I knew exactly what I was doing when I moved here. It was time for a life change, and I think perhaps I just needed a purpose to make that change."

Soon, the house and deck were filled with good food and drinks, good friends and camaraderie, laughter, and conversation. Nestled in Jorge's lap with her head on his shoulder, the sounds of the party settled into the background as she stared out over the glistening water framed by the woods. *Be still, and wait; when doubt no longer exists for you, go forward with courage.*

Turning, she held Jorge's warm gaze and smiled. "There's no doubt... I love you." His smile met hers just before she closed the distance, kissing him lightly, her heart full.

Don't miss the next Lighthouse book... Bray's story!
Bray
And I have a surprise! My new book, Home to Stay is a Lighthouse Security Investigation crossover... meet the newest LSI Keeper!
Home to Stay

Cael

Jaxon

Jayden

Asher

Zeke

Cas

Lighthouse Security Investigations

Mace

Rank

Walker

Drew

Blake

Tate

Levi

Clay

Cobb

Bray

Hope City (romantic suspense series co-developed

with Kris Michaels

Brock book 1

Sean book 2

Carter book 3

Brody book 4

Kyle book 5

Ryker book 6

Rory book 7

Killian book 8

Torin book 9

Saints Protection & Investigations

(an elite group, assigned to the cases no one else wants…or can solve)

Serial Love

Healing Love

Revealing Love

Seeing Love

Honor Love

Sacrifice Love

Protecting Love

Remember Love

Discover Love

Surviving Love

Celebrating Love

Searching Love

Follow the exciting spin-off series:

Alvarez Security (military romantic suspense)

Gabe

Tony

Vinny

Jobe

SEALs

Thin Ice (Sleeper SEAL)

SEAL Together (Silver SEAL)

Undercover Groom (Hot SEAL)

Also for a Hope City Crossover Novel / Hot SEAL...

A Forever Dad

Long Road Home

Military Romantic Suspense

Home to Stay (a Lighthouse Security Investigation crossover novel)

Letters From Home (military romance)

Class of Love

Freedom of Love

Bond of Love

The Love's Series (detectives)

Love's Taming

Love's Tempting

Love's Trusting

The Fairfield Series (small town detectives)

Emma's Home

Laurie's Time

Carol's Image

Fireworks Over Fairfield

Please take the time to leave a review of this book. Feel free to contact me, especially if you enjoyed my book. I love to hear from readers!

Facebook

Email

Website

ABOUT THE AUTHOR

I am an avid reader of romance novels, often joking that I cut my teeth on the historical romances. I have been reading and reviewing for years. In 2013, I finally gave into the characters in my head, screaming for their story to be told. From these musings, my first novel, Emma's Home, The Fairfield Series was born.

I was a high school counselor having worked in education for thirty years. I live in Virginia, having also lived in four states and two foreign countries. I have been married to a wonderfully patient man for thirty-five years. When writing, my dog or one of my four cats can generally be found in the same room if not on my lap.

Please take the time to leave a review of this book. Feel free to contact me, especially if you enjoyed my book. I love to hear from readers!

Facebook

Email

Website